Loot

Loot

Tania James

ALFRED A. KNOPF
NEW YORK   2023

THIS IS A BORZOI BOOK
PUBLISHED BY ALFRED A. KNOPF

Copyright © 2023 by Tania James

www.aaknopf.com

Knopf, Borzoi Books, and the colophon are
registered trademarks of Penguin Random House LLC.

Library of Congress Cataloging-in-Publication Data
Names: James, Tania, author.
Title: Loot / Tania James.
Description: New York : Alfred A. Knopf, 2023.
Identifiers: LCCN 2022034645 (print) | LCCN 2022034646 (ebook) |
ISBN 9780593535974 (hardcover) | ISBN 9780593535981 (ebook)
Subjects: LCSH: India—History—18th century—Fiction. |
France—History—1789–1900—Fiction. | LCGFT: Novels.
Classification: LCC PS3610.A458 L66 2023 (print) | LCC PS3610.A458
(ebook) | DDC 813/.6—dc23/eng/20220916
LC record available at https://lccn.loc.gov/2022034645
LC ebook record available at https://lccn.loc.gov/2022034646

Line drawings on pages 23 and 83 by Tania James.
Image on page 163 from *A Short History of the English People,* Vol. IV,
by John Richard Green, M.A., edited by Mrs. J. R. Green and Miss Kate Norgate.

Jacket image (tiger): studiomode/Alamy
Jacket design by Jenny Carrow

Manufactured in the United States of America
First Edition

For Luka and Sajan

SRIRANGAPATNA, MYSORE

1794

On the day he is taken from his family, Abbas is carving a peacock into a cabinet door. He drives his gouge tip through the rosewood, adjusting the pressure with his pointer finger. Grooves deepen, a beak appears. He moves on to sculpt feathers, stacked like scales. He excels at this task and has never been so bored in his life.

Seated nearby on coir mats are his father and two older brothers, Junaid and Farooq. With a post braced against the inside of his knee, Junaid knocks out nuggets of unwanted wood with the tak-*tak!* of his mallet and chisel. Farooq sketches a pair of peacocks for a headboard. Their father sands a finished post, stopping every so often to shoot Abbas a warning look.

"No more of your toys," his father has told him in private. "Beds and cabinets, that's it. The toys only bring trouble."

Pausing to arch his back, Abbas is distracted by a pigeon fluttering down from a roof across the lane. Curious, isn't it, the way birds bob their heads while they walk but never while they fly? (Abbas finds it curious, though some might say curiosity is exactly his problem.) He wonders if it's something to do with a connective mechanism between the leg and the neck. And, he wonders, if one were to construct a mechanical pigeon, how might the head be engineered to jerk with every step?

Then he recalls something a friend once told him.

Ask too many questions and next thing you know, you're the one being questioned.

Abbas is trading out one gouge for another when a man appears at the threshold, holding a bayonet that surpasses him in height. By the tiger-striped sleeves, Abbas knows him to be one of Tipu Sultan's royal guards.

"Are you Abbas, son of Yusuf Muhammad?" the guard says.

"Who's asking?" says Abbas, not as coolly as he'd like.

The guard takes a breath. "Tipu Sultan Fath Ali Khan, the Tiger of Mysore, the Padshah of Patan, Breaker of Colonel Baillie, and God-Given Overseer of the State—" Across the lane, a lathe shrieks to a stop. People lift their heads from their work. "—has summoned Abbas, son of Yusuf Muhammad, to the Summer Palace."

"Outside the city walls?" asks Abbas, who has never in his life been outside the city walls.

"Is there another Summer Palace?" says the guard. "Get up!"

Abbas stands, his legs tingling with pins and needles. He wonders if he will faint.

"Wait," says Yusuf Muhammad, following Abbas and the guard into the lane. "He's only seventeen. Let me answer for his crimes."

"What crimes?" says Junaid. "What is all this about?"

"Did I say crimes? I meant misdeeds." Yusuf Muhammad drops his voice low. "Is this about the eunuch?"

"Eunuch?" says the guard, affronted.

"I can speak for myself," Abbas says quickly. He follows the guard's instruction to walk three paces ahead but does not grant his family a backward glance, knowing it is too late to explain himself or ask their forgiveness.

It is said that in Srirangapatna, the spies outnumber the people. There are the spymasters and couriers of Tipu Sultan, ferrying messages to and from the capital city, and then there are the spies of Tipu's enemies—the Nizam of Hyderabad, the Nairs of Malabar, the

Marathas, the English, the Mangalorean Catholics. (Do not even get Tipu started on those Catholics; mention the Catholics in his presence and he will have a gold-plated fit.) Tipu has spies in the courts of his friends and enemies, too, constantly sending him intelligence, which, problematically, only excites the thirst for more intelligence.

But these are problematic times.

Tipu's kingdom barely survived the most recent war with the English, and talk of still another is always on the horizon. The people never know who is coming from where to take what from whom. All they can do is submit to power each time it changes hands, each time the powerful decide to redecorate. This one wants a new calendar. That one wants his face struck on a coin. With every alteration, large and small, the ground unfirms itself beneath their feet, making it nearly impossible for anyone to leave a lasting mark.

At the moment, Abbas has no interest in leaving a mark. All he wants is to stay out of trouble, though it is, perhaps, a little late for that.

Abbas has never been to the Summer Palace before, but he has made eight toys for Zubaida Begum, one of the high-ranking consorts of Tipu's zenana. The carved animals moved by hand crank: elephants, tigers, and horses. Soon after Abbas made one for Zubaida Begum, she ordered seven more, one after another.

To collect the toys, she sent a man by the name of Khwaja Irfan. From a distance, Abbas would watch Khwaja Irfan coming down the lane, easy to spot in his brassy cloaks of green or marigold, silks that spoke of royal places. He had a pointy chin and keen eyes, no facial hair to disguise the fineness of his features. "What's the matter?" he asked Abbas the first time they met. "Never met a eunuch before?"

Abbas shook his head.

"Then I'm your first. How fun for me." Khwaja Irfan closed the umbrella he'd been using to shield himself from the sun.

Abbas was taken with the umbrella's handle, how it curved up into the graven head of a tiger.

Khwaja Irfan noticed him staring. "Nice, isn't it. Pure elephant ivory."

Abbas eyed the cut of the teeth and said: "No."

"What do you mean, no?"

"Ivory wood, maybe. Whoever told you otherwise was lying."

Khwaja Irfan appraised him with a sly smile. "Okay, Know-It-All."

Somehow Khwaja Irfan would manage to tuck that phrase into each of his visits, a teasing that made him feel like family. Or at least like the sort of family Abbas would've requested had he any choice in the matter. His brothers were chipped from the same block of stone as their mother—blunt, judgmental, suspicious of smiley types. Of eunuchs his mother said that they were gossips and could never be trusted.

The family regarded Abbas's toys with a similar mix of disdain and skepticism. Only his father took a sheepish interest, asking for the occasional demonstration, which often ended with him saying, "How do you come up with these things?" This, to Abbas, was the highest of praise.

It made Abbas doubly proud to deliver the begum's payment to his father. The rupiya always came in a silk drawstring pouch, embroidered in gold with Tipu's tiger insignia. Before handing the pouch to his father, Abbas took a private moment to hold it to his nose and inhale.

Rosewater. Betel. Mysterious womanly smells.

"The real thing smells better," came a remark from Farooq, tailed by laughter.

Abbas shuffles ahead of the guard, down a row of artisans ordered by the nobility of their crafts: the potters, the weavers and embroiderers, the goldsmiths and blacksmiths, the muralists and miniaturists. ("At least we're not next to the leatherworkers," their father used to say about being at the far end. "We're quite a ways from them.") There is Ustad Mahfuz and deaf Bilal, Madhava the Younger and

Madhava the Disciple, Tariq and Khandan and old Ustad Saadat with his weird glass eye, tossing a bit of bread to a stringy dog.

Some of them stare. Others know better.

Though the forges are behind him now, Abbas can still hear a hammer clinking against iron, can still picture that white-orange rod wilting as if by magic, the air above it shimmering. Abbas has always liked watching the blacksmiths. It occurs to him now that he may never watch them again.

A pair of peepal trees wave him along, their leaves softly gossiping in his wake.

Soon he comes to the Water Gate, the tunnel that allows commoners to enter and leave the city. The same gate through which Yusuf Muhammad led them twelve years ago, along with a number of other woodworkers from Shimoga, all of them recruited by Tipu's father to carve the walls and columns of the Summer Palace. Yusuf Muhammad took a look around at the capital city—at the whimsical footbridges and gold-leafed fountains, at the mighty temple gopuras and the soaring minarets, not a poor person in sight, even the stray dogs lounging about with an air of satisfaction—and thought: Why leave? What reason would one have to abandon the protective walls of Srirangapatna?

Now, as Abbas passes beneath the dangling bodies of bats, he feels as though Srirangapatna is abandoning him.

"What do you call a know-it-all who knows nothing?" Khwaja Irfan asked Abbas, the last time they met.

Abbas considered the question. "European."

Khwaja Irfan laughed. "Not bad, kid."

"I'm not a kid." Abbas set his latest creation on the table. "Would a kid make this?"

It was a painted wooden horse, carrying a wooden Tipu Sultan on its back. Abbas gently turned the crank, bringing the horse to a gallop, its head easing forward and back, the legs scissoring open and closed, the tail extending like a windblown pennant.

"*Shabash,*" said Khwaja Irfan softly, all joking set aside.

Abbas offered him a turn. Khwaja Irfan guided the handle, shy at first, then transfixed. "Maybe you do know it all," he said, bringing the horse to a stop.

While packing the toy into a straw-filled crate, Abbas asked, as nonchalantly as he could, if Zubaida Begum had said anything about the last toy.

"She liked it," said Khwaja Irfan.

Abbas paused, knowing he shouldn't ask the next question. "What does she look like?"

Khwaja Irfan raised an eyebrow. "Careful."

"I'm just asking."

"Ask too many questions, my friend, and next thing you know, you're the one being questioned."

Abbas finished packing in silence and nailed the crate shut. "Here you go," he said, pushing the crate toward Khwaja Irfan, who was staring into the street, preoccupied.

When he spoke, his voice was low, almost a murmur.

> *Were an artist to choose me for his model—*
> *How could he draw the form of a sigh?*

"What is that?" Abbas asked.

"It's a poem she wrote." Khwaja Irfan paused in contemplation. "She is a poet, an artist. Like you."

Abbas waited for more, his chest beginning to thrum with a sweet sort of turbulence.

But then Khwaja Irfan turned away and stepped into the street, the package in his arms. Over his shoulder he called, "*Khuda hafiz,* Know-It-All."

Abbas muttered the poem to himself, committing it to memory.

Only later (too late) did he notice the tiger-head umbrella, roaring mutely against the wall.

. . .

At the guard's prompting, Abbas climbs a set of steps and passes through a sandstone arch that delivers them into Daria Daulat Bagh. It is an ocean of a garden, populated with fruiting and flowering plants from all over the world. Pigeons flutter and coo from a domed pigeon keep, flying in and out, messages tied to their ankles.

Down the smooth stone path he proceeds, past shrubs tamed to spheres, trees whittled to points, grass clipped tight as carpet. Beyond this lies the Summer Palace, its dark maw cut by columns. He has never seen it before, only heard it described by his father. But his father neglected to mention the enormous cages that flank the entrance, each holding a replica of a tiger. So lifelike, Abbas thinks as he nears, observing the perfect stroke of each stripe, the citrine of each eye.

One of the tigers flicks its tail, causing Abbas to leap back.

"That's Bahadur Khan," the guard says. "He gets edgy around feeding time."

As they pass, the tiger raises its head with an intent expression, as though undressing Abbas to the bone.

Inside the Summer Palace, painted battles span the walls, dizzy with red-coated soldiers being skewered by Tipu's cavalry. Still other walls are painted in delicate climbing vines, florals of carmine and blue.

No time to marvel. The guard directs him through forests of fragrance—sandalwood, teak—and around a corner, where they come upon a hidden staircase.

"Up," says the guard. Abbas is surprised, having assumed that the only direction he would be going is down. At the top of the landing, he finds himself in a grand pavilion propped by columns, every cornice frothing with scrolls and carvings. And there at the far end sits Tipu Sultan, leaning casually on a bolster pillow. Beneath him is a vast carpet. Above him is a finely dressed servant, stirring the air with a fan of white peacock feathers. The servant is wearing slippers.

Abbas presses his bony feet together, wishing he could've washed them.

"You with the yellow dhoti," says Tipu, confusing Abbas, for he had assumed his dhoti to be white. "Come forward."

As he approaches, Abbas notices a European, clad in a pyjama and turban, sitting off to the right of Tipu Sultan. The European has a long pink face that brings a mandrill to mind. His eyes are squinty and golden brown, so clear they seem capable of seeing into Abbas's thoughts, specifically the one about the mandrill. Abbas drops his gaze to the carpet, where a border of red tulips bloom, their stems leading to the circle where Tipu sits.

"Salaam," says Tipu Sultan.

Abbas bows, keeping his focus on the spurs of Tipu's leather shoes.

Tipu Sultan's face is round and mild. He has the glower of a hawk, the chin of a mouse. He lets pass a long silence.

"You are the toymaker," says Tipu, finally.

"Yes, Padshah." Abbas clasps his hands. "I am Abbas, son of Yusuf Muhammad."

"I knew an Abbas, son of Yusuf Muhammad."

Everyone knows of that Abbas, son of Yusuf Muhammad, the general and traitor recently executed by strangulation.

"No relation," says Abbas.

"But you know another traitor, I do believe. Your toys were very popular with the begum he worked for. Now we know why. She and the eunuch were in the pocket of that termite, Nana Phadnavis. What I'll never understand is why anyone would trust a Maratha. Isn't it so, Musa?"

"Indeed it is their nature," says the European—with an Arabic name?—in surprisingly smooth Kannada. "Even a Maratha will not trust a Maratha."

Tipu raises a finger. Another servant appears, carrying the wooden horse toy, the one with a painted Tipu Sultan on its back.

Abbas feels sick.

"Did you make this?" asks Tipu Sultan.

"Yes, Padshah."

Tipu rotates the hand crank, studying the gallop. Abbas catches the eye of the European Musa, who is staring not at the trotting horse but at Abbas.

"This is not how a horse runs," Tipu says flatly. "You have the back legs and hind legs running in tandem, like a dog's. When a horse gallops, each hoof meets the ground at a different moment. I am an expert on horses because of my father, praise be his memory. He could have written a treatise on horses to rival that of Xenophon."

"Forgive me, Padshah."

"Your second offense is that you've made an effigy of me." Tipu points at his wooden self. "One in which my legs have been made to appear ludicrously short. This offense is punishable by death—really anything is punishable by death if I say so."

Abbas tries to plead for his life, but the words catch in his throat. At the outskirts of his vision, the columns begin to sway.

"In spite of your failures," Tipu continues, "I see your natural capacity. So does my French friend here. This is Musa Du Leze, the greatest inventor in France. He has agreed to work with you on the making of Mysore's first *automate*." Tipu pauses. "You are jiggling your head but you do not understand. Musa?"

"You may imagine it as a great moving toy," says Musa Du Leze, in Kannada. Abbas blinks at them both, trying hard not to jiggle his head.

"This is taking forever," Tipu says. "Bring the gun."

Du Leze unfolds his long legs. A servant hands him a rifle, and for a moment, Abbas can feel the ghost of a bullet pierce his own chest. "Wait—" he says, putting up his hands. But Du Leze is turning the rifle around, inviting Abbas to look closely at the ornament on its sights.

"*Et voilà.*" Du Leze, towering over him, points to a tiny bronze man pinned by a tiny bronze tiger. The two figures are marvelously detailed, such that Abbas can distinguish the boots and hat, those trademarks of the Europeans.

"You and I will make this," says Du Leze. His voice is baritone, his breath exceptionally stale. "Out of wood and to human scale."

"I want it as tall as Musa Du Leze," says Tipu. "And I want the teeth *planted* in the neck of the infidel." Tipu points to the exact coordinates in his own throat, adding that the automaton should also emit a growling sound. "And music. It will be most amusing if the toy can play music."

Tipu and Du Leze discuss what kind of music. Abbas studies the ornament, trying to picture a musician crouched inside the tiger, perhaps playing a flute . . .

"In six weeks there will be a party for the unveiling," says Tipu. "I expect perfection."

"*Évidemment,* Padshah. I would offer no less."

"What's next, Raja Khan?"

The slippered servant bends to speak. "You have a meeting with the commissioners of the board of trade—"

"All nine?"

"All nine, Padshah. Then a meeting with the rocket master."

"*Ya Allah.* I've taken naps that were more interesting." Placing a hand on his knee, Tipu rises. "Still here?" he says to Abbas, who has been hovering at the edge of the carpet, waiting to be dismissed. "Oh, right." Tipu nods at Raja Khan, who removes a small silk purse from his pocket. Another servant transfers the purse from Raja Khan to Abbas.

"Take that to your father," Tipu says, "in recognition of his loyalty."

Receiving the purse in both hands, Abbas thanks the padshah for his infinite generosity. The purse, embroidered in gold with the tiger insignia, weighs heavily on his palm.

"One thing I notice," says Tipu. "You haven't asked me about Khwaja Irfan. Aren't you curious?"

There is an innocence to the question, the way it is offered like an open hand ready to crush the bones of another.

"I assumed he was punished, Padshah."

"Punished," Tipu says dryly. "And how do you think I should punish someone who has eaten my salt and worn my silk and acted so treacherously?"

"It is not for me to know, Padshah."

"Clever boy. Most people are not as clever as you, though. So if anyone is foolish enough to ask you what I did with Khwaja Irfan, you will tell them I said: *Who is Khwaja Irfan?*"

At last, with a nod, Tipu releases Abbas from his presence. Abbas bows and shuffles back down the entire length of the pavilion, as though walking a plank so narrow he cannot turn, can only step-by-step reverse.

When Abbas found the tiger-head umbrella, he could not help picking it up to study the craftsmanship of the handle. He especially liked the hollow of the tiger's mouth, its thornlike fangs. He dipped his fingertip into the maw and grazed the fine edge of something. Without thinking, he pulled a tightly rolled piece of paper halfway out of the mouth before stuffing it back in, his stomach churning.

"What's that?" his father said.

Abbas spun around, pressing the umbrella to his chest. "What's what?"

His father pried the umbrella from his grip and pulled the rolled paper from its hollow. Palmyra leaf. Scanning it, his face darkened. The paper was packed tight with writing, wispy letters hanging off horizontal bars.

"Marathi," his father said in a dead whisper.

"We don't know what it says."

His father rolled the note and pushed it back into the tiger's mouth. He grabbed his shawl from the shelf and wound it around the umbrella.

Abbas trotted after him, down the street. "Let me keep it for him, he'll be back any moment."

His father quickened his pace. "Who is he to you? No one."

"He is my friend!" Abbas cried after his father, uncertain if this was true, if Khwaja Irfan would've said the same.

His father stepped off the street, not looking Abbas in the eye as he cupped the back of Abbas's neck and pulled him in as if for an embrace.

"Do you want to live," he said quietly, "or do you want friends?"

The question, the touch—these stunned Abbas. He shut his eyes against a world that was forcing him to choose.

Without another word, his father walked away, clutching the umbrella like a weapon that might go off in his own hands.

Du Leze walks out of the palace in confident strides, Abbas lagging behind at a respectful distance. The sky is sullen with cloud. A sky he nearly lost.

Halfway down the stone path, the Frenchman halts to sniff a brilliant red rose. "I am sorry you lost your friend," he murmurs into the flower.

Abbas says nothing, reluctant to admit that such a friendship ever existed.

"But," says Du Leze, dipping his nose into another bloom, "you would do well to forget him now."

"Yes, Musa Sahab."

"My name is not Musa." A smile plays at the corner of the Frenchman's mouth. "I have not had the pleasure of parting the Red Sea."

"But the padshah called you Musa."

"He means *Monsieur.* It is a French term of respect. My name is Lucien Du Leze."

Abbas nods. "Moosa Loosen Doo Leez Sahab."

"Never mind, Sahab is fine. Come along."

Once they have reached the sandstone arch, Du Leze stops and exhales, as if relieved to have put distance between himself and Tipu Sultan. He turns to Abbas. "This project will require long hours of work, so I propose you to spend your nights here."

"*Inside* the palace, Sahab? With the padshah?"

"Ah, he rarely comes out here. Only to entertain foreigners. But the unveiling will be held on these grounds, so we must stay until the finish. Now I wish you to go and inform your family and return before the gate is closed."

Abbas consents with a small bow and turns to leave.

"One other thing," says Du Leze. "The spinning device beneath the platform—who taught you to make that?"

"Taught me, Sahab? No one taught me."

"Not your father?"

Abbas shakes his head. "Was it wrong?"

"Not at all." The Frenchman regards Abbas with new interest. "Hurry home, now."

Abbas dips his head, takes his leave.

Du Leze lingers, watching the boy run through the arch, pale soles flashing. He touches the side of his patka, where a slim silver flask lies in wait against his waist. Only a fool would risk a sip in the padshah's garden, eyes on all sides, the relief purely temporary.

But then, he has made foolish decisions in his life. He hopes Abbas is not one of them.

Two weeks ago, Tipu Sultan invited Du Leze to take a look at Zubaida Begum's moving toys, which had been confiscated from the zenana. It was unlikely, said Tipu, that the woodworker's boy had been involved in the plot; unlikely, or rather, just likely enough to warrant killing him off. A way of tying up loose ends.

"Unless you think he's worth keeping around, to help you with the automaton." Tipu handed Du Leze the running tiger. "That one is very fine, is it not?"

Du Leze turned the toy over, squinting at the screws and stacked discs, and wondered why he had agreed to make the automaton at all. (Not that Tipu had given him much of a choice, he being the only clockmaker at court.) In Paris, he'd made several, alongside a partner he'd worked with for decades, their history so deep each could read the other's thoughts. And now Du Leze was to choose a new partner, a stranger, fluent in the local figurative style. He had planned to ask around, to study the work of different artisans and then choose the best, but that was before Tipu put a boy's life in his hands. A boy of promise. A boy of seventeen. The precise age when Du Leze's own skills had begun to take wing, such that he could finally make a watch without assistance from his master.

In that moment, Du Leze almost wished the boy had colluded

with the eunuch. At least then, Du Leze could have put his own conscience aside.

"Well?" said Tipu. "Is it any good?"

Du Leze set down the tiger toy—praying the promise it held would bear out—and called it the work of a born master.

Most of the way home, Abbas keeps his gaze on the ground, occasionally stepping out of the path of a two-wheeled cart. The silk pouch, hidden beneath his turban, jostles atop his head. Blood money, an almost unbearable weight.

How will he explain to his family the meaning of *l'automate*? He knows he should be practicing, trying to summon the right words.

How could he draw . . . the form . . . of a sigh?

These are the only words that come to him.

He has been reciting the poem to himself ever since Khwaja Irfan's final visit. A woman wrote those lines. A woman who might be dead. He did not need to ask Tipu Sultan about her; everyone knew how Zubaida Begum was taken away, imprisoned in one of Tipu's newly named forts. And yet Abbas keeps murmuring her poem from time to time, as if it has taken up residence in his rib cage, where it flutters and stills and flutters again.

He pauses in the same spot where his father had hugged him close. He can still feel the pressure at the back of his neck.

Who is he to you? his father had said.

To his father, Khwaja Irfan was the two-faced eunuch who nearly got his boy thrown in the dungeon.

To Abbas, Khwaja Irfan was the one who said: *She is a poet, an artist. Like you.* And something thus far unseen had risen in Abbas, some want given witness.

His mind teeming, he walks straight into someone who says: "Careful."

The voice is that of Khwaja Irfan, or so it seems to Abbas for one miraculous moment.

But no, he realizes it's only the Soul, a local addict who shuffles from place to place, muttering to himself. The Soul, they call him, because his body has grown so wasted and wraithlike he may as well ascend already. Normally Abbas would hold his nose and edge past, but the Soul pins him in place with a statement:

"They chain your arms and put you in water up to your chin."

"Who?" Abbas asks, though he can already see the answer: Khwaja Irfan, panting for air, water lapping at his lower lip. Abbas shakes his head but the image remains, it will forever remain.

The Soul says, "Watch your step," and then wanders away.

In his wake, the sky seems to whiten and the very air over the road wavers from the heat, like the air over the forge, where metal is made and unmade.

And which will he be, Abbas wonders, dread rolling over him.

Made or unmade?

It is a well-known fact that of Tipu Sultan's many children, the one he loves best is Muiz-ud-din.

Muiz is five years old. His skin is fair as his father's, his eyes as wide and limpid, possessing the spirit and authority of a born monarch.

His older brother Abdul Khaliq is considered a bit less impressive. Not just because of his dark skin or his full lips or even his flattish nose; no, the problem has something to do with his doleful countenance, as if he's always on the verge of apologizing.

A prince should not make apologies, Tipu believes. Nor should a king. So Tipu did not apologize to his boys when surrendering them to Lord Cornwallis two years before, after the humiliating defeat at Bangalore. Cornwallis had demanded the boys as collateral, in case Tipu failed to hold to the terms of the peace treaty.

No Western artist was present at the moment when Tipu bade his sons goodbye, yet the scene was rendered a dozen times over by Western artists, in immense and inaccurate detail, reproduced in prints and engravings. Here was beautiful Muiz, stepping away from the gaggle of distraught brown men toward the orderly ranks of white men, Muiz's own hand growing whiter in Cornwallis's palm.

Where Abdul was included, he, too, received a whitening treatment, and so stepped the nation out of barbary, at least temporarily.

Now it is 1794, and the boys have been returned to Mysore, due to Tipu's good behavior and his timely payment of one crore and sixty lakhs, a sum extracted as tribute from the people of Mysore, many of whom, unable to submit to this "mandatory gift," have fled to neighboring districts.

What the boys saw and did in Madras, under Cornwallis's care, they have not said. Not that Tipu is asking. Expressing curiosity in this matter is out of the question, as is saying thank you. Did Tipu's own father offer thanks after Tipu, age sixteen, led Haidar Ali's forces into the Carnatic and besieged Ambur? No, he did not. It's not for the father to say thank you to the son; it is for the son to say: *Anything else I can do, Father?*

Still, Tipu is not his father. He would like to express his appreciation with a gift the likes of which his sons have never seen. (Unlike the unimaginative palanquin that Cornwallis sent back with them, which Tipu stored, still wrapped, in the deepest reaches of his vault.) The tiger automaton will be a gift of such grandeur and ferocity that it will silence all memory of the boys' exile.

And what does Abbas know of all this, of what is riding on the success of the automaton? Very little, which is perhaps as it should be. Let him sleep in the soft splendor of the palace; let him dream of flutists climbing out the mouths of live tigers. He has much to learn. For now, let him be.

III

Abbas wakes in a panic: he has no idea where he is. After the answer dawns on him—the Frenchman's suite in the Summer Palace—another panic: he has no idea where to urinate.

A quick investigation leads him to a lidded pot beneath the bed. He has heard that the wealthy relieve themselves in dishware. Until now, he has never believed it.

He sets down the pot in the center of the room. It is smooth and white, ceramic. He removes the lid to find inside the cartoon portrait of an English soldier, palms raised on either side of his frantic, pig-nosed, about-to-be-peed-upon face. On the inner wall of the bowl is a small sculpted frog, a baffling ornament until Abbas realizes this is where he's meant to aim.

After drowning the piggy Englishman (which, truth be told, does prove pleasing), Abbas closes the lid and wonders where to deposit the contents. The bowl has a handle. Presumably someone else will be grasping that handle—a mortifying thought. He slides the covered pot under his bed.

Once dressed and groomed, he stands in the middle of the room, not sure which way is the Qibla. He looks around for any sign. Junaid would say the direction in which one prays doesn't matter so long as the intention is genuine and one's mind isn't wandering. But Abbas's mind has a tendency to flit, and this is just one of his problems—so says Junaid—this is why Abbas lacks true piety.

Abbas unfurls his mat and faces the jaali-carved window. It fills with pink light, accompanied by the purest adhan he has ever heard, recited by a muezzin who must have the direct ear of Allah. And yet he misses being shoulder to shoulder with his brothers, the crack of Junaid's knees, their father's perpetual throat clearings, and there his mind goes again, flitting.

After prayer, there is a stirring outside his door. He cracks it open and peers into the sitting room.

The Frenchman's door is closed. An embroidered white cloth has been spread over the carpet, set with an array of bronze bowls, one filled with fresh water. Abbas lowers himself onto a cushion embellished with the golden figures of two dancing girls. He drinks from the rim of the water bowl and waits for Du Leze to emerge so they can eat together. Or should he eat in his own room, apart from the Frenchman? The rice is steaming hot, laden with ghee. In a fit of hunger, he swipes two handfuls of rice and rearranges the heap to appear untouched. "Know your place," his mother warned him before he left. "Don't go getting a swelled turban."

At last Du Leze opens his door and halts in the threshold. He is wearing a different set of silk pyjamas, the jama buttoned beneath his left arm in the Muslim style. Neat from the neck down, everything above has a crushed appearance: chaotic white hair, gloomy bags beneath the eyes.

"The boy from yesterday, is it?" says Du Leze, squinting.

"Abbas."

"Abbas." Du Leze scratches his stubbled cheek. "You slept in that room?"

"You told me to, Sahab."

"I remember," says the Frenchman, a bit defensively. Slowly he lowers one knee down onto the sheet. "You have eaten, yes?"

Du Leze leans across the food to rinse his hands in the bowl of water, which apparently is not for drinking.

"Sahab is not eating breakfast?"

Du Leze produces a silver flask whose clear liquid he pours into a cup of lukewarm coffee. This he stirs with his pinky and downs in three gulps, then shudders. "Breakfast," he says, then grabs the bowl of nuts. "Lunch."

Abbas wonders whether he should mention that Tipu Sultan recently abolished the consumption of alcohol, along with other intoxicants like white poppy and hemp. Surely a man like Du Leze, so fluent in Kannada, would be fluent in the rules?

Before Abbas can decide whether to open his mouth, Du Leze hoists himself up. "Much to do, *tak tak,* let's go."

Abbas follows a few paces behind as Du Leze leads them through corridors and across a courtyard. Arriving at a trim, lime-washed shed, Du Leze pushes a sliding door along a horizontal rail, allowing a trapped bird to fly out.

Of all the rooms Abbas has entered over the past two days, this—the workshop of Lucien Du Leze—is the one that steals his breath.

The walls bristle with tools, at least three of every kind and size, veiner and saw and adze and ax, gouges so small and with so many different tips that he cannot predict what all they can do. Nor does he know what to do with himself in their presence, what to touch first or not touch at all. A bouquet of long wooden planks is arranged in a bin. A lathe awaits. And on one of the two tables rests a great mass of wood, stripped of its bark and propped sideways.

Abbas runs his eyes over everything, pausing over an extraordinary contraption consisting of a flat wooden table over a little iron seat. Strung vertically through the center of the table is a serrated blade as long as a man's arm, as slim as a fingernail. Abbas approaches with care, as if the instrument might at any moment come to life.

"A mechanical scroll saw," says Du Leze, proudly. "I made it myself—but let us not get distracted."

Du Leze summons him to a table where an open notebook lies flat, a sharpened stick in the gutter. *"Un stylo,"* says Du Leze, brandishing the sharpened point, the rest of the graphite rod sheathed in wood. Abbas is still examining the *stylo* when Du Leze sets the rifle from yesterday on the table. *"Alors,"* says Du Leze, pointing to the ornament of the tiger and soldier, "see if you can draw this from the left side."

Abbas chokes the *stylo* between his fingers. He looks for as long as he can at the ornament, before setting the nib to paper. A few inquiring strokes turn to supple lines. The grain of the paper hums through his fingertips as the drawing grows into an image not of his design, yet somehow becoming his own.

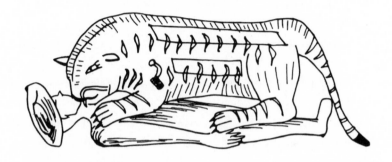

Finished, Abbas sits back, returns the *stylo* to the gutter, awaits praise.

Hastily Du Leze draws atop the sketch, explaining how the tiger will be hollow, with a bellows in the head and a pipe organ in the body. A lateral slice just above the tiger's ears will create a sort of lid, which, when removed, will expose the organ pipes. A door along its rib cage will open onto a set of ivory keys, to be operated by an organ player poised by the tiger's left flank.

"Where shall we hide?" Abbas asks.

"Why would we hide?"

"So as to make the growling sounds from inside the tiger."

"No, I told you, the bellows—" Du Leze waves a hand. "It will take too long to explain. You work on the outside, and leave the inside to me."

With a folding ruler, Du Leze chalks the dimensions of the automaton onto the great mass of wood. Abbas passes a hand over the slab. The grain is tight and consistent, the wood spongy, slightly leached of its juices, though not so much that it will crack at the first tap.

"And you," says Du Leze, handing the chalk to Abbas, who roughs the outline of the Tiger and the Soldier, making sure to stay well within Du Leze's markings. Here is the anvil of the head, the line of a haunch, the sweep of the belly, the bulb of the muzzle, the bend of a limb. He is shaky at first, but the more he draws, the steadier his hand. After they check all the measurements five times, Du Leze goes to his table. "Now I shall begin on the organ."

"And me, Sahab?"

Du Leze shrugs as if the answer is obvious. "Now you make the tiger."

Abbas tries to ignore the little lunge in his stomach as he goes to the wall of tools. His eye leaps from one to the next, dizzy with chisels, drawing a blank. He stands very still, bewildered by every second that goes by in which he has still done nothing.

"Abbas," says Du Leze. "Come here a moment."

With a sigh, Abbas joins Du Leze by the scroll saw.

Du Leze gestures with his pipe. "Pluck it. Pluck the blade."

Abbas plucks the long, thin blade. It pings, vibrating.

"If the blade is too tight, it will snap," says Du Leze. "If the blade is too loose, it will snap. It must have the proper tension. *Tu vois?*"

"You want me to use the scroll saw?"

"No, no. I am saying you must hurry up slowly. It's something my papa used to say—the only useful advice he ever gave me. *Festina lente.*"

The phrase makes little sense to Abbas, but by the time he has returned to the wall of tools, the fear has slightly loosened its hold, to the point where he can bring himself to take one of the larger gouges off the wall, its curved bit the width of his thumb. He holds the tool up to examine the handle, fine and ferruled, in perfect alignment with the tang. Next he selects a round-headed mallet, fixed tight in its handle. These tools are superior to any he has used before, but, as he well knows, the tools do not make the carver.

Armed, he approaches the mass of wood, and before he can be paralyzed once more, he studies the drawing and begins where he always begins: at the highest point. He knocks the mallet onto the chisel. Another knock, and another, the blows firm but few.

The wood begins to lose its anonymity. He learns its fragrance and grain. Straightening the chisel, he knocks toward what he imagines to be a tiger, waiting to be unleashed.

He is angling the frontal portion of the tiger, someday to be the sweeping curve of the tiger's downturned neck, when he hears a wondrous thing.

There is Du Leze, seated at the scroll saw, pedaling his feet beneath the tiny table. Its long arm is pecking at impossible speed, the thin blade moving up and down while Du Leze feeds it a slab of blond wood. Abbas goes closer, forgetting to put down his tools, watching how the shavings fly from the iron wheels, how another arm knocks beneath the table, how the slab is being sliced as simply as bread.

Du Leze stops pedaling: the scroll saw goes still. He holds up a slim rectangle. *"Joli, n'est-ce pas?"*

Abbas is awestruck. He would give anything to try it himself. Before he can ask, Du Leze resumes his pedaling.

At noon, Abbas steps outside to pray. He half expects Du Leze to join him, the Frenchman having assimilated in most other ways, but Du Leze doesn't look up from his work, does not even seem to hear the muezzin. He is pressing a ruler to a vast swath of paper, his pencil zipping straight lines into some mysterious diamond-like design.

Afterwards lunch is served in the courtyard, where a white sheet has been spread for them. The grass springs up soft beneath his soles. This time Abbas washes his hands in the proper bowl, wondering what about the water makes it feel like wealth itself.

Du Leze, meanwhile, is sitting on a low stool some distance

away from the sheet. He is holding a pale piece of hide up to the sky, frowning.

Abbas's stomach rumbles with longing for the beef flecked with coconut, the swirled nests of idiyappam. He watches Du Leze, who seems to have no idea that lunch is being served, or that Abbas is waiting for him.

"*Dommage,*" Du Leze mutters. "This hide has too many thin spots. Thin spots leak air and tear easily . . ." He looks up at Abbas. "You are waiting for me?"

Abbas nods in earnest.

With a sigh, Du Leze drapes the hides over his stool and joins him on the sheet. Abbas serves them both, but once again, Du Leze begins with his flask, which he tips into a glass of guava juice. In one go, he drinks the liquid down and closes his eyes, his face filling with ease. "I paid good money for those sheepskins."

Abbas speaks around a mouthful. "What are they for, Sahab?"

For the grunt pipe, Du Leze explains, a thing that will work like a bellows, emitting the tiger's sounds from within the head. "The hide will form the sides, but thin spots leak air, you see, and will compromise the sound. The French word for animal comes from the Latin *animus,* meaning breath. So of course, the appearance of the tiger itself should be striking, but it is sound that gives the impression of life. Ah! Is that dragon fruit? I adore dragon fruit."

"Sahab—" Abbas hesitates as Du Leze bites into a gleaming white slice. "Is it true that you are the greatest inventor in France?"

Du Leze scoffs. "Of course not."

Both of them pause, as if suddenly aware that this answer implies dishonesty on the part of Tipu Sultan.

"I was sent by His Majesty Louis XVI," Du Leze clarifies. "I came along with the three envoys from Mysore. You have heard of them?"

Abbas nods. Another subject to walk carefully around, in these surroundings.

(A brief word about the royal envoys: Tipu Sultan had sent three noblemen to Paris, with the command that they should bring back a variety of French artisans and engineers, gardeners and physicians, makers of porcelain, glass, clocks, weapons, wool, and, most important of all, the promise of a political alliance. Instead the envoys returned from France with a porcelain hookah and Du Leze. It is said that Tipu flew into a rage, for he had hookahs galore; what he'd wanted was an alliance and artisans to help him start a porcelain manufactory. Wisely, one of the envoys fled Mysore. The other two, Akbar Ali Khan and Muhammad Ousman Khan, accepted Tipu's invitation to go for a walk in the garden, where he had them killed, and word was spread throughout Mysore that all three had betrayed their sovereign.)

"They betrayed their sovereign," says Abbas.

"So I hear. I found them quite dignified." Abbas watches Du Leze stroke the underside of his chin with the back of his fingers, a contemplative gesture. "I had planned to stay in Mysore for one month only. But then . . . things became complicated in my country."

"Complicated?"

"War."

Abbas strokes his own whiskerless chin in imitation of Du Leze. "Here, we are always at war."

"That is Mysore at war with others. This is France at war with France. The king and queen were thrown in prison, the palace invaded . . ."

"By who?"

"The people of Paris."

"Common people?"

"*Insurgés.* But my friends in Paris tell me a new order is beginning. One that will give power to the class in-between."

"The class in-between?"

Du Leze stacks his palms, opening and closing them until giving up with a frustrated, "Oof, never mind. Blaque says peace is coming."

"Blaque is the new king?"

"Ha!" Du Leze flashes a smile. "He does think highly of himself. But no. He was my student at one time. Now he is my business partner, a very gifted clockmaker himself."

Du Leze curbs himself from saying more, for there is only so much Abbas needs to know. He does not need to know, for example, that Blaque is ten years younger and ten centimeters shorter than Du Leze. Or that Blaque eats raw garlic every morning and claims this to be the reason he rarely catches cold. That he has a birthmark on the inside of his thigh. That he sneezes in threes. That he denies all eye contact when he is angry with someone, which Du Leze finds effectively hurtful. None of this is of any concern to Abbas. Du Leze plucks a dried apricot from a bowlful.

"Have you tried these? They are from the Sultan of Room."

Abbas takes a bite of the apricot while Du Leze watches for his reaction.

"Nice, eh?" says Du Leze.

Abbas nods. As nice as gnawing on a sugary bit of shoe.

Du Leze reaches into the other side of his patka—a garment of surprising nooks and crannies—and removes a solid silver disc. He thumbs a button on the side of the disc, causing a door to flip open. Without trespassing into the Frenchman's space, Abbas strains to see what is within.

"L'horloge," says Du Leze extending his palm, in which the object fits snugly. "It tells time, like the sundial atop the mosque, but with much greater accuracy."

Abbas studies the circular arrangement of black markings against a white face. Two lines extend from the center of the clock, one line longer than the other, and a third, fine as an eyelash, marches haltingly around the circle.

But how can it move without someone to move it? Abbas wonders.

As if anticipating the question, Du Leze turns the watch around and flips open another door, exposing a series of delicate golden gears turning against one another. They churn of their own accord, teeth fitting perfectly into gaps. How strange that this is the side being concealed, when the back is far more wondrous than the front.

"I made a clock like this for Tipu," says Du Leze. "Between you and me, this one is better."

"How so, Sahab?"

"More precise, more elegant. Blaque made it, you see. He is good to me." Du Leze tilts his head quizzically. "Good to me?"

"Better than me."

"Better than me, *oui*."

Du Leze gazes into the clockface, as if reading a story inscribed by the ticking hands. "In January I came to Mysore. In July Paris fell."

"Bad timing," says Abbas.

Du Leze looks up with a surprised laugh. Abbas beams, proud of having prompted it.

IV

The next three days proceed without calamity.

During this period, Abbas learns that there are two versions of Du Leze. The preferable version tends to surface sometime after noon, following the second dose of "breakfast," when the Frenchman's cheeks turn rosy and his eyes take on a glassy shine. The less preferable Du Leze, pale and puffy-eyed, grunts by way of greeting.

He always starts the day by sketching in his little book, his pipe clamped between his back teeth. The pipe—never lit during work hours—seems crucial to his process, as is the *stylo*. Abbas can spy little else from his own table. He wishes to go closer, to see what Du Leze is sketching in that notebook with such furious concentration. And why is he slicing the leather into those wide bands? Why is he folding them back and forth into narrow fans? Now he is clamping the fans with little vises, maybe to train them to hold their folds. But what are the fans for?

"Pas de temps à perdre!" says Du Leze, when he catches Abbas staring. "Back to work."

Abbas returns his attention to the block of wood. It's still something of a stranger to him, this piece of tree, something he is coming to know through continued conversation. And as with any conversation between strangers, their talk begins tentatively. Tap of mallet against wood, loosening forefinger and thumb, gaining speed as he goes, wood chips shooting this way and that as he dissolves into the work, until he is no longer a toymaker serving Tipu Sultan. He is wood and mallet and chisel. A nutty aroma rises from the flesh of the wood, its surface as dappled as windblown water.

All is going well until a beastly grunt rips through the silence, a sound so ragged and unnatural it makes his mallet slip, his chisel skidding—

Pain rakes the back of his wrist. And there: a white gash as long as his thumb, welling thickly with blood. Du Leze is hurrying over, yelling in French. *"Ta main! Que t'est-il arrivé?"* Blood throbs warmly down the wrist.

"I heard something . . ." Abbas murmurs, his vision populated with tiny black points.

And now Du Leze is wrapping his red patka around the gash, then walking Abbas to the wall, then instructing him to sit down and keep his hand raised. Du Leze stands, scratching the back of his head. His jama floats ghostly around his form. "Sahab," Abbas says dimly, "your patka . . ."

"That can be replaced, unlike your hand."

"What was that sound?"

"Quoi? The pipe?"

From his worktable, Du Leze brings over a box with a curved lid. On the bottom of the box is a bellows, attached by fan-folded pieces of hide. With two fingers, Du Leze presses up on the underside of the bellows. The box emits a throaty grunt, the same as Abbas heard moments before. "It is this you heard," says Du Leze. "This box will go inside the tiger's head."

"Once more," says Abbas, amazed.

Du Leze presses the bellows: a tiger grumbles.

"It is a kind of pipe," says Du Leze, exposing the open end of the box, through which Abbas can see a thin wall separating the hollow into two uneven chambers. "I should have warned you."

Abbas looks down: his blood freckles the floor. A memory runs through his mind, someone, maybe a cousin, lifting him up to show where a tiger had sharpened its claws on a tree trunk, a frenzy of gashes, each one deep enough to fit two fingers.

Abbas winces as Du Leze peels back the fabric, tiny threads clinging to raw flesh. "Too deep," says Du Leze, exhaling through his nose. "I shall have to sew you back together."

Abbas hopes something in that sentence has been lost in translation.

Moments later, Du Leze is threading a needle over a bowl of water.

Abbas looks until the very last minute, then screws his eyes shut. The first piercing makes him cringe, though he finds his breath eventually. More unsettling than the pain is the sound of being sewn, the needle whispering through the fabric of himself, the wound sealed in neat white stitches.

"Finished," says Du Leze, setting the bowl of bloodied water aside. "You will need to rest it for a week."

"But who will finish the tiger, Sahab?" Another question occurs to him with a touch of panic: "Am I to be replaced?"

Du Leze rubs the back of his neck, a pained expression on his face. "If I dismissed you now, I fear you would not be going home." Before Abbas can ask where else he would go, Du Leze supplies the answer: "Perhaps to the dungeon. Or worse."

Abbas flinches; surely he has misheard. "What for—what have I done?"

"For making effigies. For conspiring with a traitor. Did you not hear your king?"

"But I was released—he rewarded me—"

"He rewarded your father. About you, he is undecided."

Abbas looks to the grindstone. Just this morning, he'd thought himself lucky, for he hadn't nicked the blade in days.

"Rest your hand for a time," says Du Leze. "Then we can decide."

. . .

For the next five days, Du Leze forbids Abbas from gripping any tool with his wounded hand. In that time, Abbas tries to make himself useful, accepting every simple task, however tedious. Snipping a piece of leather. Carving screws. He is determined to do anything—even transport the Frenchman's piss pot—to prevent himself from being replaced (or worse), and to learn what he can along the way.

Eventually Du Leze seems to grow used to Abbas's presence and even narrates his own actions. He explains, for example, how a wooden cogwheel and its four iron vanes will be mounted in the tiger's neck, and how the cogwheel will be driven by the worm gear on the crank, and how the four vanes will engage the lifting piece of the grunt pipe.

When Abbas pretends to understand what a worm gear is, Du Leze sucks his teeth with all the tetchiness of a local. "You learn nothing from nodding along, yes? If you do not understand, then ask. Learn."

And so Abbas begins to ask and ask. Astonishingly, the Frenchman's patience extends without end. Rather than sucking his teeth at a question, Du Leze simply reaches for his sketchbook. He cannot translate the exact terms for *reciprocator* and *spill valve, crankshaft* and *connecting rod,* but what he lacks in language he makes up for in his detailed schematics.

Abbas will always remember this time, the daily ferment and thrill of learning. Still, much remains mysterious. Whenever he verges on grasping a concept—the motion of a cam and lever, for example—Du Leze complicates the picture with two more mechanical additions, and once again, whatever Abbas has begun to understand sinks into darkness.

"You cannot learn everything in a week," says Du Leze, after finding Abbas bent over a sketch, trying to decode a crankshaft. "Young men study for years."

Abbas looks up at him, full of hope.

"Regretfully," says Du Leze, taken aback, "I plan to leave soon."

"How soon, Sahab?"

"In a few months. Back to Paris."

"But the war?"

"The war can kiss my left buttock."

Abbas is perplexed by this imagery.

"War or no war," says Du Leze, "my life is there."

That night, Abbas flops from side to side in the bed. He has not yet grown accustomed to sleeping on a mattress above the floor. He prefers the pallet at home, on the verandah, surrounded by the snores of his brothers, both of whom refuse to believe they snore at all. ("Prove it," says Farooq, the more empirical of the two.) For a time Abbas stares at the opposite wall, where the jaali-carved window has made a puzzle of the moonlight.

His agitation, he knows, has nothing to do with the mattress or the silence. It is something else, a sense of indignation, of incompletion, something left unsaid or undone, crowding out the air in his lungs. *My life is there.* What about my life? Abbas thinks, then chides himself, for he has a life, one he would have been happy to return to the week before, if that had been an option.

Yet something has shifted in him, the emergence of some new possibility, a future of making more than toys and figurines. Is it the effect of living in the Summer Palace, of witnessing the grandeur of so much sky? Of gazing out at the horizon and wondering what lies beyond that line?

There was a time when the figurines were more than enough, full of accidental discoveries and discarded failures, and sometimes delight. The best ones he gave to Farooq, who was twelve at the time, Abbas two years behind, so close in both age and mind that Abbas usually knew what Farooq was thinking. Farooq had favored the animal figurines, including a goat, a peacock, an elephant, and a crocodile, each one more refined than the last. He'd lined them up against the wall by his pallet and talked to them in the dark. But when Abbas brought him a human figurine—a small wooden boy— Farooq fell quiet, turning the boy in his fingers.

Abbas had been expecting his brother's eyes to widen at the peculiar life-likeness of the face, which had come as some surprise to

Abbas. The refinement of the nose, the symmetry of each eye. Even the smirk. He'd been so proud of the wooden boy he'd almost wanted to keep it, to remind himself of what he was capable of doing.

But Farooq had no compliments. His gaze was fixed yet distant, as if seeing something in the figurine that Abbas could not.

"Did you want something different?" Abbas asked.

Farooq said finally: "I want what you have."

Then Farooq returned the wooden boy, which Abbas threw away, embarrassed and somehow guilty. A few days later, all the figurines were gone from the wall where they'd stood. Farooq had given them to some neighborhood children who were younger, he said, and more suited to playing with toys.

At the time, it had seemed to Abbas a thankless response. Now he understands. What Farooq told him that day is precisely what Abbas would say to Du Leze, if he could muster the honesty. *I want what you have.*

In the morning, at the workshop, Abbas allows Du Leze to snip him free of the stitches with a small pair of scissors. The scab is a fresh pink. Du Leze covers it with gauze.

Abbas goes immediately to work on the tiger, knowing he has no more time to spare. The surface is all dappled, a bloated shape, like a great beast trapped in a bag. He takes up the mallet and chisel, wincing at the sting.

As the day goes on, he stops himself from glancing over at whatever Du Leze is doing. He trains his mind on the task at hand, whether the shaping of an ear or the honing of the muzzle. This, and only this, is his business.

Usually, when the workday is done, Du Leze reads his books or writes letters while Abbas takes a simple meal in his room. Afterwards Abbas prays, then prepares for an early bedtime.

But on this evening, Du Leze calls Abbas into the sitting room. Du Leze is in the teak armchair, a thick red book in his lap. "From now on," he says, "we will spend every evening in tutelage."

"Tutelage, Sahab?"

"I mean to teach you French. Then, after I am gone, you can teach yourself a great deal from the books I intend to leave you. I have a fine translation of Turiano's treatise on the Mechanical Monk—that one was completed sometime in the late sixteenth century—as well as a good horology book. Good to start with, anyway. If you can begin to understand clockwork, a whole world will open up to you. The Silver Swan *par exemple,* that one is all clockwork beneath the feathers and fine finish." Du Leze stops. "Why are you so quiet?"

"You mean to leave me books, Sahab?"

"Just two, yes. I cannot bring them all back to France."

Abbas hardly knows how to respond, what words could befit the magnitude of the gift. He has never owned a book in his life. He learned his letters in a slate of sand.

"I have here *Contes de ma mère l'Oye.*" Du Leze holds up the book, displaying a cover with letters of gleaming gold. "King Louis had sent it with me as a gift to Tipu, but Tipu found it too silly. It is called Tales of a . . . a mother called Goose."

"A female goose?"

"No, it is a woman *called* Goose Mother. A human woman."

Abbas and Du Leze blink at one another, daunted by the chasm between languages.

"*Alors,* shall we?" says Du Leze.

Abbas takes the settee and receives the tome into his lap. The language will not come easily to him, but he will long remember lifting the cover for the first time and inhaling the fragrance that escapes these pages, like the summoning breath of France itself.

V

One morning, Du Leze awakes in the grip of a belligerent hang-over. The only cure—more wine—is in the armoire, but upon opening the doors and sorting the bottles (empty, empty) he can only curse himself. Some vinegary stuff trickles pitifully down his gullet.

Set on replenishing his stock, he dresses quickly in a jama and patka. The mirror on the door confronts him with his reflection. Generally he prefers not to look until noon, if he must look at all, for looking always provokes the same question: *What happened to you?* He is fifty-seven years old, all the ease chiseled from his face. He grins experimentally, and there he is, the old gap-toothed rake, or some of him anyway. Blaque was the first person who claimed to like the gap between his two front teeth. Not just like. *I miss dipping my tongue in it,* he wrote. That was in Paris. Blaque's recent letters have been dry as chalk, mindful of Tipu's spies and censors, though the last contained a little sketch of a gap-toothed smile.

That letter arrived one year ago, along with a bottle of Arma-gnac. Nothing since.

Hastily dressed, Du Leze passes through the sitting room. Abbas has already finished breakfast. Now he sits in the armchair, examin-ing an illustration from *The Tales of Mother Goose.*

They abandoned the book after the first session, when Du Leze realized that more progress could be made through simple words and phrases, which could be stacked to build sentences. *Bonjour. Bonsoir. Quel est votre nom? Bonne nuit.* Now Du Leze wonders whether he was too ambitious with his predictions—Turiano and the rest of it. But who knows what the boy is capable of with that dogged cast of mind, that set to his jaw?

Abbas looks up. *"Bonne matin, monsieur."*

"I have errands to run," says Du Leze, helplessly rude on his way to the door. "You go on without me today."

"But, Sahab, we have only two weeks . . ."

"Work hard, then. I shall return shortly." Du Leze can feel the boy's frown follow him out the door.

Du Leze borrows a drowsy mare from the stable and deposits his empty bottles in the saddlebag. Together they clank along the narrow dirt road that leads to the French Rocks—the French cantonment at the foot of the Hirodi Hills.

The road curves around rain trees that offer passing shade, canopies fine as Brittany lace. Puddles glisten with last night's rain. At least the heat is not yet oppressive, he thinks, until he emerges from the tree cover and into the sunless white heat; in minutes, a pond of sweat collects in the small of his back. The horse stumbles from time to time, her neck as damp as his own.

Out here, there are few to no people. A woman in pink milking a cow. Another hacking at a fistful of plants with a long curved knife. A boy sitting on the grass, leaning back onto his palms, surrounded by four white buffalo in various states of browsing and rest. The boy stares at Du Leze, who tips his hat in passing, to no response.

An hour later the hills are before him, wind-polished boulders piled to peaks. Below them are rows upon rows of gray tents, sprouted and stolid as mushrooms.

After baiting his horse, Du Leze makes his way through the camp, breathing solely through his mouth, though there is no way of escaping the foulness in the air. "Where is the latrine?" Du Leze asked when he first visited so many years ago. "You're standing in it!" a soldier laughed. That was the moment Du Leze decided to limit his visits to the French Rocks.

He walks directly to a shed standing apart from the tents and hung with a sign that reads in Kannada and French: *For sale of spirituous liquors TO FRENCH ONLY.* The vendor, Gourcuff, is already engaged with a soldier, nodding periodically as the soldier declaims to the invisible masses: ". . . Just look what happened to our silk sellers! You can't get any better than Lyonnaise silk, my mother always said. But once the elite catches Indomania, it'll spread like the bloody flux, I promise you that. They'll be clamoring for *Indian* muslin, *Indian* cotton, and using Lyonnaise silk to wipe their arses! Maybe it's already happening, and we don't know because we're stuck on this rock, for God knows what reason . . ."

Du Leze plunks his empty bottles on the counter. The soldier is silenced by the sight of Du Leze's turban, jama, and sandals, the sum of which leads the soldier to utter softly, "Heaven help us."

"Good morning," says Du Leze to Gourcuff.

"Monsieur Du Leze," says Gourcuff, glancing over the bottles. "Are you drinking the stuff or bathing in it?"

"A private question for you," Du Leze says quietly. "You wouldn't happen to have any brandy squirreled away somewhere? Some personal stock of your own?"

"Do you see any vineyards behind me?"

"Imported, obviously. I would pay extra."

"I have cashew feni. Just arrived from Goa."

Reluctantly Du Leze settles for a bottle of palm wine and four bottles of feni.

"Have you met Lieutenant Laurent?" asks Gourcuff, retreating to the shelves. "Laurent, this is Monsieur Du Leze."

Du Leze nods quickly at Laurent, a sunburned fellow with bad teeth in a fine face. Du Leze is no mood for small talk. He cracks his knuckles to hide the trembling in his hands.

"Does Tipu make you wear that dress?" asks Laurent.

"By pain of death," says Du Leze, eyes forward. "But my knickers are pure Lyonnaise silk."

"Are you joking? Is he joking?" Laurent calls to Gourcuff, who is squatting among crates, tipping bottles to squint at the labels.

Du Leze puts his beating head in his hands. "My God, man, are you just now learning to read?"

"Don't mind him," Gourcuff tells Laurent. "Life at court has given him airs."

"Where are you from?" Laurent asks Du Leze.

"Rouen," he says eventually.

"So you're a Norman and Gourcuff is a Breton!" Laurent grins. "You know the one about—"

"The Norman baby and the Breton baby, yes."

"If you throw them both in the air, both will survive. The Breton because he's so hardheaded he'll bounce. And the Norman because he's so stingy his little fingers will grab the eaves."

Du Leze scowls at the man. "If you must know, I lived in Paris for twenty years, in the Marais."

"Ah, the Marais," Laurent says in a voice of longing. "I proposed to my wife on the promenade." He leans an elbow on the counter and heaves a sigh toward the sky. "*Oh là,* someday soon."

"Soon what?"

"I'll go back."

"I used to say the same. And here I am, five years later."

Laurent straightens. "I will. I mean it."

"No need to get hot. I intend to go back as well."

"You?" Laurent stares. "How?"

"By ship, same as anyone."

"But you can't."

Du Leze and Laurent frown at one another, as if they're no longer speaking the same language.

"What do you mean I can't?" Du Leze tries to sound cavalier. Gourcuff has arrived with an armful of bottles, which he sets upon the counter. "What the hell is he talking about?"

"How should I know, you sent me looking for your precious swill . . ."

Laurent speaks in the brisk, bloodless voice of a bureaucrat. "The Alien Act bars all nonmilitary emigrants from returning to France. Their assets have been confiscated, their property nationalized and sold. If an emigrant should return, the death penalty awaits him."

"Oh, that," says Gourcuff, unbothered. "You didn't know about that?"

Du Leze says no, he did not.

Gourcuff fills a small glass with milky palm wine. "You should come around more often, Du Leze. If you did, you'd know certain things. Me, I'm not worried. They can't keep track of every old bastard who ever left."

"They can," says Laurent. "There are lists of emigrants in every community across the nation, departments created just to keep track."

"I assure you, no one is keeping track of old Gourcuff. I'm not nearly that important."

At once, the two men look to Du Leze.

A surge of laughter at his back, a sharp whiff of piss. He is not going home, then. He has no home.

Gourcuff nudges the glass toward Du Leze, who takes a deep breath and drains what will be the first of many.

There is the France *dedans* and the France *dehors*. Of the latter, there are the emigrants and exiles and aliens, now lumped together by law. There are the ones who know everything about the situation back home, and there are the ones who know even more. And no one is better at arguing over the motherland—about priorities and policies and progress and its opposite—than those who are no longer in the motherland. From a distance, all becomes clear.

Except to Lucien Du Leze, who is standing atop the taller Hirodi Hill. From here, the edges of the world bend away from him, baffling.

It was a clumsy, drunken climb, Du Leze grasping at the tall grasses between boulders, willing himself to the top. The mare waits down below, laden with bottles. If only he'd lessened her load by taking one with him.

Now he pants with exhaustion, drenched in sweat. He massages his hands, which are raw from the climb. When he was a little boy, his father would sit across from him and crack each one of his knuckles, right hand then left. If Du Leze were to wince, his father would denounce him for being "thin-skinned," warning that if Lucien didn't stop whimpering he'd reacquaint him with the cane. And so Du Leze practiced the habit on his own time, on his own hands, so that he could meet his father's eye throughout the test without flinching.

As a youth, he apprenticed with his father, a bitter fellow who embittered anyone who worked for him. Quickly Du Leze outgrew his father's skills and moved on to work with other masters of clockmaking, yet some things he will never outgrow: his whole hot ear in his father's hand, hearing his own teeth rattle inside his head. All this, supposedly, for failing to fully clean a tool. Lucien knew there was some other reason, something about him that could ignite his father's fury at any time, whether the tools were clean or not.

He remembers Blaque, many years later, kissing his knuckles and saying, "It's still a disgusting habit, Lucien. Please stop."

Blaque. This is all his fault, really, for refusing to come along, for insisting on staying and supporting a doomed monarchy, and then a constitutional monarchy, and then, when there was no longer a monarch, going into hiding from whence he wrote letters devoid of humor and larded with quotations, as if meant to be read by a student of history some hundred years hence.

Duquesnoy says neither the magnates nor the brigands are the people. He says it is composed of the bourgeoisie, that throng of busy, virtuous men who are corrupted neither by opulence nor poverty; they truly are the nation, the people.

So Blaque had written in his last letter. To which Du Leze had wanted to reply: *If I wanted to hear from Duquesnoy, I would be fucking Dusquesnoy.*

And: *We are not the people he's talking about.*
But: *You are my person.*
Also: *More about my gap teeth.*

They had first met at a fête for the queen. She was wearing a headdress that Lucien had designed—a towering, cloudlike wig through which two blue bird automata flew in circles. Her charisma was such that she could be wearing a mob cap and still command the attention of a room. (Her eyes danced when meeting his, the same eyes, Lucien later heard, that scanned the mob when the executioner held up her severed head.) And there was a young man, standing by himself in private rumination, watching not the bird wig nor the queen. Who are you? Lucien thought, glimpsing Blaque that day. Who could be so self-contained?

Du Leze has written to mutual friends and yet has learned nothing of Blaque's whereabouts, has no idea if his beloved is alive or dead. Once—only once—at the height of his homesickness and heartache, did Lucien chance a quick fuck in his palace apartment. A courtier, compact in size, with a trowel-shaped face. Lucien then spent weeks in agony, certain he would be discovered, executed for those ten sweet minutes with the compact courtier, that gasp in the luminous dark.

And he had survived, but for what? How tiring it is, life in so foreign a land, where even time is subject to different rules, the day divided not by sixty-minute hours but twenty-four-minute ghatis. It took him a full year to comprehend, without making mental calculations, the meaning of *Come have dinner with me three ghatis after sunset.* And still so many ungraspable words, so many misinterpreted jokes. Most unbearable is being the joke, the clockmaker with bad timing, bereft of a home.

It seems to him now, from the top of the Hirodi Hill, that death is the only home still available to him.

He draws a parched breath and peers over the edge of a boulder. Far down below is a slab as flat as a headstone. He wonders how to engineer his fall so that his crown may meet with it.

· · ·

For hours, he paces the top of the hill, every so often approaching a different edge. Seated, he scoots to the verge and turns onto his side, lowering himself down the rockface. His feet find purchase in two different holds. He leans onto his elbows. He takes shallow, vigorous breaths. He scrambles back onto the flat surface and lies facedown on his forearms, the sun scorching the back of his neck. He feels weak, his muscles turned to curd.

A bee zips past his ear. He flinches, then snorts at the fact that his fear of bees exceeds his fear of death.

The bee returns to harass him. He rolls onto his side and swats the air, baffled when the bee becomes two, then three. And then he understands:

It is a swarm. There are hundreds of them.

Scrambling to his feet, he stumbles down into a crevice between rocks, cowering. A foolish move, he realizes. He has nowhere to go. He waits for the swarm to flow through the crevice and destroy him. Instead the black cloud hovers. He watches, frightened yet spellbound. The swarm seems a single sentient creature, filling every hollow of his body with its unearthly drone until he begins to wonder whether the drone contains a secret message intended for him.

"Blaque?" he whispers.

And then the swarm begins to thin, like veils drawn away, until, all at once, it departs.

Du Leze does not believe in ghosts or God-sent bees, in the sort of superstition that seems to govern the lives of every native he meets. The bees simply interrupted his mission to end his own life, just as he must have interrupted their migratory route, sending them into a frenzy. That is all, Du Leze thinks, blundering down the hill, a buzzing in his bones.

On horseback, he sobers. Next time, no dizzying cliffsides. Poison, perhaps, or a whetted blade across the wrists.

A voice in him says to wait, to consider the boy, Abbas, who is in no position to finish the automaton himself. What would it mean to abandon him now, to leave him a loose end? What does he owe a boy he has only just met?

Du Leze closes his eyes and tries to think. Surrenders to the rhythm of the horse, the rattle of the bottles. Imagines the aviary that once crowned the queen, those two birds tunneling into and out of her wig. He is certain it was destroyed, scavenged or burned along with his other creations. Why not, then, complete the tiger, and be survived by something of his making?

A few more weeks, this he can do. He can see the project through and then see himself out, in that order. At least he can try.

VI

To our dear son Abbas, peace be upon you and our Padshah Tipu Sultan.

We write in the hopes that you are in good health and good spirits. Are you? We have received no word in the weeks since you left home. No doubt you must be working hard and getting fat on palace food. We are grateful to Allah, blessed be His name, and to the Padshah and to the French Sahab for bestowing on you this honor.

Your mother says you should look into becoming a scribe while you are at the Summer Palace. She says it is simply a matter of asking around and if you don't ask around you will go nowhere. I would rather you come home. The shop is too quiet these days. Also Junaid's peacocks look like pelicans and as you know he does not take well to criticism.

We hope to see you soon. Until then, may Allah guide you and keep you safe.

Abba

After reading the letter, Abbas jots a quick response: *Everything fine, Abba. Very busy. Will come home soon. Your son Abbas.*

Du Leze agrees to send the letter for him, enclosed by his own seal. "I am sure this will be opened somewhere along the way," says Du Leze, blowing on the wax. "But more likely to reach your father."

After handing the letter to a servant, Du Leze leads the way to the workshop.

"And how are your parents?" Du Leze calls over his shoulder.

"They are well, Sahab."

"Are they worried about you?"

"As much as any parent, I suppose."

"There is no such thing as any parent," says Du Leze. "Only your own."

The silence expands between them. Abbas wonders if he has overstepped some personal boundary, though it was Du Leze who stepped first.

As they pass a monkey tail plant, Du Leze reaches out and runs his hands through the downy catkins, as if he and the flowers are on friendly terms.

"*En tout cas,*" he says, "tell them it will all be over soon."

All week at the workshop, Abbas stays later than Du Leze, sometimes dozing on his table, head in his arms, waking at the clatter of his chisel on the floor. And while he is pleased, overall, with the look of the tiger, at other times he feels estranged from the thing he is making, almost convinced of a dark energy pulsing from the grain. It happens once while he is inking the line of the tiger's brow. And again, after he removes the top half to sand the insides: he finds he can see out of the tiger's mouth, as if he is no more than a live meal in its belly.

In the evenings, Du Leze conducts the French lessons with patience and a glass of tea, never losing his temper. Abbas wonders whether all these slippery words will be of use someday. He lies awake, muttering the French he has learned from Du Leze, imagining a land that, curiously, has only one word for rain.

. . .

At least Abbas is proud of the tiger taking shape between his hands. Tigers he can do. They live in folktales and forests, in statues and paintings, everywhere and nowhere at once.

Of English soldiers, he knows little and feels less. The prospect of carving one worries him.

In any case, there is always more to do for the tiger: claws to be sharpened, limbs to be laminated, a tongue to shape and tuck into the mouth. And so he keeps perfecting the enemy he knows and putting off the one he doesn't.

Before embarking on the soldier, Abbas gains permission to view the murals along the inner walls of the palace, specifically the Battle of Pollilur.

Sketchbook in hand, he stands several steps back from the painting, his vision swimming with figures. Here are Haidar and Tipu, father and son calmly presiding over the violence from the backs of elephants. There is Colonel Baillie in a palanquin, biting his knuckle at the sight of his own powder tumbril exploding while the Mysorean cavalry swirl about, galloping on horseback, loosing arrows, plunging lances. Meanwhile the English forces are frozen in three tight rows, guns pointed this way and that. One of their severed heads lies on the grass.

After making his sketches, a guard escorts him out. Abbas runs his eyes over the carvings along columns and under jarokhas, all the wooden foliage that seems to grow from the walls. He is almost certain he knows which flowers were carved by his father, the ones whose petals are dimpled with three fine lines. Six years of his father's life were spent on the Summer Palace, and yet he has never seen it, and likely never will.

Halfway through the garden, Abbas catches sight of a nautch girl in white, dancing barefoot on the grass. He slows to a stop. He has seen folk dancers during festivals, women stepping lightly while palming small clay lamps, but no one so artful as the nautch girl.

He could reach her in three strides, if he dared. The tunnel of his vision narrows to her alone.

She moves with slow, somber deliberation, in keeping with Tipu's directives that the nautch girls refrain from wanton looks or movements. Her own look is one of boredom. It's not the dance she is bored with, but the guard, who is running his tongue over his sharpest tooth. Countless times he has silently tongued her while standing behind this or that guest of the palace. It's a gesture meant to disarm her, make her stumble or lose her composure. Little does he know she has borne butt grabs and cock adjustments and any number of humiliations while performing; little does he know that while she slowly sweeps a delicate, henna-red foot across the grass, she is mentally slashing his neck with a kitchen knife and hearing in her own ears the sound of him drowning in his blood.

Water gurgles serenely from a stone fountain.

She glances at the young guest, who nods briefly, as if embarrassed, and walks away.

Virgin, she thinks, turning slowly on the grass.

Only ten days remain: nowhere near enough time for Abbas to carve the soldier from a single piece of jackwood, as he did with the tiger. Instead he puzzles the soldier together from an assortment of blocks.

Abbas and Du Leze are in the midst of fitting the pipe hole in the mouth when someone raps a cane against the threshold of the workshop.

"Here you are, you rascal!" The man in the doorway doffs his hat to reveal a bald head hugged by a thin fringe of hair. "Hiding away from the world, no surprise."

Understanding little of the visitor's French, Abbas looks to Du Leze. Du Leze closes his eyes and sighs, as if hoping, by the time he opens his eyes, the visitor will be gone. "My dear Martine," says Du Leze, "what brings you away from the forges?"

"Oh, don't play the dotard—you invited me!" Martine hangs his hat upon the lathe.

Du Leze knows Martine only slightly, both men having trained at the same horology school in Paris. But where Du Leze pursued a career in clocks, Martine switched to engineering, and has been serving in Tipu's armory for the last ten years. Once, over a lengthy meal at a cabinet minister's house, Martine confided in Du Leze the sad particulars of his marriage, how he'd fallen in love with a well-to-do Muslim girl, then persuaded her family to accept his marriage proposal, against the wishes of his own, only for his beloved Shaheena bibi to die two days after giving birth to their daughter, Jehanne. "A lovelier lady you never saw," he said, a tear plopping into the dregs of his buttermilk. Du Leze offered condolences while privately vowing never again to sit beside Monsieur Martine.

"My daughter wanted to see the creation," Martine says now, running a palm over his head as he surveys the space. "As do I, to be honest."

Only then does Du Leze notice a girl of nine or ten hovering in the doorway. She rustles into the workshop, shy and careful in a yellow silk skirt. Martine mutters something to her. Quickly she curtsies at Du Leze, then scans the walls, her honey-brown hair in two oiled plaits, her hands clasped as if she's been warned in advance not to touch anything.

In Kannada, Du Leze tells Abbas to make her a spinning top from the piece already mounted in the lathe. Abbas nods and removes Martine's hat from the lathe, holding it in both hands, waiting for Martine to take it elsewhere.

Martine fails to notice. "Incredible how you've picked up the local tongue," he says to Du Leze, in French. "Eyes closed, one would mistake you for a native."

"Not if that one were a native," says Du Leze.

Martine lets out a bombastic laugh. Abbas hangs the hat on the wall.

As Du Leze leads the visitors to the tiger, Abbas sits down to the lathe. Today he'd planned to fashion the mounted piece into the soldier's forearm, one of seventeen other pressing tasks that await him, such as refining the soldier's chin. And the nose. Also the mouth. The mouth is not even really a mouth, just a hole to fit the opening of the curved pipe. It is a far cry from the mouth on Vaucanson's Flutist, an automaton whose subtle lips are so intricately built that, according to Du Leze, she can play a whole song.

Pumping the foot pedal, Abbas sets the piece spinning. He trains his roughing gouge against the wood, angling the piece, then narrows the handle with a spindle gouge. Shavings fly and fur the back of his hand. He is only vaguely aware of the little girl, who watches from the opposite side.

Over the screech and hum, the girl shouts at him in Kannada: "Papa calls me Jehanne but my true name is Jehan!"

Abbas only nods. He knows better than to call her anything, considering her status.

She tilts her head in study of the man. "He's funny-looking. Not in a bad way," she adds. "Funny like a joke. I like jokes."

He pumps the pedal harder, hoping the din will drown out further conversation.

The girl leans forward, her nose nearing the spinning piece until he warns: "Not so close—it will take your nose off!"

She jumps back, a hand over her nose.

He smiles to reassure her. "Want to see something?"

She releases her nose and nods.

He applies a stick of red lacquer to the tip, flushing it a vivid crimson. Another stick whips a ring of marigold around the rest. He works the color up to a fine smooth gloss, keeping his gaze on the top, aware of her growing interest.

At last he severs the handle and sets the top spinning—a blur of yellow and red. She watches, lips parted, as he watches her. Never has he seen a child of her coloring: amber skin, gray eyes, heavy brows. It occurs to him that these features must be the confluence of Monsieur Martine and a Mysorean wife.

The top whirls off the table and into his hand. He holds it out to the girl. She takes it into the cradle of her palm, looking up at him as if he has transformed from a woodworker to a wizard in a tale.

Later, after Monsieur Martine and his daughter have left, Du Leze fits the pipe hole in the mouth. Then he and Abbas stand back and evaluate . . . what? What is this creature with a peachy slab for a face, a wedge of a nose, and round blue eyes bereft of pupils? It is nothing close to what Abbas had intended or imagined, after making so many faces in the Frenchman's mirror, sketching so many anguished mouths and eyes. Now the anguish is his own.

"It will do," says Du Leze, mysteriously impassive.

"It barely looks human, Sahab."

"Nor should it. Otherwise we would pity him. No, we should despise the man, we should wish for him to suffer."

Abbas frowns up at Du Leze.

"Perhaps we can turn him so he is facing the wall," says Du Leze.

Last week, at Du Leze's instruction, Abbas had carved a series of French letters on the underside of the grunt pipe. Only after carving did Du Leze explain what they meant. *Faite par L. Du Leze & Abbas.* Abbas was overwhelmed. His name? On the same line, in the same breath, as that of Du Leze? He dared to believe he deserved the honor.

"*Tak tak,*" says Du Leze, giving him a pat on the back.

Abbas interprets this as a gesture of extreme pity, and is not reassured.

VII

On the morning of the unveiling, Abbas wears an outfit much
too fine for a man of his station. It is a gift from Du Leze, who
insists. The jama is short, a fine white muslin that fastens beneath
his left arm. The green silk pyjamas hug his ankles in neat diagonal
pleats. As a final touch, Du Leze presents him with a pair of mojari.

"Camel-skin," says Du Leze, when Abbas shakes his head at the
slippers. "What? They don't spit."

"It wouldn't look right, Sahab."

"Who would notice what you are wearing on your feet?"

Abbas raises an eyebrow.

"Well, yes," says Du Leze, setting the slippers aside. "There is
him."

Du Leze, on the other hand, dresses with the purpose of attract-
ing notice. His entire outfit is an atlas of textiles, from the Afghani
brocade qaba that cinches his waist, patterned with blossoms and
fastened with pearls, to the shahtu draped over his shoulder, its soft
wool collected from thorns where Kashmiri mountain goats brushed
their underbellies in passing—so claimed the seller, at any rate.

"And this?" says Du Leze, sliding a turquoise ring onto his
thumb. "It is too much?"

"No, Sahab. Turquoise protects the wearer from bad luck."

"A little late for that," says Du Leze. Abbas doesn't know how to interpret the remark and doesn't have time to ask, for the guard has arrived to usher them to the party.

The Rag Mahal sits in the southwest corner of the royal garden, a humble little hall that could fit within a pocket of the palace. Inside, the hall abandons all humility, decorated to resemble an exuberant jungle. Fan palms and birds of paradise framing plates of flatbreads and biscuits, rasgullah eggs in spun-sugar nests fanned by attendants so the sugar won't melt, balls of caramel flame, parrots of pista barfi, marzipan bees hovering over floral confection. Abbas has never seen anything like this room, and as he steps close to a marzipan bee, noting each perfect stripe, he knows he will never forget it.

"Pah!" says Jehanne, poking her face between the bees. "I scared you."

"*Bonjour, mademoiselle.*" He dips his head. She beams up at him as if he is the only person in the room.

"I have the top you made me." She takes a bite of the laddu in her hand and adds: "It's in my pocket."

"Very good, mademoiselle."

She stuffs the rest of the laddu in her mouth and speaks from behind her wrist. "I want to be a toymaker when I grow up. Papa says only a fool would be a toymaker." She chews thoughtfully, then swallows. "But you don't look like a fool."

"Thank you. And where is your papa?"

"I shall fetch him for you!" she says, hurrying off.

To his relief, Abbas is called away to help the three servants tasked with lowering the tiger's bottom half onto the body of the soldier. Du Leze directs them slowly until, at last, the four holes in the soldier—two in the thighs, two in the shoulders—receive the long wooden screws lodged in the tiger's paws.

Abbas wishes the screws weren't so visible. He wishes he'd jointed the soldier's arm at the elbow, instead of below the elbow. And maybe it was a bad idea to adorn the red coat with golden florals. He thought the red coat looked too drab without, that perhaps the florals would distract from the plainness of the face. Now he plucks at the front of his new jama, aware of the sweat stains already blooming beneath his arms.

The automaton is draped with a sheet of glazed white cotton, rippling over the shape of its hidden object.

Du Leze and Abbas flank the automaton as the guests begin to trickle in, announced one by one by a mace-bearing chobdar. Among them are the most distinguished of Tipu's officers: Sayyid Ghaffur, Mir Sadiq, Muhammad Raza, Khan Jehan Khan, and Purnaiya, allegedly the only remaining Brahmin in whom Tipu places trust.

(It is well known in this company that Purnaiya, at present, is plagued by controversy. There are those who say Tipu should get rid of Purnaiya, that Tipu should not put trust in a Hindu. Others say Purnaiya's bona fides are unquestionable, citing his service to Tipu's father, Haidar Ali. When Haidar died in a tent on the battlefield, it was Purnaiya who knew better than to allow the rumor of the dead ruler to spread, which would have prompted others to take his seat. It was Purnaiya who dispatched a secret message to Tipu—*Ride for Srirangapatna and declare your inheritance.* And it was Purnaiya who folded Haidar's body into an ornate chest and filled it with marigolds and carnations and aromatics, so that all along its journey, none would suspect it was carrying a rotting corpse. If Tipu can't trust Purnaiya, whom can he trust?)

Of all the richly dressed guests gliding into the room, all the warriors and heroes of the field, only one causes Abbas to forget his own name, only one whose title he has known from childhood:

The Wonder Hand, superintendent of goldsmiths, perhaps the greatest of the century, a legend among craftsmen. In greeting, Du Leze clasps the Wonder Hand's hands. Abbas stands by, dumb with astonishment. (He had expected the Wonder Hand to be taller.) Abbas may not seem the type to know much about gold, but he knows good craftsmanship; he knows the Wonder Hand made the ring that now encircles Tipu's thumb, its interior inlaid with Tipu's title in a calligraphy of tiny rubies ground flat, the very creation that led Tipu to anoint him *aja'ib-dast.* The Wonder Hand.

"So, Musa," says the Wonder Hand, peering around Du Leze's shoulder, "what is it you're hiding under that sheet?"

"A creation that will surely fall short of your own, *mon cher*." Du Leze inclines his head toward Abbas. "This is my accomplice."

Both Du Leze and the Wonder Hand look to him. Speechless, Abbas can only press a hand to his heart and bow.

"He is quite gifted at woodcarving," says Du Leze. "I wager he is the finest Mysorean woodcarver I have ever met, and I expect the tiger is only the beginning of his accomplishments."

That Abbas might be the only Mysorean woodcarver Du Leze has ever met is a fact that will only occur later to Abbas. At the moment, he is moved.

More officials and ministers and their families arrive. Here are the twelve sons of Tipu and their retinue, the servants in matching maroon livery. The sons come in a range of heights, each bearing a different resemblance to the father. This son has Tipu's chin. That son has Tipu's short legs. The smallest one, Ghulam Muhammad, favors his mother, but to make up for it, he has adopted Tipu's royal stare. All of them wear the same long white jama, the same swollen ruby in their turbans, from which a white peacock feather grows. The honored sons, Abdul Khaliq and Muiz, stand conjoined at all times, stiff and perfect in their finery.

As for Tipu's wives and daughters, they are confined to the zenana, behind windows of jaali-worked teak meant to keep them from seeing and being seen. (And yet they know how to see what they are not meant to see; they've been seeing this way for ages, see-ing inwardly, and if you try the same method, you just might see the fingertip of a little girl, tracing a hollow in the jaali-work that seems, to her, tapered exactly like the tiger's eye of her imaginings.)

Tipu Sultan is the last to be announced.

The guests turn toward the entrance, watching the padshah ascend the carpeted steps, a royal fan gyring slowly over his head. Upon reaching the automaton, he greets Du Leze with a swift salaam and turns to address the audience.

All is quiet in the Rag Mahal.

"Behold," says Tipu Sultan, reaching into his patka to remove a small glass wand, which he holds up in the air. "The barometer."

Everyone stares at the wand, no taller than Tipu's hand.

"It is a device for shewing the air, as indicated by the quicksilver in this narrow central tube." Tipu points to the quicksilver with his pinky. "A barometer—or *howarnuman*, as I have coined it—allows us to precisely read air pressure. Unfortunately, this particular barometer, which was sent to me by the French governor of Pondicherry, is defective due to the oldness of the quicksilver. So I have requested from him a good one, made in the present year, as well as a European treatise on its use, which I intend to personally translate into Persian."

Tipu hands the faulty barometer to the servant Raja Khan, who passes it around the room.

"Now," he continues, "I believe it is no accident that the governor of Pondicherry has sent the padshah of Mysore an old and broken howarnuman. Why such trickery, you may ask, when we are allies with France; France is our friend! This is almost true. But when all is said and done, Europe will never want us on footing equal to theirs."

A murmur of affirmation spreads through the room.

"Under my leadership," Tipu continues, his voice lifting to fill the Rag Mahal, "we will not only equal but exceed their scientific advancements. This is the only way to secure our borders from the greed and corruption of the Nazarenes. To that end, the kingdom of Mysore is developing new inventions and creations in all fields, from medicine to botany to metalsmithing. I have employed French and English artisans to show us how to copy all variety of their devices, from improved muskets to scissors to hourglasses to barometers that actually work.

"And now, to celebrate the birth of Prince Muiz-ud-din, and to commemorate his glorious return and that of Prince Abdul Khaliq, I present another innovation, made by a Frenchman some of you may know. He is Musa Lucien Du Leze, the greatest clockmaker in France and a true friend of Mysore. In fact, he looks more and more Mysorean by the day! That's very good. I shall not spoil the surprise, but suffice to say that this fantastical curiosity serves a purpose different from that of all the other innovations I have commissioned—yet equally important." Tipu pauses meaningfully. "This one extends the imagination."

Tipu moves to take his place between Abdul and Muiz, who part to make space for him.

Throughout the speech Abbas has remained motionless, unable to understand any of it, for the speech was in Persian. No matter. To Abbas's ear, the sounds were sophisticated and luxurious, lulling him into the sleepy belief that he is watching a drama that has nothing to do with him, and only to do with a person of divine presence. Abbas is reminded of their first meeting, the vast carpet of crimson tulips on which Tipu had been sitting. Now every head in the Rag Mahal is such a tulip, all their gazes running toward the padshah like stems to the sole source of water.

"We present," says Du Leze, pinching the sheet between his fingers, jolting Abbas from the spell, "the Tiger of Mysore."

Off goes the sheet.

The room draws a breath.

Du Leze moves to his position between the tiger and the wall. He opens the door along the flank to expose the organ keys, which the audience will not be able to see. Abbas takes hold of the crank in his sweaty palm. Prompted by a nod from Du Leze, Abbas turns the crank and Du Leze presses the keys, but aside from the *thunk* of the soldier's hand to his mouth, no sound comes out.

A sick feeling takes hold of his stomach. It is a failure, they have failed.

Unperturbed, Du Leze walks around to the rear of the tiger and pushes the two wind stops located in the tiger's left buttock, earning a snort from one of the guests. Resuming his post, Du Leze begins again.

Whenever Du Leze has practiced playing in the workshop, Abbas has found the organ music to be nasal and discordant, a sort of whiny harmonium. Now he realizes the organ notes were trapped by the workshop's low ceiling. In the Rag Mahal, they soar.

Meanwhile Abbas turns the crank, trying not to grow distracted by the chain of cause and effect: how the turning of the crank spins the rotary valve that squeezes the bellows that activates the mechanism that flaps the soldier's arm. After every fourth grunt from the tiger, the soldier groans.

Abbas watches Du Leze for any signal to stop. The Frenchman keeps his eyes on the keys, seed pearls of sweat on his nose.

"That's enough," says Tipu Sultan.

Du Leze releases a long last chord, then resumes his place at the head of the tiger. As practiced, he and Abbas face Tipu and bow.

Few people in the kingdom of Mysore have seen Tipu smile with all his teeth, not in person or in paintings. He is not easily beguiled. And yet, that day in the Rag Mahal, he is grinning, freed from the fear that the toy would not turn out as he'd hoped, that the audience would find it too bizarre, too eccentric. Tipu brings his hands together in one loud clap, like the first crack of thunder, opening the sky and bringing down a rain of applause, cries of *Shabash!*

Only now does Abbas register the sweat streaming down his back, the exultation so intense that he closes his hands into fists. He will never forget this—the pleasure of surprising everyone, even himself.

Abbas is lost in the swirl of well-wishers until Tipu approaches, his arms around Abdul Khaliq and Muiz. Their presence rattles Abbas. He reminds himself that the hard part is over; Tipu is pleased.

"You were right about the toymaker," Tipu tells Du Leze, in Kannada.

"I thank you for your trust, Padshah."

Tipu lowers his voice, his face turning grave. "It is a shame about the new law in France."

Du Leze blinks, unprepared. "Yes. Indeed it is."

"Here you have a home." Tipu nods at Abbas. "And now, an apprentice."

Abbas looks to Du Leze for explanation, but the Frenchman is bending low to address Abdul Khaliq and Muiz. "I sincerely hope the princes are pleased with their gift."

"Well?" Tipu says. "Are you pleased, Muiz?"

"Yes, Father, thank you."

Tipu turns to the older boy. "These men can make you whatever you want for your birthday as well. What do you want, Abdul? *Abdul.*"

At the second mention of his name, Abdul snaps to attention. "Yes, Father? What do I want?"

"For your birthday."

Thinking, Abdul tucks his tongue behind his lower lip.

"Stop that," Tipu says. Abdul stops. "So what is it you want for your birthday?"

Abdul considers the question. With every added second, the silence distends, the entire room tightening with expectation until, desperate for release, he blurts:

"Trifle."

Tipu frowns. "What?"

"I'd like—" Abdul swallows. "I would like trifle?"

Tipu looks to Du Leze, who shrugs.

"It is cake, then custard, then cake," says Abdul, doomed Abdul, depicting the layers by stacking his hands.

"Then custard," adds Muiz, trying to help. Abdul's hands fall to his sides.

"Where have you eaten this food?" Tipu says.

"Lord Cornwallis gave it to us."

By now all other conversations have dragged to a halt. Tipu's face has turned cold.

"Did you know," says Tipu, "that this person you call a *lord* led an army into America, only to be chased out by a band of farmers? Is that the conduct of a lord? Or perhaps he didn't tell you that story— perhaps he simply stuffed your faces with truffle!"

It seems to just about everyone in the hall that Abdul is going to cry, so still is his face. Half the men in that room would have crumbled from such a scolding. Yet these men are not Abdul Khaliq; they don't carry the blood of Haidar Ali in their veins. This is the only way to explain how a boy of eight can endure a public lashing with such composure and say without hesitation: "Father, a truffle is a mushroom."

Tipu glowers at Abdul, then Muiz, who bites his lip, not quite suppressing his smile. He is on the verge of banishing both sons from the party. But then some other notion goes fluttering through his rage. When did they get so fidgety, his sons? He used to breakfast every morning with Abdul and Muiz, and it was easy and good to be with them; he felt closer to his own father somehow, gently chiding them with Haidar's exact words. But these days he has no idea what to say to Abdul and Muiz. More than once, since their return, he has found them not quite the same, more like replicas of his real sons, who are at this moment trapped in the house of Cornwallis, refusing all offers of trifle and declaring loyalty to the Tiger of Mysore.

A silly notion, one with no actual stake in reality.

And now Purnaiya slides into view, loyal Purnaiya, armed with good sense and sangfroid, always at the ready to bail him out of an unpleasant situation. "Lunch is ready on the lawn," Purnaiya says. Tipu allows himself to be led away from the boys and makes a mental note to tell their mothers about the fidgeting.

Everyone sits around the edges of a vast white tablecloth spread across the lawn, beneath a tent whose silver embroidery dances with sunlight. Seated beside Du Leze, Abbas surveys the scene. Two bubbling cauldrons, their fires sustained by a man waving a wicker fan. Another man blistering chapati on a grill. Two cooks turning a giant shish kebab of mutton over an open fire while two others shoulder poles to transport a massive pot of rice, which they set in the center of the sheet. All the servants wear white masks over their mouths, to protect the food from their breath. Their faces glisten with sweat they do not dare to wipe publicly.

Every time a server comes by with a bowl of this or a platter of that, Abbas nods for more. His boredom makes him greedy and so he eats past the brim of his appetite, too quickly to realize that two kebabs ago he was already full.

Conversation flows around him. Absently he tears a marigold between his fingers, trying to catch Du Leze's attention, but Du Leze is deep in discussion with the Wonder Hand. What was the new law Tipu had referred to? And why did the mention of it bring a pinched look to the Frenchman's face? Is he really staying in Mysore and taking Abbas as his apprentice? Abbas waits for the opportunity to ask, but as the meal goes on, it becomes clear that Du Leze is avoiding him.

After the departure of the dignified guests, a few young men invite Abbas to smoke shisha. These men wear showy clothes, the tips of their mustaches waxed to spurs. They seem to assume that Abbas is on his way up in the world, or at least in Tipu's court, and thus are eager to get in at the ground level.

Abbas finds Du Leze fingering one of the marzipan bees with a grave look.

"Ah, no," says Du Leze, in response to Abbas's invitation. "I am to retire early. And I would prefer that you sleep at your father's house tonight."

"Tonight, Sahab? But my things—"

"You may pick them up on the morrow. Forgive me, but I must insist."

Du Leze looks away. There's something strange in his manner, a concealed agitation. Abbas can keep quiet no longer.

"Sahab," he says forcefully, "are you not going back to France?"

Regret flickers across the Frenchman's face. "No, I am not. And I am not taking on an apprentice at this time."

"At another time?"

Du Leze gently shakes his head.

"Sahab . . ." Abbas feels the moment slipping away from him. "I may not have the talent of your usual students, but I would work very hard—"

"You have bushels of talent, Abbas. It is not that."

"Then what, may I ask?"

Du Leze pauses for a breath. "No, you may not."

Abbas begins to protest, then, seeing the futility in trying, mutters "Very well," and shuts his mouth.

Du Leze plants his hands on Abbas's shoulders and goes on to say encouraging things. Half listening, Abbas clenches his toes against the grass. There is nothing to mourn here, he reminds himself. How can he mourn a thing that never was? Though he does wish he'd accepted the mojari, not to wear but to remind himself that he had, at one time, risen past his station.

And so Abbas follows his newfound friends through the Water Gate, retracing the same steps he took a lifetime ago. They gather on the rooftop of a haveli, three stories high, allowing him a view of the city washed in sunset, the familiar gullies and lanes, the smiling strings of drying laundry, the Brahmin houses with their shuttered doors, the Muslim eateries, open late. Dogs bay in the growing dark. The city has never seemed so small.

The roof fills with more men. Abbas is toasted and praised as the one who built Tipu's Tiger, the automaton described in hyperbolic terms. He tries to explain that he was only an assistant to the great French inventor Lucien Du Leze. No one cares to listen. They exhale smoky plumes and tell mystifying jokes. "Every man should have four wives," declares the fellow who invited Abbas. "A Persian to converse with, a Turk to do the housework, a Hindu to raise the kids, and an Uzbek to beat as a warning to the others." (Why an Uzbek? Abbas wonders, having always thought them a race of invaders; presumably you couldn't walk away from beating an Uzbek woman without a broken limb of your own.)

The man beside him offers a draught from his silver flask.

Abbas refuses. "It's haram."

"Haram, haram," the man groans. "Harun al-Rashid loved his women and his drink. Who is more righteous than he was, tell me, who has more taqwa? The guy who goes around saying *haram, haram* or the guy who started the Golden Age of Islam?"

Abbas says little after that, but the next time the flask comes to him, he tips it into his glass of lemon juice. The sweet tang takes on a punishing aftertaste. Embers spark as the coals are turned. Watching them, he grows morose.

It's not the al-Rashid lecture that bothers him but the parting words of Du Leze. *Bushels of talent.* This is the greatest compliment Abbas has ever received. And yet. Bushels aren't enough to merit the Frenchman's tutelage. For this Abbas would need . . . what? Boatloads? Mustn't one begin with bushels before advancing to boatloads? He wonders if he'd be happier with no bushels at all, dull yet unencumbered.

The sky over the city darkens. Exhausted, he closes his eyes, just a moment's rest before he will get up and head home. Nodding off, he feels a hand atop his own, accompanied by a warm voice:

"Why the long face, Know-It-All?"

Abbas looks in amazement at Khwaja Irfan, sitting across from him. The candlelight reveals the changes in his face: sharper cheekbones, sunken eyes. A tight pink scar sickles his cheek. His silk robe gleams with shifting hues—teal in one light, violet in another—his resplendence unchanged.

"My friend," says Abbas, finding his voice. "I thought you were dead."

"A fair assumption."

"But what happened, where have you been? Tell me."

Khwaja Irfan subjects him to a cool appraisal. His eyes appear glazed, pupils so large and black they swallow the candlelight, not a flicker to be seen within them. "No point in looking back," he says. "Believe me, life is too short."

"Whose life?" Abbas asks, but Khwaja Irfan doesn't hear. Instead he is surveying the other men, his gaze coming to settle on Abbas. *"Whose life?"* Abbas demands.

Khwaja Irfan tilts his head, his face filled with pity.

"No," Abbas whispers. "Not yet—"

He feels a jab in his side and startles awake.

"Not yet for what?" says a guard, scowling over him.

Abbas sits up straight. He is surrounded by inscrutable stares, none of them belonging to Khwaja Irfan.

"Pull yourself together," says the guard. "You've been summoned."

Abbas rides on the back of the royal horse, trying to stay balanced as they gallop through a different gate—this one for important people—and arrive in quick time at the Rag Mahal.

Abbas enters to find Tipu frowning down at the organ keys of the automaton.

"The keys are not yielding sound," Tipu says, irritated. "Even when I pull out the wind stops."

"May I, Padshah?" With a nod from Tipu, Abbas takes hold of the hand crank, explaining how the turning crank powers the internal bellows, which pumps air through the pipes, all the while trying not to focus on the fact that he is speaking to Tipu Sultan.

"Turn it, then," says Tipu. "Let me see."

Abbas turns the crank. Tipu presses a few keys, producing a high, discordant sound. He grunts his approval.

Stepping back with a bow, Abbas feels a ripple of gas move through his lower abdomen. He blames the shisha, the kebabs, the lecturing man with the flask.

"Do you play?" Tipu asks.

"Forgive me, Padshah. Monsieur Du Leze knows—shall I bring him?"

"No, no. I was only seeking a distraction."

Tipu rests a hand on the hump of the tiger's neck and ponders one of the blazes. The whites of his eyes are red from sleeplessness, Abbas presumes, though presuming anything about the padshah feels wrong, so he focuses on controlling his own flatulence, though the more he thinks about controlling it, the less control he seems to possess. He clenches his whole self and prays the meeting will be brief.

"I had this night a dream," Tipu begins, dashing all hopes of brevity. "A handsome young man, a stranger, came and sat down beside me. I chatted him up, rather playfully, cutting jokes the way I would with a woman, you know. Eventually this man—he rose and took off his turban, and all this long, fragrant, frankly very feminine hair went spilling down his shoulders. That was the first strange thing. And then he opened his robe and revealed a woman's bosom." Tipu turns his bloodshot eyes on Abbas. "A bosom. What does it mean?"

Abbas has no idea how to reply.

"Why do I ask a toymaker," Tipu says, just as Abbas feels his body rebelling, the gas descending, which he can only think to cover by saying what first comes to mind: "The English wear wigs."

Tipu looks at him, affronted. Whether by the answer or the gas Abbas cannot tell.

"Englishmen wear ladylike wigs," Abbas proceeds haltingly. "So even while they may wear a soldier's clothing, in the end, they will only flee the fight, like women."

Tipu's face remains expressionless, sealed against overt displays of emotion. Yet his slow nod feels to Abbas as incredible as an embrace. "That makes some sense."

"It's as in the painting, Padshah. Colonel Baillie didn't even ride in on a horse, isn't that so? He came in on some sort of covered palanquin, like a bride."

"A hideous bride."

"About to be taken by the tiger."

Tipu frowns. "I don't like lewdness."

"Forgive me, Padshah."

"No, but your theory is a clever one. Very clever. I can see why Du Leze chose you as his apprentice."

"Thank you, Padshah."

"You must learn from him how to play this thing. A few songs would suffice. The bulk of your time should go to learning the mechanics of the automaton, until you can conceive and produce them yourself, without him."

Abbas tries to object, but Tipu is already gazing past him, into the middle distance. "Right now, in Europe, automata are being constructed to do things beyond your wildest dreams. There is one automaton in the form of a Turk, seated before a chessboard, able to win against any human opponent that challenges him. There is another automaton, from the past century, a duck that could both eat from the ground and then digest and excrete, exactly as a duck in flesh! But we must not be lured by the hubris of the hat-wearers, making things just to compete with the Almighty. This is heresy. What I want are automata that can do the work of twenty toymakers, or embroiderers, or metalsmiths. With these creations, we will not be competing with Allah, but elevating His Kingdom through industry and trade, until none would dare try to master us again."

Tipu stops, staring out into an imaginary audience, then scratches the side of his nose. "Still working on the ending. Not quite there yet."

"I found it very rousing, Padshah."

"Good for you." Tipu releases Abbas with a small scuppering gesture of the fingers. "Tomorrow you begin again with Du Leze."

"Forgive me, Padshah, but—" Abbas hesitates. "Sahab has said he will not be taking me as his student."

A wrinkle deepens between Tipu's brows. "But he gave me his word."

"Maybe, Padshah, he misunderstood?"

"Or he lied."

"Perhaps I am the one who misunderstood, Padshah."

"Are you lying to me?"

Abbas is held still. "No, Padshah."

"Then go in peace."

By the time Abbas is escorted to the Frenchman's apartment, he has reached a conclusion: Du Leze will not be there. He will be halfway to Mangalore or Pondicherry by now, possibly on horseback, perhaps aided by one of Tipu's enemies. No one rejects a request made by Tipu Sultan and remains within his borders. Du Leze is gone. Abbas will be questioned. Or worse. He thinks of the Khwaja Irfan from his dream—was it a dream?—and his stomach turns.

He stands before Du Leze's bedroom door. Not ajar as usual, but closed. *Au revoir,* Du Leze said at the party. Never before had he said goodbye in French, deploying Kannada instead: *See you later.*

All signs point to a final departure.

Abbas knocks, waits, then knocks again. No answer. He dares to open the door.

There is Du Leze, asleep in his bed. He lies on his side atop the quilt, still in his fine clothes, presumably too drunk or exhausted to change into his nightdress. His head rests on his arm, his one knee drawn up. In sleep he is serene, a glisten of spittle at the corner of his mouth.

Abbas sighs, relieved, yet bewildered.

Turning to leave, he catches sight of something silver in Du Leze's grip. He takes a few steps closer—Du Leze is holding a spoon.

Why a spoon?

This question leads him to others:

Has the Frenchman's skin always been so pale?

Are his lips tinted purple?

Is that vomit at the corner of his mouth?

Is he breathing?

This final question, when Abbas bends close to Du Leze and picks up a sour whiff, appears to be no.

Abbas jerks back from the bed, bumping into a side table. On the table is a piece of paper, held in place by a cup of water. The paper contains several lines jotted in French. The only part he can read are the final three words, whose letters match the ones he carved into the bellows.

L. Du Leze.

A note.

He hates notes.

His vision dapples with shadow. He is tingling all over, numb with realization. The spoon served a purpose—Du Leze has poisoned himself.

Without another thought, Abbas grabs the cup from the side table and dashes water against the Frenchman's face. Nothing. He slaps him hard across the mouth. Another slap, still nothing. He once witnessed someone slap the Soul under similar circumstances, and when that failed to wake the Soul, who lay near-dead beneath the awning of a beeda shop, the beeda seller—a heavyset fellow infuriated that the Soul had brought death to his threshold—knelt and ground his knuckles into the dying man's chest, making circular motions with his fist. How the beeda seller knew to do this was a mystery to Abbas, a mystery that does not matter now as he climbs aboard the bed and does the same, knuckling the Frenchman's sternum, kneading life into the lungs, demanding the body do its job. Du Leze does not respond. Abbas pours his fury into his fist, cursing and praying and apologizing and grinding his knuckles in bumpy circles until maybe, just maybe, he hears the faintest trace of a groan.

"How do you feel?" asks Abbas.

Wincing, Du Leze touches his sternum. "Like my lungs are wet dough."

Abbas strokes his own knuckles, which are rubbery, still ringing.

They are in the sitting room now. After a long period on the floor, Du Leze allowed himself to be helped to a chair. He limped heavily, his breath sodden with vomit, and beneath that scent: sesame. Haltingly, he confessed his plan to Abbas, how he'd heard of a bibi who took her own life by ingesting a large quantity of opium along with several spoonfuls of sesame oil. How much opium, he had not known. All he'd heard was that she'd eaten the opium like cheese, bite after bite. Doing the same, he drifted off.

Now Du Leze sits on the sofa, his palms facedown on the cushions. Abbas is slumped in an armchair.

"I would do anything for a piece of country bread at the moment." Du Leze stares vaguely ahead. "Warm with butter."

"Sahab, why are we talking of bread?"

Du Leze's stomach makes a burbling sound. "That is why. I never realized how dying can so whet the appetite." When Abbas does not answer, Du Leze adds, warily: "I must have been a sight."

Abbas gives him a hard look.

"Well, but who told you to come back here? I told you to go home, did I not?"

"If I had gone home, you would be in hell by now!"

Abbas falls silent. He had intended to save his master's soul—yes, this would be the charitable explanation for why he intervened. Yet another nags at him, the inchoate anger, the indignation he felt as he saw Du Leze, and the note, as the pieces fell into place. No, his own heroism was not untouched by self-interest. Du Leze is his teacher. He is also a ticket to greater things.

"Have you never thought of it?" Du Leze asks at last.

"My life is not mine to take."

"That is no answer."

Abbas tries to imagine wanting to end his own life. "If I could, I would live forever."

Du Leze scoffs, then presses a palm to his sternum. "Terrible," he says, though Abbas isn't sure if he is referring to his pain or the prospect of immortality.

"Will you do it again, Sahab?"

Du Leze listens to his own breath going in and out, in spite of his earlier efforts. When he looks at Abbas, he sees a boy who doesn't want the truth in this moment, does not want to know that Lucien has no idea what he will do five days or five minutes from now, whether the same despair that dragged him to the top of the Hirodi Hill will pull him down once and for all. Abbas scowls like a child. He has down on his upper lip. He would not understand.

"No," says Du Leze. "I will not."

A twitch of guilt accompanies what might be a lie. Or the truth. Who is to say at this particular moment?

Abbas releases a breath and sits back. Together they listen to the twang of frogs. Outside, beyond their line of hearing or sight, a turtle emerges from a pond and snaps an egret by the leg into the water, an event that comes to them only as a gentle splash.

SRIRANGAPATNA, MYSORE

1798–1799

I

It is a calm winter morning, swollen with fog, when Abbas's mother serves him a cup of coffee and says it is time for him to marry.

The coffee shoots up his nose, making his eyes water.

"You don't have to cry about it," his mother says.

He tells her he is too young. Past twenty, she reminds him.

"But what about my apprenticeship with Musa Sahab?" he says. "I've barely begun!"

His mother sighs. (Really, it should be her husband saying these things, but this has always been his problem, in her opinion: his almost zealous avoidance of serious discussion.) "My son," she says in a voice of gentle urgency, "what are you learning that requires you to stop living? And where will this learning take you after that Musa has gone back to his people?"

In reply, Abbas describes a prospective future, wherein he will finish his apprenticeship with Du Leze and become the first clock-maker in all of Mysore, perhaps even the subcontinent. In that future, every town will boast a clock tower, every pocket will cradle a watch. And in addition to clocks, Abbas will build automata of his own design; there has even been talk of Tipu creating a Ministry of Technical Advancement and granting Abbas a title. (Scant talk, but still.) How, then, can Abbas move home and marry at this critical juncture?

His mother absorbs all this with a candid squint and finally asks: "Do you have someone on the side?"

"Of course not."

"Abbas," says his mother, firm. But he insists he does not.

The truth—about his future, anyway—is that Tipu Sultan seems to have lost interest in automata. For months after the unveiling, Abbas and Du Leze were invited to play the Musical Tiger from time to time. Du Leze even learned to play four additional tunes. How fortunate those days, how fraught with anxiety, a desire to please! But Tipu rarely showed pleasure. He simply stared at the feasting tiger as if into a void.

Then, abruptly, the invitations came to a halt. It was said that Tipu was appearing less frequently at court, that he was busy building up his arsenal, mining metal to fashion flintlocks, perfecting his rockets, and building warships in the port of Mangalore. For all Abbas knows, the beast has been forgotten, left to grow a pelt of dust.

Another truth: Thus far, Abbas has found his apprenticeship to be slow going. The entire first week was spent on the fundamentals of proper working posture. His table had to be chest high, one that he built expressly for this purpose. He was to steady the sides of his hands against the tabletop. "Sit up straight," Du Leze kept saying, but years of sitting and working on the floor had sickled his posture irrevocably.

And then were months of simply learning how to clean various timepieces. Who knew cleaning required so much concentration? Tweezing away the hour and minute hands, the display and the dial. Digging dirt out of the jewel holes with a pointy stick. Fussing over the clock plate with a brush whose bristles are fine as a child's eyelashes.

In exchange for room and board in Du Leze's house, Abbas makes deliveries, does small repairs, and helps Devi, the cook, by handling market trips. Devi excites him: the tuneless bhajans she hums, the flat of her back as she weeds. The sidewise look she gives him when she catches him watching. Not affronted, but mildly interested. According to Lucien, she was widowed at sixteen but ran away from home before she could be confined to an ashram. Abbas wonders at that wildness, how it hides within the forest of her silence. How long ago did she run? How old is she now? She has the taut umber skin of a woman who might be thirty or fifty, but he cannot find the courage to ask the question, not even after they make love in the master's bed, while Du Leze is away.

"What's wrong?" she says, as he lies quiet and winded in the aftermath. "Scared you'll go to hell for sleeping with my kind?"

"No," he says uncertainly, and turns to hold her. He thumbs a blue vein at her wrist, thick as a stalk beneath the skin. "Nothing scares you, does it?"

She considers. "Heaven scares me. I wouldn't know a soul."

He has never met a woman like her, one who shrugs off all notions of shyness and shame. She believes that all bodies need relief, that she and Abbas are simply providing that relief for one another. They provide it in the pantry. They provide it in the kitchen, on the pallet where she usually sleeps. They provide it on the rooftop where, one night, she lets out a moan that prompts a dog to howl back. They break apart, laughing, and soon enough he wants her all over again.

For a time, Abbas takes pleasure in this sweet secret life, beyond the eagle-eyed attention of his mother. She has been busy arranging the weddings of Junaid and Farooq to a pair of sisters, each woman endowed with a parcel of land by their father, a rice merchant from Somnathpur. Abbas's earnings from the automaton financed both weddings, in addition to a new coat of paint for the house made from limestone and jaggery. Now the walls blaze so white Abbas hardly recognizes the house and quite often walks past it, looking for the ashen mud walls he remembers.

After the weddings have settled, life takes on an easy rhythm between day and night, Devi and the rest—until one day a man arrives panting at the door, telling Abbas there has been an accident, no time to explain, his father is dying. The stranger, a man, has a terrible growth flowering at the base of his neck, and for a moment, it is this that has Abbas transfixed, until Du Leze shoves him in the back and tells him to get up and go home—*go!*

Earlier that day, his father received a horse-kick to the head, the result of standing slightly too close to a horse that was mean and skittish, unaccustomed to the screech of the whetstone. Several bystanders helped him up. He seemed well enough to walk home, albeit stiffly. Then he lay down on his pallet, dozed off, and awoke without any sensation in his legs.

In the ensuing days, Abbas presses his father's legs for hours on end, listening to him describe the accident multiple times in a soft and fumbling voice. All the kneading in the world restores neither mind nor foot. His father—the one they knew—is dissolving.

Abbas's mother consults healers and imams and astrologers. She sleeps beside her husband all night, disturbed by all the fitful sounds he now makes, the whistling and wheezing as if trying to breathe around rubble embedded in his chest. During the day, she moves in a silent, red-eyed rage, barely hearing when Abbas tells her he must return to work.

"I was not expecting you back so soon," says Du Leze, upon Abbas's return a week later. Du Leze is sitting on the verandah, an open book in his lap. "How is your father?"

Abbas gives a brief report.

"Good Lord." Du Leze studies him. "Why don't you spend another week or two at home? It's quite all right. Sukumaran is here to keep me company."

"Sukumaran?"

"Devi's replacement."

"Devi left?"

"Without any notice at all. She simply stopped coming." Du Leze lowers his voice. "I miss her fish fry but what can you do."

Later, in the kitchen, Abbas is confronted by the saggy-chested Sukumaran, whose eagerness to please is almost aggressive. Coffee,

Sukumaran offers, or tea? Juice? Lemon? Minty lemon? Cucumber? What?

Abbas flees the battery of beverage offerings and goes to the workshop at the back of the house.

The clocks wait with bland white faces, but he is too disoriented to sit. For a while he stands very still, holding his elbows.

In time, he will regard her from a new angle, bewildered by her coldness, by his own naivete. Her absence will lose its sting. For now he can feel every pound of his heart, can still hear the echo of her laughter on the roof.

··

Six months later, on a sweltering morning in July, Abbas goes with Du Leze to the parade grounds, to attend the celebration of a new French organization—the Srirangapatna Jacobin Club. The crowd is almost entirely French, bobbing with heads of varied hues: orange, brown, ash, straw. From the periphery, Abbas can just make out the figure of Tipu Sultan, standing on a raised platform. He wears a simple muslin jama and turban, playing to the tastes of his unaristocratic audience.

Abbas is uncertain who the Jacobins are, other than a convoy of radical Frenchmen who have sailed to Mysore in order to make an alliance with Tipu. In private, Du Leze has made clear to Abbas what he thinks of the Jacobins ("lazy, loud, dirty") and of their leader, Admiral Ripaud. "He is no admiral, he is a pirate," said Du Leze. "It was a storm that blew him onto these shores but as the *admiral* would have it, he has come with the sole motive of answering Tipu's every prayer and raising up a French army. He could no sooner raise the dead from their tombs!"

"How do you know all this, Sahab?" Abbas asked quietly, glancing over his shoulder. They were striding down the promenade alone, but, as Du Leze likes to say, even the air has ears.

"My friends at the French Rocks." Du Leze paused. "From what I hear, no good can come of so public an alliance."

At the celebration, Du Leze keeps these opinions to himself, his face blank and benign as Tipu addresses the crowd in French.

Abbas spots the stout figure of Monsieur Martine at the front of the crowd, fanning his face with his hat. Martine, who engineered for Tipu a new boring machine for the increased production of cannons. Martine, who displaced Du Leze as Tipu's favorite Frenchman. Abbas wonders if Martine's daughter is running around the grounds, though probably not, at such a shabby gathering of men.

Ripaud comes forward and presides over the planting of a tree festooned with ribbons. When the last shovelful of dirt has been tamped over the roots, a breeze takes up the tricolored ribbons, making them flare and fly as if the heavens approve.

"Where the wind blows," Du Leze says quietly, "so goes Ripaud."

Ripaud raises his arms to the crowd. *"Citoyens!"* he yells. "Do you swear hatred to all kings except Tipu Sultan the Victorious, Ally of the French Republic?"

The crowd yells a variety of affirmations.

"Do you declare war against all tyrants and love toward your country, and that of Citizen Tipu?"

More affirmations.

"Then repeat after me: We Jacobins swear to live free or die!"

"We swear to live free or die!"

"Let them hear you in Calcutta, in Madras!"

"WE SWEAR TO LIVE FREE OR DIE!"

Now Tipu slashes his finger through the air. Tiger-headed cannons fire and reel, smoking from open jaws. At last the rocket men, dressed in babri stripe, kneel to angle their rockets toward the sky. The rockets go soaring, farther than any projectile Abbas has ever seen, filling him with awe and fear, as if whatever Tipu Sultan hurls at the heavens will one day come hurtling back.

Having the rest of the day off, Abbas goes home to visit with his family. They receive him like the rare guest that he is, watching him pinch off pieces of ragi ball to dip in a bowl of mutton gravy. He has missed his old breakfast. The only thing slowing his appetite is the sight of his father on a charpai by the wall, legs like a pair of parsnips under a quilt.

"Sahra made the mutton," his mother says. Sahra Bhabhi, Junaid's wife, leans against the doorway. She is a petite woman with a protuberant belly who has yet to forgive Abbas for asking at their second meeting if she was pregnant. (She wasn't.)

"The mutton is delicious," says Abbas.

"Ammi taught me," Sahra says curtly. "She has many specifications."

"Count yourself lucky," his mother says. "Some old crones won't let their daughters-in-law step foot in the kitchen."

"Don't call my mother a crone." Everyone looks at Yusuf Muhammad, who has just spoken with rare lucidity though his eyes are still closed.

"I thought you were sleeping," says Abbas's mother.

"You always think that," he replies.

Whispers draw their attention to the window, where two of the neighbor children are gripping the bars. "*Ei,* what are you both staring at?" his mother says playfully. "Is he Bahadur Khan?"

Abbas growls at the children. They drop down beneath the sill, squealing.

"Abbas is famous," Sahra says. He can never tell when Sahra is teasing him, which he finds mildly annoying. "What is the French sahab teaching you now?"

"Clockwork," he says.

"Still?"

Before he can take offense, his mother cuts in. "Abbas, have you asked around about scribe work? You might have to start at the bottom as an ink man, but you can work your way up to being a Farsi scribe—their wages are three times that of the Kannada scribes."

Abbas is exasperated. "Shall I tell the padshah I am to quit my apprenticeship—the one he gave me—because my mother wants me to be an ink man?"

"I doubt he would notice," his mother says. "I hear Tipu spends all his time on rockets and warships."

"The padshah does many things with his time," Abbas says. "Sometimes five things at once."

"Every day we hear the rockets," says his father. His eyes open with revelation. "Maybe it was Tipu's rocket that frightened the horse."

"It wasn't," says Abbas.

"No, it wasn't," his father agrees solemnly. "It was that eunuch who cursed me."

Abbas twists around to look at his father.

"What?" his father says. "It must be."

His mother drops her voice to a whisper. "He keeps talking about some eunuch. Where he gets these ideas, I don't know."

"You can never trust a eunuch," his father says.

"Enough about eunuchs!" says his mother. "The neighbors will hear."

"Abbas knows what I'm talking about. Tell her, Abbas, tell about the eunuch that cursed me."

Abbas tries to reason with his father, tries to remind him that the injury was the result of sheer bad luck. He reaches out to place a hand on his father's arm, but his father elbows him away.

"Oh, so now you know all?" says his father. "You can't even remember the bloody eunuch!"

Sahra retreats to the kitchen.

To Abbas's surprise, it is his mother who intervenes in a strong, soothing voice, urging his father not to cry, for crying will only dry him up, leading him to drink too much water, which will mean getting the bowl, and no one wants to deal with the bowl, do they? Well, do they? No, says his father, no bowl. She reaches out and gives his blanketed toes a squeeze; it is the first time Abbas has ever seen her touch him. But his father is unmoved, frowning as resolutely as when he carried off the tiger-headed umbrella in search of someone to tell, and none could stop those legs, that will.

II

In the early months of 1797, one of Tipu's envoys returns from Persia, not with an army but with a tome. It is a copy of *The Book of Knowledge of Ingenious Mechanical Devices* written in the thirteenth century by Badiʿ al-Zaman ibn al-Razzaz al-Jazari, also known as the Prodigy of the Age, also known as the Son of a Rice Merchant, and most widely known as Al-Jazari.

Days and nights Tipu spends with *The Book of Knowledge,* forgoing all company in favor of the engineering feats detailed within: camshafts and crankshafts and crank-slider mechanisms, segmental gears, chain pumps, double-action suction pumps with valves and reciprocating piston motions, candle clocks, castle clocks, weight-driven water clocks, and humanoid automata that are hundreds of years ahead of Vaucanson's Duck, and, in Tipu's opinion, far superior, for Al-Jazari's automata actually served a purpose!

Take the hand-washing automaton, designed to aid the king in his ritual ablutions. Built of jointed copper, the automaton held in its right hand a brass peacock-shaped pitcher. At the proper time, the automaton would smoothly pour a stream of clean water from the pitcher, without sputtering, into the basin. When the basin was full, the automaton would straighten up and extend with its left arm a towel, comb, and mirror so that the king could dry his face and tend to his beard.

It is enough to make any other king, however beardless, sigh with envy.

Accompanying every device and creation is a perfect miniature painting, also done by Al-Jazari, rich with plum purples and gleaming golds, with marginal notes to explain each mechanism. The most ingenious of the ingenious mechanical devices is the Elephant Clock, two stories high and consisting of a tower atop a life-sized elephant and including a cymbal-playing mahout, a rotating scribe, two dragons, a snake, a phoenix, and a turbaned Arab on top. At the turn of each hour, these figures would spring to life, not only entertaining the spectator but also keeping accurate time. The painting is enchanting, yet what makes the Elephant Clock take hold of Tipu, what makes it feel like an idea sprung from his very own mind, are the accompanying words of Al-Jazari:

> The elephant represents the Indian and African cultures, the phoenix represents Persian culture, the water work represents Greek culture, and the turban represents Islamic culture.

Al-Jazari is speaking to him across time and space and otherworldly dimension, writing of the past but also a possible future, in which Europe does not even merit a footnote.

Tipu instructs his scribes to translate the page from Persian to French and deliver the translation to Monsieur Du Leze. Through Purnaiya, he informs Du Leze that Mysore's Elephant Clock must be completed for display at the Dasara Festival in September. They have six months. A tall order to finish in so little time, but the people need a distraction. Tipu is eager to get them talking about something other than the untimely death of their Wodeyar king.

It is said that over the last five hundred years, the line of Wodeyar kings has never been broken, one Wodeyar blissfully succeeding the last. (According to the royal record, at any rate.) Then Tipu's father, Haidar Ali, came along and slid into the ruling position. Of course a Muslim could not displace a Hindu—a son of the soil, no less— without problems. So Haidar allowed the king to remain a king in name and to retain certain customs, as on the first evening of Dasara, when the king would appear on the verandah of his palace, seated on his throne, surrounded by attendants who took turns fanning him and scattering perfume and petals on his long, lustrously oiled hair. That sort of tradition wasn't Haidar's cup of tea, nor Tipu's, but fine. Live and let live, they decided, when it came to peaceable Hindus and Christians within the kingdom.

Then, in the spring of '96, the most recent king, Khasa-Chamaraja Wodeyar, died. That he was twenty-three at the time of death, a death that came suddenly and without explanation, invited the suggestion of foul play. Tipu would not answer to these rumors, nor to criticism of his next move: to expel the Wodeyar family from their palace, ignore all claims of succession, and make himself sole ruler of the Mysore kingdom.

A bold move? Certainly. But does history favor the bold or does it favor the petaled and perfumed?

Two years later, the Royalists are still grumbling about their dead king. To drown out the noise, Tipu will bring to the festival a new main attraction, one that he hopes will provoke among the masses a sense of awe and its close cousin— obedience.

On a sheet of paper, Abbas draws the Elephant Clock, his heart thumping hard with every glance at Al-Jazari's text. He knows this is only a copy of a copy of a copy, and yet it feels as though his pencil marks are summoning up the soul of the legend himself.

He and Du Leze begin by building a prototype, this one hip-high. The prototype allows them to see how the mechanisms within form an elaborate chain of cause and effect, all of which is tethered, remarkably, to something as simple as a bowl with a hole in its bottom.

Hidden within the elephant's belly is a tank of water. Floating in the water is the perforated bowl. Over the course of exactly thirty minutes, the bowl fills with water, tips, and sinks, engaging a pulley system that runs up to the top of the cupola, which tips a hidden channel of balls, a stopper lifting to release a single one, which drops against the paddle of a wheel, sending the phoenix atop the cupola spinning.

Yet the ball is not finished. Still hidden, it slinks down another channel, and then emerges from the mouth of a falcon, released from the beak into the mouth of a serpent, which then rears back from the weight of the ball, tugging on a hidden rope that pulls the perforated bowl within the belly of the elephant back to the surface of the water to begin the process all over again.

Has it been mentioned that the ball drops into a vase, causing the mahout to beat a cymbal, sounding the half hour? Or that the rotating scribe has been marking the minutes by his pen all the while? Or that the rate of water flow must be daily changed through a flow-control regulator to match the uneven length of days throughout the year?

And this is only the prototype. Mistakes and measurements are made again and again, so many that Du Leze has taken on a hassled look, his beard unkempt, stubble crawling down his neck, mumbling into the gutter of Al-Jazari's book as if to draw out its secrets.

On the plus side, Abbas now has two carvers working for him. The old one has a droopy face and coffee breath. The younger one is vain about his mustache, often petting the corner with his pinky. And indeed it is a covetable fringe, the kind Abbas can only dream of growing. Yet in the most important sense, Abbas is living his dream. How many young men of mean origins can claim an association with Tipu Sultan? If the other two carvers are resentful of working for someone so young, they conceal their feelings.

There was one instance of disharmony, when Abbas stepped out for a breath of fresh air and returned to find the carvers talking about Tipu's breakfast. "I hear he eats a spoonful of sparrow brains every morning," the younger man was saying, enacting the reason by holding a pencil at his groin, then lifting the pencil to a horizontal position. "Bet you a hundred mohurs it's true."

Abbas took up his gouge. "I wouldn't make such bets."

"He was joking," said the old man. "He's never even seen a mohur."

With the gouge, Abbas lifted a long curling tendril of wood. "If the padshah were to hear you talking of his gifts, he might make some changes to your own."

The gouge went *zzzzip zzzzip.* The men said not a word for the rest of the day.

Abbas doesn't mind the silence; in fact he prefers the sole company of carving, the sanctity of it. The way the wood almost displays a wit of its own, how it makes and unmakes its own rules. That a cut cannot be undone. That the grain may change depending on the cut. That you might expect a line to go one way only for it to swerve. That total control will never be yours.

At night, in bed, Abbas thinks of Al-Jazari, a man who began humbly, the son of a rice merchant. This detail, for Abbas, holds mystery and meaning, and invites him to imagine himself in the great man's place. Of course he knows he is no Al-Jazari and never will be. He has no head for conceiving ingenious devices, though in the minutes before sleep, he imagines a fleet of mechanical horses, perfectly jointed and galloping across a battlefield, blasting bullets from their flaring, fist-sized nostrils. Or a row of mechanical nautch girls who twirl with the turning of the hour. The nautch girls would be identical in feature, with high foreheads and wide-set eyes, like the one he witnessed dancing in Tipu's gardens years ago. Though he hasn't seen her since, he remembers her still. Some nights he reinvents her in explicit detail, and Devi, too, so much so that he ends up disgracing his sheets.

Never mind that he lacks the skill to make a nautch girl clock or a battle horse. At night, his future feels to him expansive, oceanic. The future has yet to test him, yet to present him with the most difficult decision of his life. His mind glitters with ideas, yet he has no idea of how much luck he will need.

III

Harvest season arrives and with it, the festival of Dasara, honoring the triumph of good over evil, of the goddess over the buffalo demon, their painted effigies as tall as teak trees facing off in perpetual battle.

Outside the arena, where most of the festivities are taking place, a stilt-walker stumbles among the people. The stilt-walker is dressed as an Englishman, with a black hat on his head, white paint on his face, and giant black pants to cloak the stilts. He pretends to drink from a liquor bottle and inhale snuff from a tin, occasionally improvising acts of buffoonery. People flow past him to get a seat inside the arena, where the real drama transpires: great stags clacking horns; elephants fighting hind-legged; wrestlers throwing flower garlands in one another's faces before the first steel-taloned punch; drunken donkeys sent stumbling into a tiger's pen—a bit of comic relief before the tiger fight, a battle that has everyone flinching until the winning tiger is coaxed back into its cage, and the losing tiger, hemorrhaging out the mouth, has its head crushed by an elephant's foot.

These spectacles are no different from the ones that have been held on these grounds for the past hundred years. The only difference is the Elephant Clock. It towers in a courtyard of its own, the height of two tuskers standing one atop the other.

Abbas no longer watches the Elephant Clock in action. He finds the audience more interesting, how awe can transfigure a person, can make a man escape his own life in the space of seconds, can do this for a whole group of men and women and children, so that all their faces turn young with wonder.

There is one spectator who watches him more than she watches the Elephant Clock. A fair-skinned girl, her bun hung with jasmine. She stares as though they know one another.

As soon as the Elephant Clock stills, people approach him with questions, wanting to know what the phoenix means and what the gold ball weighs. The girl hovers until they are alone, then steps forward with a little curtsy.

"Do you know me?" she asks, with a half-smile he recognizes instantly.

"Mademoiselle Jehanne," he says. He notes that her cheekbones are steeper now, that her height has leapt to equal his own. "You've grown taller."

A trite thing to say, but she nods energetically. "I am nearly as tall as my father."

"How is Monsieur Martine? Is he here?"

"No, he swore off melas after someone snatched his wig." She says this with pleasure, as if she'd snatched the wig herself. "And your family, did they come?"

He is reluctant to tell of his father's tattered mind, his mother's hair, gone white within the space of a year. "They prefer not to travel."

She nods slowly and reaches for her bun, as if to make sure it's still in one piece. For a moment, it seems they have nothing more to say. This would be the natural time to part ways, but between them is a mutual unwillingness.

"Are you tired of explaining how it works?" she says.

"How what works?"

"The Elephant Clock."

Embarrassed, he glances over his shoulder and begins to describe, in detail, the entire chain of reaction and the story of Al-Jazari, all the while standing within the fragrant radius of her hair.

At last she says: "What a thing you've made."

"Well, it was Al-Jazari who designed it. Lucien Sahab and I, we merely replicated the original."

"Perhaps one day you'll make a thing that will be replicated centuries hence."

He says nothing, her remark landing too close to his most self-indulgent dreams.

A man in passing interrupts to ask when the next showing will be. When the scribe's pen falls in line with the elephant's trunk, says Abbas. Before walking on, the man nods and flicks a glance between Jehanne and Abbas, as if detecting something untoward in the two of them, alone together.

"I should find my aunt," says Jehanne, and then, hesitating, she thrusts something at him in her outstretched hand. "This is for you. In exchange for the top you gave me."

It is a folded kerchief of white cotton, which he opens to find four embroidered florals, fine beneath his fingertip.

"I made it myself," she says. "Even the pattern."

"It's very pretty," he says, looking up at her. A pinkish color is creeping up her throat. With a brisk nod and a curtsy, she leaves him.

Abbas has yet to get a glimpse of Tipu Sultan at the festival. "Ah, well," says Du Leze, walking through the mela with Abbas, "it has only been two weeks."

(Two weeks since the death of Tipu's wife Khadijah Begum. Of his four wives, she had been his third favorite. The first and second favorites are also dead, leaving him with his first wife, who was neither his choice nor a favorite but still insists on being called Tipu Begum.)

Du Leze has drawn Abbas away from the Elephant Clock on a matter of urgency—good urgency, not bad urgency, he said. Now he leads the way to the food stalls in a leisurely manner, scratching at the bites on the backs of his hands, where mosquitos have found room to dine too.

"Did you see Jehanne Martine?" Du Leze asks slyly. "She saw you. I doubt she saw much else."

Abbas pretends not to hear as they pass through smells of fried batter, rows of milk sweets shaped as balls and boxes and flowers. Roses and jasmine hang in damp garlands so fresh that bees still swarm the blooms for nectar. Du Leze pauses to buy two paper cones of warm peanuts. Beneath a banyan tree, at some remove from the mela, he hands a cone to Abbas and raises his own in the air. "To a fresh start!" he says.

Abbas is growing impatient. Du Leze tosses a few peanuts into his grinning mouth, drawing out the drama.

Du Leze has received a letter from his sister in France. The sister is a pious woman who goes each Sunday to a Christian church, where she prays for his safe return, then goes into town and checks the émigré lists, to see if her God has been listening. "She has been doing this every week for three years now, and for several weeks in January, she said there has been a line through my name. Then in February she said my name was gone."

"What does it mean?"

"Perhaps there were two Lucien Du Lezes. Perhaps the other one died, who knows? Isabelle says mistakes happen all the time with these lists." His eyes are bright, shining. "She believes it is safe for me now to go home."

Abbas searches for the right words. *"Mashallah."*

"And I wish you to come with me."

"To France?"

"Yes, to Rouen."

Rouen? Abbas has only heard Du Leze speak of Paris. "Rou . . ." Abbas attempts.

"Rouen." Du Leze utters the word as if trying to rid his voice of some stuck thing. "A beautiful town. You would carry on studying with me—a little more horology wouldn't hurt. After that, some basic engineering, physics, mechanics, building automata, and then . . ." Du Leze shrugs. "You decide if you wish to stay or return to your home."

"But when . . ."

"There are two trade ships leaving from Pondicherry—one is leaving in a month, another six months hence. I intend to take the earlier ship, and I would prefer you come with me."

"In a month, Sahab?"

"Soon, I know. But I cannot lose my chance this time. Surely you can say your farewells in the next few weeks?"

Abbas stares at the ground, his mind racing toward the future, over land, across the sea.

And then he remembers his father. His father, who is dying. Abbas has never allowed himself to think of his father as dying, but what else to call his continual diminishment, the way the family circles him, serves him, waiting for what they cannot name?

When Abbas mentions this, Du Leze's face falls. "Your father. Of course." Du Leze pinches his chin, pulling, thinking. "Would his condition be any different in six months? Would he wish you to lose the opportunity altogether?"

Abbas falls silent, thinking of his father, who, at his most peaceful moments, stares into the wall by his cot, his wishes known only to him.

"Then come on the second ship, if you must," says Du Leze. "I warn you, it will not be easy on your own. The voyage itself takes a year, with many stops in between. And you have so little French—"

"But what did Tipu say? About my leaving?"

Du Leze opens his mouth, exhales.

"You did not ask?" says Abbas.

"It would be best to leave without asking. He would not know."

"He would know when I came back and asked for my old job."

"I highly doubt he would keep such a close eye on one wood-carver. He has bigger problems, in case you haven't noticed."

With this talk they are edging toward treason. The realization is dizzying.

"The East India Company has a new governor," Du Leze continues. "And from what I hear, he has a heavier hand than his predecessor. The smallest provocation, such as this business with the Jacobin Club and Ripaud . . ." Du Leze falls quiet, waiting for a stranger to pass. Then he takes a step forward, this great and towering tree of a man, in whose shade Abbas has walked safely these past five years. "You do not have to decide now, my boy. Spend a few days with the idea, then tell me."

A heavy pat on the shoulder, and Du Leze disappears into the crowd.

Abbas sinks to a crouch between the banyan roots. He watches people go by. There is a man—the stilt-walker, still in costume minus the stilts—trying to close his mouth around a whole sweet. The man's face is still painted white, yet he has neglected to paint the backs of his hands, which are dark brown. (Something about this discrepancy unsettles Abbas.) There is a child picking his teeth with the shaft of a feather until his mother knocks it from his hands, telling him "*Chee!* It's dirty, leave it." Far beyond them, on top of a wall, is a crow, standing in the perfect spot from which an English soldier could aim his rifle and shoot the child in the back of the head.

The thought comes as a shock, as though he has willed violence on the child, when there is no violence at all in the cloudless blue sky, no violence in the mother cupping the back of the boy's head as they stroll blithely along.

IV

Du Leze stands on the beach in his oilcloth coat, mesmerized by the Bay of Bengal. His eye follows the folds of water crashing against the shore, a puzzle of dark rocks honed flat by the tide. At his back is Pondicherry, a city that gives off a heady splendor, if not a little weariness at being so attractive to centuries of conquerors and would-be conquerors. At this early-morning hour, Pondicherry lets out a blue sigh. Du Leze can feel it on the air. He feels some of the same, though mostly what he feels is bewilderment.

He is going home.

When he first arrived eleven years ago, Pondicherry belonged to France. Now English flags fly from every possible rampart. What these waters must have looked like, thick with English frigates, the sky black with mortar fire. His guide told him the French had barely put up a fight. In fact, the guide added dryly, the only thing the French garrison seized was a tankard of ale, leaving them too sozzled to surrender properly.

The guide had been courteous, his French unusually smooth. He rode with Du Leze for two days on horseback, then delivered him to a hotel in White Town, the sea-facing part of the city that had been claimed by French rulers, leaving Black Town for the ruled. All this the guide explained without a glint of resentment or resignation, a skilled performance. He even made sure to point out the two landmarks that mattered most to the people he guided—the closest church and the French bakery across the street. And though Du Leze found that he'd grown fond of his guide, the man accepted the money with curt gratitude and left for Black Town without a backward glance.

For several days Du Leze has been walking the streets of White Town, which feels to him foreign and familiar, all angles and order, pediments and pillars, the seriousness of the architecture leavened by hues of pale pink, butter yellow, light blue. Last night he listened to the crash of tides through the window and wondered if he would ever see Abbas again.

Did he try hard enough to persuade the boy? Did he explain how difficult the journey would be with no companion or interpreter? No, he spent most of his persuasive powers on the merchants in the bazaar, running around buying gifts to take with him to Rouen. Never could he find such textiles in Europe, iridescent silks embroidered with mirrorwork, pashmina shawls of luminous hue. He can only imagine how his sister, Isabelle, will receive a Kanchipuram sari; probably squint at it and ask whether all Indians dress in circus colors.

Blaque would know what to do with such fabrics—turn them into lavish waistcoats or curtains or some other head-turning piece. But Blaque, he has heard, is somewhere in Austria, if not dead. And Paris is too risky to revisit, his workshop and apartment likely inhabited by strangers.

Du Leze tells himself he has lost all desire for Paris, for Blaque. He used to imagine not his own death, but how the news of his death would reach his beloved. Here was Blaque, falling to his knees on the Austrian cobbles. Here was Blaque, rooting through Lucien's letters, all of which he had kept; here he was reading over them with tenderness and tears. How would that other Lucien have died? By opening his veins? Borrowing a gun? The despair that nearly sent him plummeting seems somehow to have vanished; he knows not how or why. Yet, even though death itself is no longer so alluring, the fascination remains.

Lately he has been drawn to the possibilities of his new life. In Rouen, he can begin again, maybe rent a room from Isabelle and begin with basic clock repair. He wouldn't mind a country life, work that quiets the mind. And if all goes to plan, Abbas will arrive six months later. The guild will give him trouble for taking a foreigner as an apprentice. Not to mention objections from Isabelle for housing an Indian, apprentice or not. Only temporary, he finds himself reassuring her in his mind.

The question is whether Abbas will come at all.

"Why are you so invested in his future?" This is the question Isabelle will pose, or something along the lines of "What is he to you?"

Meaning: Are you in love with this person? She's always had her suspicions.

Love, no. And yet from the day they met, Du Leze felt drawn to Abbas, as curious about the boy and his talent as the rest of the world was indifferent to it.

Du Leze never thought he would like being a teacher. Only now, at the miraculous age of sixty-three, does he realize how it can revive a person, can restore the old thrill. And what delight there has been in watching Abbas grow in all ways, height and skill and worldliness, from tentative questions to candid opinions. But what comes next?

Instead of buying silks, he should've requested one more meeting with Abbas. He should have told him: I was once a boy like you, toiling in my father's shop until my uncle plucked me out and planted me with a horologist in Paris. I never saw my father again—he died before I could return—but I had already let him go. So must you with yours. Talent will take you only so far now that Tipu has turned his eye elsewhere. You need time and tutelage. You need my help, and I need to know I have done something of use before I die.

· · ·

After breakfast, the guide brings Du Leze to the Port Office, trunks in tow. They avoid the piazza, which is already hectic with merchants. Du Leze takes note of the orderly design: the slim colonnades along the chunam-plaster wall, the saplings planted at even intervals. The guide points out Du Leze's corvette among the other vessels lining the dock. A placard at the helm reads *Aurore*. A red pennant snaps from the tallest mast.

Du Leze feels a tug of exhilaration. And dread.

First the *Aurore* will stop at Isle de France, off the coast of Madagascar, then the Cape of Good Hope then Ascension Island then Gorée Island then Malaga then Toulon, before the overland journey to Rouen. He recalls what he witnessed years ago on the way to Mysore. Bad winds. Ruffians. Scurvy. Of the latter, he gave Abbas a precise explanation, every symptom causing the boy's face to contort with disgust. "Take several tins of lemon pickle," said Du Leze, "in case you find yourself on a ship that has run out of scorbutics." Du Leze also gave Abbas a cloth pouch of money—four times the amount needed to buy passage to France. Abbas objected weakly, but Du Leze overrode him. "You simply ask for directions to the Port Office, wearing clean clothes, mind you—preferably trousers, I shall obtain them for you—and request a one-way ticket to Toulon. *Et voilà.*"

Is it so simple? Du Leze thinks to himself, scanning the harbor. Was this place always so frenzied with people, lascars in motion, loading crates into holds, sails unfurling, clapping with the wind? How in God's name will Abbas find his way?

A horn sounds, inviting the passengers to board.

On the deckhouse, Du Leze shakes hands with Monsieur Martine. "I'd almost forgotten you were coming!" says Martine, his cheeks pink with excitement or sunburn. "But where is Abbas?"

"He will be on the next ship. Six months hence."

"Alone?"

"He is quite capable," Du Leze says sharply.

"Ah, well," says Martine with a shrug. "Poor Jehanne, she will be disappointed."

"Disappointed why?" says Jehanne, joining them. Du Leze is struck by the heavy black kohl rimming her pale gray eyes and the black dot on her cheek, making her seem older than fourteen. She wears a white frock, and seems as uncomfortable in that getup as Du Leze feels in his breeches. "Where is Abbas?"

"He is not coming, my dear," says Martine.

"But he will," Du Leze adds. "On a later ship."

She looks from one man to the other. "You left him behind?" she says, her voice softly incredulous.

The question stings. "He will come," repeats Du Leze, with less certainty. "Eventually."

Her gaze drops to his hands; only then does he realize he has been cracking his knuckles. She walks away.

"Jehanne," says Martine, chidingly.

She turns back, curtsies. "Excuse me," she says, and goes to stand broadside, her eyes on the shore.

"Be glad you don't have a daughter," Martine says. "They're a stew of emotions at this age. Still, I'll have someone to look after me when I'm old."

Du Leze observes Jehanne. Her back is straight, her figure still.

"One moment," he says to Martine, and joins her broadside.

At first Du Leze stands apart, wanting to grant her the privacy to wipe away her tears. But she does not move, not even when he looks at her, surprised to find that she has not been crying. Hers is an expression of sad disbelief. Du Leze follows her eyeline to the shore and wishes, suddenly, that he'd pocketed a stone, even a handful of dirt.

He forgets why he has joined her here, what he'd intended to say. Something to reassure her or to reassure himself?

As the *Aurore* pulls away, he turns his gaze up to the clouds. A flock of birds, too far and too tiny to name, are crossing the blue. The longer he looks, the more birds keep emerging like pinpoints from the clouds, faint as pencil marks at first, flickering into being.

"Look at that," he says, pointing at the sky.

She looks, but is quiet for so long he assumes she is simply humoring him and sees nothing.

Then she says, "Oh."

"You see them?"

"Yes."

And they both go quiet, watching bird after bird materializing from thin air.

The Final Months of Tipu Sultan

1799

Two months before his death, Tipu Sultan does his dawn prayer. The rest of the impious world is asleep, allowing Tipu to feel as though he's having a one-to-one with Allah. His belly is empty, his mind clean. Usually the surah flows through him, but this morning, there are stops and starts. Other words are clotting his mind, the words of that walking hemorrhoid, Governor Wellesley.

> *It is impossible that you should suppose me to be ignorant of the intercourse which subsists between you and the French . . .*

Tipu draws a deep dismissive breath and stands taller, tweaking a nerve in his back. He touches his lower spine, pained, then annoyed. His back, that unruly subject. He senses Raja Khan behind him, shifting his weight, always at the ready to provide a hot-water bottle. Tipu doesn't want a hot-water bottle. He wants to continue with the rakah.

Guide us in the straight way.

You cannot imagine me to be indifferent . . .

His own unwritten reply breaks unbidden through his mind. *You know what I cannot imagine? I cannot imagine that you are try-*

ing to concoct a war with no specific charge other than a hundred ugly Frenchmen having landed on my shore if you call that "intercourse" then why don't you write to all the other princes the French have been "intercoursing" with and

He coughs; a pain goes pulsing through his chest. Breathing lightly, he puts his forehead to the carpet.

Most of the blame belongs to the governor of Isle de France, a French colony and supposedly an ally. Tipu had sent his envoys to the island for a secret meeting in hopes of raising a secret French army, and what does the governor of Isle de France do? He publishes a bloody proclamation in the newspaper! SOLDIERS WANTED BY TIPU SULTAN—ANYONE INTERESTED? (Wellesley was very interested.) And the entire effort resulted in only a boatful of Frenchmen sent to Mysore—pale, flea-bitten "volunteers" most likely culled from the pits of prison.

A mistake to trust the French. A lesson Tipu has learned time and time again. Perhaps he should've checked in with that makeshift consulate in Paris, should've realized that they were far too preoccupied with fighting wars in the Mediterranean to spend even a pittance on Tipu.

Mistakes have been made. And no doubt his father is in heaven, counting each and every one, so they can spend all eternity talking about what Haidar would have done instead.

A letter to the caliph. A letter to Wellesley. A letter to the shah. A letter to Major Doveton. A letter to Baji Rao. A letter to the peshwa. He trusts no one but himself to write these letters, none but himself to stamp his personal seal on the page.

It's not the writing that tires him. It's the sense that he is more salesman than sultan, going kingdom to kingdom with a product no one seems to want to buy. Everyone agrees, more or less, with the fact that the English must be chased out of India. Everyone claims to love the gifts Tipu sends along with the letters. Yet no one is quite capable of saying no, preferring polite indecision over outright rejection. And quite a few wish him to fail because he is descended not from kings but from an illiterate mercenary.

Only the Americans seem to appreciate that sort of origin story. Their first president once raised a toast to Tipu's father; they even named one of their naval ships the *Hyder Ally*. But now the Americans have their piracy troubles, and the French have their Mediterranean troubles, and Tipu has no one.

And so he continues to send letters and gifts, his last going to the shah of Persia, along with exotic birds, jewelry, dresses, ivory, sandalwood, and spices.

To His Greatness Fath-Ali Shah Qajar, writes Tipu, consulting the scribe's notes for all of the shah's royal titles, Lord of This, That, and the Next . . .

At the final claim, Tipu pauses.

Aloud he reads: "Most Formidable Lord and Master of the *Encyclopaedia Britannica*?" He looks to Raja Khan for confirmation.

"A European reference book," supplies Raja Khan. "His Greatness has read all eighteen volumes."

"Persians," Tipu says, though not without a touch of respect. What he would do with so much time on his hands. His whole library awaits, neglected.

For the time being, he puts the nib of his pen to paper.

Most Formidable Lord and Master of the Encyclopaedia Britannica . . .

The shah will be moved by the letter, specifically its message that the English plan to conquer India and then continue on through Arabia, destroying Islam along the way. In return, the shah will send back to Mysore an embassy of men to negotiate an alliance with Tipu, who will be dead by the time they arrive.

Tipu takes breakfast with Sayyid Ghaffur, his finest general. Tipu drafted Ghaffur many years ago, while passing through Honnali.

There, Tipu had witnessed a man riding a horse, hands free, when suddenly the man reached up and grabbed a tree branch and, using only the strength of his legs, made the horse stop and swivel this way and that, this way and that. As a general, Ghaffur no longer does horse tricks, but his thighs are still thick as two barrel drums.

Also present is Purnaiya, a stringy fellow by comparison, though he seems not the least bit intimidated by Ghaffur. They sit on either side of the meal laid before them: dal and roti, pigeon eggs, buttermilk. Tipu's own plates and cups are covered by squares of white cloth, to convey that the taster has done his job and survived.

They speak of Harris's army, twenty-one thousand men marching from Vellore toward Mysore. They speak of the sixteen thousand English troops from Hyderabad, poised to join at Ambur. Not to mention the forces at Trichinpoly, rising from the south.

They discuss attacking at night, stealing cannons, letting the light cavalry loose on the enemy while they dream.

"But how will these guerrilla tactics stop an army of so many?" says Purnaiya.

"Half their armies are bullocks," says Ghaffur, his mustache fringed with buttermilk. Tipu brushes at his own mustache, but Ghaffur doesn't get the hint. "With their camels and cooks and wives and children, they're moving so slow, the rains will outrun them."

"We hope," says Purnaiya.

Ghaffur registers Purnaiya's remark with a twitch of his mouth. An angry twitch. An I-don't-trust-you sort of twitch. "We have only to harass them along the way. Burn the forage before their horses can get to it."

"I can monitor the movements of Harris," says Purnaiya. "Myself and Sayyid Saheb."

"We don't need monitors," Ghaffur says. "We need warriors. Loyal ones."

Purnaiya says nothing, as though Ghaffur's implication has sailed right over his head. (Of course, nothing sails past Purnaiya; he has simply perfected the art of pretending not to hear.) "General," says Purnaiya, "you have buttermilk on your mustache."

Glowering, the general wipes his mustache.

And so begins an argument Tipu has no interest in mediating. He is focused on the ruins of their meal. A white cloth is neatly folded beside his plate, but beside his teacup, no cloth. Did it arrive with a cloth? He can't remember. He has already finished the tea. He can't remember whether the teacup arrived with its white covering cloth.

"Was this teacup covered when it came?" he asks abruptly.

Purnaiya and Ghaffur look at him, then at the teacup that holds his attention.

"It was," says Purnaiya.

Tipu nods. The moment seems to have passed. Ghaffur is turning back to Purnaiya when Tipu says, "And the taster—what is his name?"

Ghaffur smirks. "Why should the Tiger of Mysore need to know the name of some lowly taster?"

Tipu looks at Ghaffur, who is silenced. "Because I require it."

Purnaiya gives Tipu a name: Riyad.

"And this Riyad," says Tipu, "he has been with us for how many years?"

"Ten at least. He was hired by the superintendent of the Imperial Kitchen, who, as the padshah knows, has an impeccable reputation and insists on the same for all the kitchen workers he hires."

Tipu allows his guests to carry on with the discussion of military strategy. But privately he is considering his father, who was almost killed by a poisoned meal in Bednur, a city he had invaded but not properly subdued. By the next afternoon, mostly recovered, Haidar was rounding up his men and heading back to the capital city, where he could eat meals prepared by people he trusted. Behind him, in Bednur, he left three hundred men and women, alleged conspirators, hanging from the city gates.

Tomorrow Tipu marches for Maddur; from there he will march east and surprise General Stuart.

Today he takes a walk in Daria Daulat Bagh. Cypress trees line the walk, offering shade. Here is the pomegranate tree, bejeweled with fruit. Here are the more exotic trees, apple and peach, stubbornly refusing to prosper. He tells Raja Khan to have the apple and the peach replanted in a shadier section. They continue on through herbs and orchids and purple riots of hydrangea.

Upon reaching the far end of the promenade, Tipu turns and gazes at the palace. He imagines a herd of redcoats tromping up the path. He pictures the palace aflame behind castrated pillars, and only the rain trees still standing, trembling with terrible visions.

These are mutinous thoughts, ones that assume his own defeat.

But he must prepare himself for the possibility.

He has also been preparing the city. Ganjam evacuated. Men conscripted, their families sent to other parts of Mysore. Experience is no matter. He calls on those skilled and unskilled in war, on cooks and blacksmiths and basket weavers, boys as young as fourteen, men who've only ever held the tools of their trade in their fists. He has had the walls of the fort whitewashed, all the caricatures erased, in case the English storm the fort and he must negotiate another treaty. Pig-nosed effigies will not help his cause. Nor will an automaton of a tiger feeding on the throat of an Englishman. But this item shall remain where it is in the Rag Mahal. Let them see the extent of his hatred, should they get so far within his walls. Let them know.

He turns the ruby around his pinky, the ring looser than usual. His appetite has lessened these past few days, his dreams feeding him troubling visions of that traitorous eunuch. The one who aided the begum Zubaida. In the dream, the eunuch stands in a vat of water up to his chin, his arms chained up behind him, the same conditions in which he likely died. And yet, in the dream, Tipu is the one pleading his case to the eunuch, admitting to the fact that, yes, he has done brutal things, many brutal things, but isn't brutality a condition of war? And is it not obvious what will happen if we give in to the Nazarenes, how their brutality will extend for centuries, their boots forever on our necks until our every breath goes to building their wealth across the sea?

But the eunuch never lifts his head.

Tipu thumbs the ruby, which is said to dispel self-doubt.

Aloud he says, "They will stable their horses in our masjid."

Raja Khan asks carefully: "Who, Padshah?"

Tipu gives him a sidelong glance, waiting for Raja Khan to say the same things that everyone says, that the rains will come early, that the river will rise, that the English will drown trying to cross it.

Instead, quite out of character, Raja Khan breaks his master's gaze to look at the garden. "If they haven't eaten them all by now."

"Eaten?"

"It's true, Padshah—the heathens eat horse."

"They do not eat horse."

"They do other things with their horses, too, I hear."

"Raja Khan," says Tipu, in a tone of light censure. But for the first time in a long time, he chuckles.

Since the disasters at Maddur and Malavalli, Tipu has been having bad dreams. To fend them off, he finds comfort in the verse where Allah told Muhammad through Gibreel: *We have created man for toil and trial. Does he think no one will have power over him?*

As soon as Tipu rises from his prayer rug, pain stabs him in the side of his knee, a pale shadow of the original pain, dealt by the enemy's sword. He stands with his hands on his thighs, breathing deeply. You were made to be humbled, he thinks. You were made for this pain.

He received the sword cut at Malavalli. Everything was going so well at first, early in the morning, as he and his troops snuck through the jungle. They split into halves, and then, with serendipitous timing, the two halves attacked Montresor from the rear and the front. Just as the carnage was wrapping up, Stuart arrived, bloody Stuart informed by his bloody spies that Tipu's green tent had been spotted near Maddur. More carnage, more confusion; Tipu retreated with what remained of his force.

Someone said Tipu's cousin Benki was among the dead. Last seen lying on the ground, eyes still and skyward.

It is said he roared like a lion while he fought, surrounded by

English horses that fell screaming on Mysorean bayonets. Benki Nawab, his fat and faithful cousin, who earned his fiery name for burning Malabar. Always up for a rout. Sometimes going a bit too far, as with the Malabar situation, but that's Benki being Benki.

Was Benki being Benki.

There is no time to mourn. Tipu must appoint a replacement for the head of his personal bodyguard. His first thought is to assign this task to Purnaiya, yet he hesitates, and settles on Raja Khan instead. Not that he doesn't trust Purnaiya; surely not that. Presumably Purnaiya is at this very moment on horseback, along with Sayyid Saheb and a handful of troops, burning the forage along General Harris's march so that his retinue of bulls and goats and horses will have nothing to nibble but ash. Presumably.

In recent days, Mysorean rockets have been keening across the sky, music to Tipu's ears. He watches from the southern ramparts, where he has pitched his tent. With every blast, he grits his teeth. He knows how they must seem to the English, wondrous and terrible, soaring a whole kilometer farther than expected. Tipu is proud of his rockets. It was Tipu who conceived of crafting iron combustion chambers, wherein the bursting energy would build to unparalleled heights, the schematics recorded in his treatise on rocketry.

A few years later, Sir William Congreve will make a replica of Tipu's rocket and call it the Congreve. For now, though, the rockets are Tipu Sultan's, tipped with swords and spiraling toward the enemy.

The rockets are being dispatched from Sultanpet, a grove on the outskirts of the fort. Harris orders his men to subdue the rocket artillery. His men are weak, practically starving on their half-portions of rice, all that is left of their provisions. A strong wind could push them over.

Many of Harris's men die that night, trying to take Sultanpet.

By morning, fortune turns in his favor. Wellesley has arrived—the younger brother, not the walking hemorrhoid, though this Wellesley will soon prove for Tipu just as bothersome.

Fed, reinforced, they take Sultanpet.

They now stand within sixteen hundred meters of the fort.

Traitors, traitors everywhere. Tipu counts them on his fingers. Purnaiya and Sayyid Saheb. How easily they could have destroyed the forage, debilitating the sixty thousand bullocks that accompanied Harris's army. But no, Harris is here, proof that Purnaiya and Sayyid Saheb did nothing. And what about Qamar-uddin Khan, that four-legged fiend? If he'd done his job, the armies of Floyd and Stuart would never have met, would never have crossed the Kaveri. And the rains, when will they come? Is the natural world conspiring against him, too?

He thinks to ask Ghaffur for advice, but Ghaffur is dead. His best general, his oldest friend, who could make a horse swivel between his legs while laughing. Killed by cannon shot yesterday. Or was it the day before? Time bleeds. The fact remains: Ghaffur is dead.

Meanwhile Harris has sent his terms in the form of a handwritten letter, delivered by Tipu's vakils:

Half of Mysore.

Two crore rupees within six months.

Four of his sons and four of his generals to be taken as hostages.

Twenty-four hours in which to accept.

Tipu stares at the letter in his hands, at the English writing trooping across the page. A cold fire enters his chest. They have no desire to make peace. They have no interest in taming him, as they have with weaker kings. He controls the southwestern ports, the spices that flow out, the wealth that flows in. They have never had any ambition but to crush him.

Ghaffur, who always knew when to leave a party, is dead.

The paper trembles in his hands.

He considers writing one last letter to his sons, just as Haidar wrote to him. But then he remembers the weight of that letter. *Do this. Do that. Buy France. Save Mysore.* Saddling him in the way one saddles a horse, and then—boom. Gone.

He won't do the same to his own sons. Not one of them has the guts or cunning to foment a real rebellion. They are too content to be rebels, and that's okay, when he thinks about it. In public he likes to say: "Better to live two days as a tiger than two hundred days as a sheep." One drawback to being a tiger: it walks alone.

He sets the letter aside. He has no more to write. Now the Almighty holds the pen.

He tells Raja Khan to arrange his quarters in the choultry on the northern ramparts. Raja Khan balks. The small stone shrine is meant for passing travelers; it's no place for royalty. But Tipu wants to keep an eye on the English advance, and he doesn't mind a humble shelter. He has always liked the smell of stone, the cool welcome of a crypt.

THE SIEGE

The fort has known violence in its lifetime. Tipu Sultan took it from the Nawab of Arcot, who took it from the Peshwas, who took it from the Wodeyars, who took it from Timmana Nayaka, who took it from the earth somewhere in the fourteenth century. Even its birth, like all births, was a violence.

But no one has sent a cannonball at the walls before. No enemy has known—as the English know—that the northwest wall of the fort is the weakest. This is the sort of knowledge that could only be granted from someone on the inside. And there are many on the inside who might have granted it.

So the cannon fires; so the northwest wall breaks like biscuit.

Mines are laid beneath the breach. They explode, even as the Mysoreans are rushing to plug the hole with broken stone, their own bodies broken to rubble.

For the first time in its life, the fort is unstable, uneven. Mysorean troops guard the breach overnight. If these fort walls could talk, they would say that the head of these troops—Mir Sadiq—is in the pocket of General Harris.

. . .

By morning the English forces are flowing through the breach. They wade through the Kaveri River, which is only hip-high at its deepest point. The men cannot believe they are crossing the river. It has always seemed impossible until, suddenly, it isn't.

The men have barely the strength to keep their weapons hoisted over their heads. But they are distracted from their hunger. They notice the way the honey-hued light falls in swaths over the water, burnishing the riverbed, turning stones large and small into golden eggs.

Another miracle: no one fires at them from the opposite bank. No one resists their advance.

Seven minutes later, they have planted a flag in the southern rampart. Now the fort is theirs. And so, they believe, is everything in it.

The armies of the East India Company—the Light Dragoons and Regiments of Foot, the Swiss mercenaries and Scotch brigades, the sepoy forces of Madras and Bengal—pour into the streets. They shoot every Mysorean in sight, primed on stories of Tipu's dungeons, tales of nails being driven into innocent eyes (no proof of this, but proof, at present, is beside the point). It's all so bloody easy. The give of stone walls, of sternum against steel. Thousands of dying Mysoreans. Any one of them could be Tipu Sultan. They don't know what he looks like, having only heard reports of a wild-eyed fat man with a black mouth and a bloodthirsty laugh.

There is Tipu's personal palace with its tall, ribbed columns, untold treasures for the taking.

Also for the taking: the women and girls of the zenana.

Four will be immortalized in a popular English engraving, lips thin and smirking, torsos twisted in protest against the soldiers who are carrying them off. In the engraving, the men appear lusty and leering. In reality, they are efficient in their taking, tactical and cold.

Of the women, some scream and some don't. Some proffer jewels in exchange for immunity. One, for whom it's too late to proffer anything, staggers around a corner, clutching the torn drawstring of her skirt. Know that she will survive this night and many to come. What will sustain her is the story that will form in her mind, in which she is not the spoils of war but a fallen warrior.

By nightfall, the victors discover near the Water Gate the dead body of Tipu Sultan. It is Raja Khan who points the finger; pointing and wheezing is all Raja Khan can do as he lies nearby, bleeding out from a stomach wound.

Tipu Sultan was seen firing from the ramparts with a series of hunting rifles, handed to him one after another by his servants, until a gunshot felled him. As he lay dying, an English soldier tried to steal his sword belt. Tipu took a swipe with his own sword, slicing the soldier's knee. For this the soldier put a gun to his temple.

And so passed the Tiger of Mysore.

In death he lies on a palanquin, his body still warm. Shorter and lighter-skinned than they were expecting, dressed casually in a linen jacket over flowery trousers. Also odd is the expression on his face, filled with a peaceable calm none would expect of a tyrant.

While the officers mull over the body, a soldier snips the corner of the dead king's mustache with the edge of his bayonet. He gives his appalled superiors a sheepish smile. "A little prize, sirs. Everyone's doing it."

••

Of the nine paintings imagining the final moments of Tipu Sultan, exactly zero contain Abbas, cowering behind a broken pillar, hand in hand with the Wonder Hand. An odd pair, these two. And yet each man is all the other has, an alliance born of sheer happenstance.

Ten minutes earlier, Abbas had been staggering down an alley, trying to find his way out of the fort, when a distant cannon blast shuddered through the soles of his feet. A charging horse sheared past him, its rider dragged along by a leg. Where was Munir? Munir was his fellow stretcher bearer with whom he'd trained for a week, learning how to bear away the dead. (Of the training he recalled only step one: Position the casualty to be lifted.) Munir had shouted, "How are we to carry the stretcher when they've shot us full of holes?"— and fled his post.

Their training had not readied them for the breaching of the fort. Chaos outside the walls? Maybe. Ganjam invaded? Quite possibly. That possibility had led Tipu to evacuate the industrial suburbs, empty the Gun House, hide all supplies lest they be melted down for munitions.

In preparation for leaving, Abbas helped his family load their bullock cart with possessions. Farooq had already fled with his wife and children to her brother's house in Somnathpur. Junaid had received a delay on the start of his service so he could deliver the rest of the family to Shimoga, from where he would not be returning. Abbas refused to go along with either of these plans, no matter how his mother cursed and cried and how his brothers threatened to knock him unconscious and carry him off. (At this Abbas had laughed; his brothers had not.)

"Sit next to me," his father said, patting the space beside himself in the bullock cart.

Abbas reminded his father that he wasn't coming along. His father asked why not. His mother looked at Abbas, her eyes red from crying, wild with the hope that he might change his mind.

Abbas told his father, as he had told him before, that he was staying behind to serve in Tipu's army.

His father was bewildered by the notion. "But you are not the fighting kind," he said softly. "You couldn't beat an egg."

Abbas took a deep breath. What the deep breath meant was unclear to Yusuf Muhammad, but he could see that his son was frustrated, and assumed that he himself was the cause, which he regretted, because there was no one in the world he loved more than his youngest. It used to be that he could hide his preference behind a stoic face, pretending not to watch the boy as he carved some trinket so exquisite it belonged on a shelf. Where did you come from? Yusuf Muhammad wondered at moments like those, not without a hint of fear. What will you become? It now occurred to Yusuf Muhammad that he would never find out.

From the driver's seat, Junaid said coldly, "Let him go, Abba."

Yusuf Muhammad squeezed his son's hand very tight and released it.

Abbas stayed to watch the bullock cart trundle away, Junaid in the seat, the rest of the family walking alongside. Only Yusuf Muhammad was facing Abbas, and how backwards it felt, to be leaving his youngest behind. He stared as Abbas grew small in the distance, as lost as a child in need of a father's hand, and prayed that someone, anyone at all, would provide it.

A man shoves past Abbas, holding the side of his blasted face together, only to run straight into a bayonet that comes out his lower back, and maybe Abbas imagined it, but the sound it makes is that of a quiet pop, and his own bladder drains reflexively.

He runs in the opposite direction of the skewered man. Which way he is bound, he does not know.

He rounds a corner to find the Wonder Hand slumped against a wall, vaguely kicking at a crow that seems to have him confused for a corpse. His turban is gone, his head very small without it.

He meets Abbas's eye. "Help," he says so quietly, so plainly, he could be asking for directions. "Help me, son."

A horde of yelling men is rounding the corner.

Abbas flings himself over the Wonder Hand, toppling them both, his back turned against the onrush. His only hope: that the soldiers will make the same mistake as the raven and think them a pair of dead bodies.

For the next eleven seconds, his nose in the stubble of the Wonder Hand's neck, Abbas does not breathe.

The clamor rises and rounds the corner, filled with maniacal yelling, footfalls pulsing through the stones.

After the sounds have mostly passed, Abbas opens his eyes. He is nose to nose with the Wonder Hand, whose right eye is clotted with blood.

"My son," says the Wonder Hand, his frailty causing Abbas to surge with strength and certainty.

Abbas slings the Wonder Hand's arm over his shoulders. Together they cut through an alley, the Wonder Hand slow on his twisted leg but able to keep moving. The air is thick with char and smoke, walls turned to a white mist on the air, clouding his vision and stuffing his lungs, yet when he glimpses the banyan through the white, he knows the Delhi Gate is near. If he can get them through the Delhi Gate, they will know the glory of another hour, another year, maybe even the rest of a regular life.

There are sparks and smells of metal, sprays of broken rock. Dragging the Wonder Hand, he lumbers over fallen bodies—here a limb, there a face—fine bones breaking beneath his weight. At the keening of a rocket, he yanks the Wonder Hand behind a slab.

Crouching, peering over the slab, he sees Delhi Gate. An enemy soldier is kneeling on top, pointing a rifle and firing at anyone attempting to pass. The sky behind the soldier is a flare of orange, a blur of possibility.

Abbas tightens his grip on the Wonder Hand, preparing to run.

"Oh," says the Wonder Hand.

Slowly—for everything seems to be moving slowly—Abbas looks to the Wonder Hand. But the Wonder Hand is wrenching his hand free and running away, why is he running away, *why are you running away*, Abbas is about to say when the whole world jolts at once and he is knocked to the ground.

A shrill sound in his ears. Blood in his mouth. He is pinned beneath something. His cheek pressed to the ground, he sees the Wonder Hand limping away in a crouch, making it almost to the gate before gunfire drops him flat.

All sound turns distant, submerged. His own breathing recedes to an animal wheeze. His mind flicks past visions—

A field of bright red tulips. A silken pouch. A wasp inside a fig.

Abba, cupping the back of his neck.

Garlands of wedding carnations.

A little wooden boy.

The Brahmagiri Mountains. The Kaveri and all her tributaries swelling into the Bay of Bengal.

Burning ships on a sea of ash.

These visions grow farther apart as darkness consumes him.

••

Here comes the first rain of the season—the very rain Tipu had been praying for, the rain that might have saved him— hurtling in torrents, tearing up the dirt, dousing the piles of stinking bodies. The sky throbs with lightning; thunder rolls through the earth. Relentless, the storm folds the rot into itself. Not erasing it entirely; that will take time.

The fort has time. The rain washes the cracks between its stones, the breakage in the wall. The water mixes with blood, and carries it down gutters and drains. The Water Gate swells, the river rises. Smoke moves over Srirangapatna, seething from flattened homes, christening the city, which will thenceforward go by a name that its conquerors can (sort of) pronounce: Seringapatam.

The looting begins. Soldiers are tucking jewels into pockets, sleeves, armpits. Someone has the bust of Louis XVI on his shoulder, its fine smile carved in bisque. ("I asked for troops," Tipu told Pur- naiya, when the gifts arrived, "and he sends me his head.") They carry chintz drapes, blazed silks, rubies pried from finials. They carry howdah cushions, firearms, jeweled swords, silver maces, sheet gold of the highest touch. General Harris orders the city gates locked, to prevent soldiers from escaping with the spoils, so the soldiers take to throwing their loot over the walls, or rigging up simple pulleys.

In turn Harris rigs up a simple gallows and has four of his own men hung. More flogged. And though the tigers had nothing to do with the thieving—had simply been starving to death in their cages—that same day, their cage doors are opened. Bahadur Khan limps into a freedom he knew twenty years before, when he was first taken from the forest. His fur mangy, ribs like claws. He gazes up at the unbarred sky, having barely the energy to draw a breath before he is shot.

The rain has receded, order mostly restored.

On the parade grounds in front of Tipu's personal palace, General Harris sets up a prize committee. Plunder is chaos; prize is organized.

Three long tables are arranged in a row, where seven prize agents and one Hindu goldsmith can study each object being removed from Tipu's tosh-khana, register the object in a ledger, assign the object a value, and assign the prize to a recipient according to rank.

Throngs of white men wait their turn. Among them is Colonel Horace Selwyn. Attending the colonel is Rangappa Rao, his aide-de-camp and a sepoy with the Madras Infantry.

It seems a haphazard way of doing things, at least to Rangappa, or Rum, as he is called. But Rum keeps his opinion to himself. His only job is to stand by until Colonel Selwyn's name is announced and keep his own head together. Difficult, what with the stink of dead bodies in the air, piled out of sight yet accusing in their odor.

Ever since becoming Colonel Selwyn's aide-de-camp, Rum has kept no friends among the other sepoys. Which leaves him a bit lonesome at times. But there are perks. At least he isn't one of those wretched fellows tasked with dragging the dead bodies into heaps. So many bodies. Two hours it took to cut them all down. Two hours.

(But he will not allow himself to pity these men, oh no, he has waited decades for Tipu's fall, has imagined driving his own thumbs into Tipu's eyes, plunging a rusted knife into that flabby fucker's heart . . .)

"Would she like a brooch, do you think?" asks Colonel Selwyn.

Rum turns alert. "Has my lord ever seen Lady Selwyn wearing a brooch?"

Colonel Selwyn squints, as if trying to summon a memory of his wife wearing a brooch. Rum has never met Lady Selwyn, yet throughout his months of service, he has received from Colonel Selwyn an overall negative impression.

"Incorrigible woman," Colonel Selwyn once said, bent over a letter on his makeshift desk. They were in a tent on the outskirts of Porto Novo. "She just bought a wooden cravat carved by Grinling Gibbons. What on earth do we need with a wooden cravat? Mind you, not asking if she can buy it. Informing me. And that's not to mention all the whatnots she isn't telling me about. Like that ghastly painting of Lady Digby on her deathbed!" Colonel Selwyn passed a hand across his face. "The Twickenham paper ran a cartoon of myself and Lady Selwyn, sitting atop a mountain of curios, which included—what was it?—oh, yes: the bones of a mouse that had run across Shakespeare's foot. And a pimple from Oliver Cromwell's nose—a pimple, Rum!"

"Another drink, sir?" Rum poured the Scotch.

"God knows what else she will have acquired by the time I get back."

Colonel Selwyn has a severe way of talking about her, yet at times like this, while he is quietly debating pearls or pendants, Rum wonders whether the man is a little afraid of his wife.

There are greater things to be afraid of, Rum thinks, looking up at the bruisy clouds, which look as though they could, at any moment, explode.

When Colonel Selwyn is called to the prize committee table, he is presented with a choice of either a silver filigreed casket, studded with semiprecious gems, or two palanquin pole ends, gilt silver, cast and chased into the shape of tiger heads.

Colonel Selwyn bends to peer at each object. He can just imagine what Lady Selwyn's first question will be, if he presents her with either the casket or the pole ends: What else was on offer? What did other people get? And then she will pout about the fact that he did not know her well enough, after thirty-three years of marriage, to get her what she really wanted—an object of genuine flair and drama.

"Colonel?" says the prize agent, pen poised over the ledger.

Colonel Selwyn scans the objects gathered on the platform behind the prize agents. Turquoise brooch: no. Rosewater sprinkler, whatever that is: no. Telescope and case . . . ?

"What about that thing?" he says, pointing to an enormous wood sculpture of a tiger feeding on a man.

"The Musical Tiger?" says the prize agent, frowning. "Why, it's only wood and glue. We have here—"

"A casket and pole ends, yes, I know. What makes the music?"

The prize agent expels air through his nostrils. "Allan," he says, calling to the prize agent at the adjacent table, "what makes the music in the Musical Tiger?"

"I believe there's an organ inside," says Allan.

"And it was Tipu's?" asks Selwyn.

"Allan, was it Tipu's?" asks the prize agent.

"Whose else would it be?" says Allan, who flattens his tone in the face of Selwyn's frown. "Excuse me, sir, it was discovered in the Music Hall. Crude, if you ask me."

"I'll take it," says Selwyn. "The Musical Tiger, not the pole ends or whatever."

And so, for his loyal service in the Anglo-Mysore Wars, the prize committee awards Colonel Horace Selwyn the gift of one Musical Tiger. The longer Selwyn looks at the Musical Tiger, the giddier he feels. His wife has a penchant for crusader tales, Moors and knights, blood and tragedy. For once, he feels one step ahead of her.

A feeling that will not last very long, for in two weeks he will die of dysentery, and be, per his wishes, cremated.

Rum will be the one to deliver the remains to Lady Selwyn, along with Colonel Selwyn's uniform, his silver medal from the Battle of

Seringapatam, and a wooden box of such heft and proportion that for one delirious moment, she will think it contains her husband, ready to spring out and surprise her.

Tipu's books will take time to evaluate. They reside in the library, a dim and musty room in the southeastern section of the upper verandah. The library is filled with chests, the chests filled with books, thousands elegantly leather bound by his order. Most books bear the name of their previously plundered owners, kings of the Deccan or Carnatic, Tipu's seal above their own. A team of munshis pores over the pages, translating titles. Of the four thousand volumes in the library, eight hundred will be sent to London and Calcutta.

Yet what of the remaining manuscripts considered poor in shape, lacking covers or names? What of the manuals on gardening and horsemanship, the advice dictated from deathbeds, the memoirs of the noblewomen confined to the zenana? What of the poetry of Hafiz and Firdawsi? What of the Persian treatise on magic? What of the chronicles of court life, the notebooks on rocketry and botany? What of the anthology of prayers and charms, the old Qurans, the exposition on ragas and raginis? It would be safe to assume that most of these will go up in flames when, a decade later, Wellesley orders Tipu's personal palace to be razed.

Three days after the siege and now the bodies are being heaped onto carts and dragged to the river.

The sepoys work steadily to clear the ground, though it seems an impossible task, so many bodies piled on bodies, arms thrown over necks, a sea of boys and men.

Evening falls. The youngest sepoy, a boy of sixteen, works quickly, no longer tying a cloth around his nose, for the reek will penetrate anything. He smells it while he sleeps. Perhaps, he thinks, taking hold of two knobby ankles, he will smell it forever. Just as he will forever see these faces, the depthless eyes, the opened throats.

The lower half of a leg, covered in down. The ridges on a fingernail. A buzzard relieving a man of his intestines.

To witness such things and feel neither fear nor awe, not even a shudder: this is what it is to be cursed. The sepoy bends and lifts, dragging with him a sense of doom, knowing he will never come back from where he is now.

With the knobby ankles in his hands, the sepoy throws his weight back.

Then stops. Drops the ankles. Stares.

There, by the Delhi Gate, a jinn is staggering up from the field of bodies. The jinn is too far away to be perceived in detail, yet what else could it be? A jinn in the form of a slight young man.

The jinn sways in place for a moment. In the fading light, the sepoy cannot tell if the jinn is looking back at him.

The sepoy has never met a jinn before, but his childhood best friend was a big believer; the friend told wild tales of what a jinn could do: slide up your nostrils, puppet your body, kill you from within.

The sepoy summons his courage. He hisses at the jinn, waves it off with both hands.

To his astonishment, the jinn turns and limps toward the Delhi Gate. The sepoy watches, relieved at first, then unsure; his friend never said anything about limping jinns.

Could be the jinn is no jinn, he thinks. Could be what he thinks to be a jinn is, in fact, a man. A man who has been lying for three nights beneath a corpse, a man silent yet alive, sweltering in his thirst, sucking rainwater from puddles when no one was looking, wetting himself, blacking out, waking and waiting for the moment to rise.

But who would believe a thing like that?

The sepoy watches until the figure disappears through the Delhi Gate, glad to see it gone, though certain it will surface in some other place, some other form.

A Journal of My Time in the Liquid World

Observations and Adventures of the
Seaman Thomas Beddicker

1802 July.—It is said that Englishmen are born with a love of the sea. Some say it is to do with our stoutness of character and lust for adventure. My mother says England is a tiny island with bad weather. Small wonder the English are obsessed with getting away from it.

My mother is from Calais. My father was an officer with the East India Company when he met her, promising her his hand and his fortune. (She says she was quite the eye-trap back then.) But by the time she joined him in Suffolk, she found that he had already run through much of his so-called fortune. Two months into her arrival he was felled by some illness, leaving her sixteen years old and with child.

Yet with that strength of spirit that had brought her to Suffolk, she raised me up on her own. And I, having known her sacrifice and suffering, was proud to tell her, at the age of seventeen, that I wished to be, like my own departed father, a seaman with the East India Company.

She received my news with a sigh and said, "Stop pulling my leg, Thomas, and peel those potatoes." I suppose she still saw me as a child, the same one who, when sent to fetch something from the root cellar, would call her name with every step into the dark.

She reminded me of the perils involved: disease, boredom, storms, to say nothing of Dutch and French privateers, their own Companies disbanded, sore losers in the game of trade. All my young life she had fed me tales of the most infamous pirate ships—the *Preneuse* and her cruel captain Dujardin, the *Confiance* with her black and yellow sides, knifing through the waters. Even then those tales held some dark allure.

When my mother saw I was decided, she threw her arms around my ankles and begged me to stay. She has only myself in the world. Yet what is a man if he has only his mother? I was determined to work hard, to gain the learning and friendship of men, and to earn enough such that one day a cook would be peeling potatoes for my mother.

So it was that I visited a banker friend of my father's—a teaman at 420 Strand, London—who obtained for me a berth in the Honourable East India Company's maritime service. By his generosity I was hired to the crew of the *Peppercorn,* a fine sailing ship of some 840 tons and 151 men in all.

Before setting sail, I was initiated by my future messmates. One of them, William Lowden, had secretly advised me to bring a gallon of grog to the mizzen-top, otherwise my future messmates would tie me to the rigging as per custom. At first my messmates were annoyed with Lowden's intervention, his kindliness having prevented their havoc. However, I surprised them with three gallons instead of one, which pleased and impressed them. Still now I remember William Lowden, giving me a warm wallop on the back and saying, "This lad's going places."

On we sailed to Madras and Bengal, and are now in the port town of Pondicherry, making repairs and caulking seams for the next five days.

We have not seen much of Pondicherry, our time belonging to the Company. Sometimes the black children linger at the edges of the dockyard, watching us at our work. When we look their way, they whoop and disperse like a flock of starlings.

Samuel Lowden disdains me for waving at the children, saying they are pick-pockets one and all.

Here I refer to two very different Lowdens. There is William Lowden, the messmate who rescued me from a proper initiation, and then there is his elder brother, Samuel Lowden, the boatswain, who has only a sliver of his sibling's kindness.

Samuel Lowden was not always of such a surly disposition. The brothers Lowden used to entertain us every Sunday dinner with their singing voices. But then William Lowden died of an abscess on our way through the Mozambique Passage and Samuel Lowden never sang another note.

It was William Lowden's death that inspired me to keep a diary as he did. "Even if I have gained little in money," he told me, "I shall have some record of my time in the liquid world." I thought it a fine phrase—the liquid world. But that was William. Everywhere he set his eye took on a radiance.

7 July 1802.—Careened the *Peppercorn* today. Was surprised to find a Hindustani among us. I am told he will serve as carpenter's assistant to Mr. Grimmer, an Irishman of few words until he has a cup of grog and then he is a church bell.

Samuel Lowden was livid, saying in earshot of the Hindustani that theirs is a feeble and lazy race, not much better than the Mandarin or Manila men. "Fifty lascars," he proclaimed, "do not equal the worth of a single British seaman."

Mr. Grimmer told Lowden to go wag his tail elsewhere.

Either the Hindustani does not understand English or he is very skilled at playing deaf. By my lights he lugged as much as anyone that day, removing from her holds the cargo, anchor, dunnage &c. We dragged twenty cannons onto the sand and roped the *Peppercorn*'s masts.

Then began the dangerous work. We lined up and gripped the rope, the Hindustani in front of me, stripped to the waist—he had a mulatto's hue—all of us grinding our heels into the sand and pulling as one, groaning and hoping we wouldn't be smashed like those poor souls in Java, until, at last, with a great suck of water, she tilted and bellied up toward the sky.

Only once did I catch the Hindustani idling, and that was when we gathered at the upended hull. Below the waterline of the boat: a dense, dripping forest of seaweed and plant growth, brittle wings of mollusk shell, barnacles like gleaming white teeth. I watched the Hindustani tap a fingernail against a barnacle. He seemed deeply curious as to its structure, as if his attention might unlock a secret. The spell was broken when Mr. Grimmer handed him a chisel and told us all to start scraping for if we wanted to keep to our Company schedules, we couldn't have such stowaways slowing us down.

1802 August.—At five p.m. we weighed and made sail to the tune of our own cannon-fire. The echo was felt through our bones if not our boot soles, being so harried with setting the sails and trimming the sheets and braces. The sea was high and the wind was gusting mightily from the NW. Normally we would be joined by a convoy of other ships, there being safety in numbers, but given the Peace at Amiens between France and England, our ship has been dispatched on her own.

6th—Bid goodbye to the last sighting of the land. . . .
7th—Unbent the anchors and coiled the cables for stowage below . . .
8th—Today I was mopping the deck when I discovered the Hindustani slumped at the rail, clutching his head as if to keep it attached to his neck. He has been vomiting for two days. Well do I remember that hell, having suffered to the same extent on my voyage out of Deptford. I advised the Hindustani to keep his eye on the horizon, feet hip-width apart. He gave me a dull look so I demonstrated. "Do that and you'll soon get your sea legs," I said.

He straightened, still gripping the railing but heeding my suggestions. *Merci,* he said to me. *Du rien,* I said surprised and wondering if he spoke more French than that. (I am the only French speaker among my messmates.) But I hurried on with my mopping before Samuel Lowden could accuse me of taking liberties with my time.

10th—Rudely awakened this morning by Samuel Lowden, who used his knife to cut down our hammocks. Apparently we had not leapt out of our hammocks at the requisite second—hence the drop. A number of us considered complaining to Captain Northcote who is fair of mind, known to treat his mids the same as he treats his officers. (Though we are not midshipmen, not yet.) Two problems with this plan: Captain Northcote is always moving from one place to the next, and therefore difficult to have a word with. (Purposefully so, I reckon.) The other problem is our own remaining sympathy for Samuel Lowden.

When William Lowden was alive, we'd looked on Samuel Lowden as an older brother. He could be stern with us but also sparred and joked. Now he has hardened against us, his inferiors, and checks our smallest infractions with heavy punishments. We have agreed to say nothing against him to the captain, but my messmate Bunn says if the hammock-cutting be a sign of things to come, it will be a sore journey.

1 September 1802.—Five days of vicious storms. I have never worked so endlessly in my life, repairing wind-split sails until my fingers were stiff. On the worst night, I could only grip the nearest post on deck as our *Peppercorn* tossed on the waves, as light as her namesake.

At one point, lightning struck and exploded onto the surface of the sea like thousands of tiny white beads, dropped from the heavens. The storm has passed now and the sky is clear and blue, yet when I close my eyes I can still see that beaded light, marbles of fire dropping and bouncing as I never knew fire could do. When I asked Bunn if he'd seen what I'd seen, he said, "I think those marbles are the ones you've lost, Thomas."

I do not know when I acquired a reputation for having my head in the heavens, but it is not a reputation I enjoy. Just because a man is quiet in the company of friends does not mean he is given to dreaming. William Lowden understood this. On night watch we were equally content to talk or fall quiet, and somehow he knew when a certain lonely feeling was eating me from within. "Bad weather?" he'd say, referring to my own internal state. But he never tried to talk me out of such spells, for he suffered them himself at times, as we all did, and do, try as we might to conceal ourselves.

10 September 1802.—This morning, we were awoken from our hammocks to the sound of screaming. It was the assistant surgeon, claiming that there was a hole in the ship, that the ship was sinking!

The captain went down to assess the damage, along with the first mate, the master carpenter, and the carpenter's first and second mates—the latter being the Hindustani. The rest I heard from eye witnesses:

The assistant surgeon made a great fuss, pointing to a puddle by his bed. He knelt and searched the wall, revealing the sullied soles of his feet for he hadn't taken the time to don shoes before running abovedeck. He insisted that the wall had been punctured in the night and shrieked at the Hindustani to help him locate the leak.

The Hindustani located an empty jug that had been lying on its side on the floor.

Everyone stared at the jug. One can only imagine the silence that ensued.

It was quickly ascertained that the assistant surgeon had knocked the jug over in the night, quite likely during a vivid dream of a leaky ship. After some choice words from Captain Northcote, the party trailed out of the cabin, the assistant surgeon hugging the empty jug to his chest. As much as I pity the poor man, I am also indebted to him for giving the rest of us a good yarn.

1 October 1802.—I have been irregular in my writings but poor weather conditions have not left me a minute to myself. At least the gales have kept the cruisers away, though we are now blown 30 miles off course.

To my own surprise I have found a friend in the Hindustani. For two night watches this week we have been assigned to the lee side of quarterdeck. Last night was so cloudy and starless you could not see the hand on the end of your own arm. Neither could we light a candle, all flames and whistles forbidden after seven p.m. so as not to attract the attention of privateers. With little else to do we talked. The Hindustani was only too happy to have a fellow conversant in French. All throughout our conversation, his hands were busy carving a small block of wood, the blade making a *scritch-scritch* sound I found somehow pleasing.

Abbas, as he calls himself, was originally a woodworker in the kingdom of Tipu Sultan. (I have heard of Tipu the Treacherous of course, but not knowing Abbas's loyalties, I merely nodded along.) Whilst there, Abbas learned French from a great inventor named Lucien Du Leze. (He spoke the name inquisitively as though I might recognize it, but I did not.) From Mysore he traveled a fortnight—by foot or any cart that would have him—and found his way to Pondicherry, where he sold little trinkets and teak boxes that he himself had carved. When desperate, he begged. He learned English from a missionary at a Catholic church where he was also given one meal a day so long as he agreed to hold hands with other Native Christians and pray. In fact he is a Mahommedan.

One day, when Abbas had had enough of the watery lentils and clammy hands, he went to the wharves and studied the ships, memorizing the strange creatures carved onto their sides. One had the tail of a scaly fish, the body of a man. Another prow featured a woman in blowing robes, the folds frozen in place. Some ships had no such embellishments. Many featured lions. "Is England a land of many lions?" he asked me, to which I said not a one.

He spent three days carving a lion's head with girlish ringlets, something like the ones he'd seen on the ship side. When he brought this to the master carpenter, Mr. Grimmer was most impressed, especially when he saw the little switchblade Abbas had carved it with. The master carpenter needed a second mate for the return journey, his previous one having deserted in Calcutta. (I never knew the deserter, but I doubt he has gone on to better things. Only degradation shall follow one so disloyal.)

So it was that Abbas was sent on his very first day to career the *Peppercorn*. His contract has him serving for five years, like myself.

We shared our greatest wishes. Mine: to captain a ship of my own. His: to create a thing that would outlast him, and for which he would be remembered.

When I asked what kind of thing, he handed me the small object he had been carving. "Not that," he said sheepishly.

By then the sky had begun to lighten. I could see that the object was a small whale, with smooth sides and perfect flukes. How he did this in the dark I don't know, but I will remember him for it.

3 October 1802.—Samuel Lowden cornered me while I was greasing a mast and, feigning a casual air, asked me what it was that had me so chummy with the Hindustani. I said nothing, for the question seemed not a question at all. Still he wanted to know what we were talking about. I said we talked of our lives and our families same as any pair of men would do when faced with four hours of night watch and the whole liquid world ahead of us.

"Liquid what?" said Samuel Lowden, making a face as if I had just farted out my mouth.

He then told me that Easterners could not be trusted, that they would bobble their head and do the opposite of whatever they promised. And too the lascars were becoming an eyesore in the streets of London, begging and debasing themselves on our land when they should be going back to theirs.

I told Samuel Lowden that Abbas was a world apart from those Easterners because, in the first place, he could speak both English and French—

At this revelation—that Abbas and I had spoken French to one another—Samuel Lowden accused me of being overly familiar with the Hindustani. "Oh for the love of God," I said, at which Samuel

Lowden threatened me with a dozen for insolence. He used to say such things in a jovial manner when his brother was alive. Nowadays, with that certain glint in his eye, one cannot be too careful.

20 October 1802.—Having successfully crossed the Equator, we are allowed a Saturday evening of celebration. A cow and her calf provided ample beef and veal to go along with the pork. We mustered our best clothes and raised our cups for Mr. Morrison's toast: *To sweethearts and wives!* Our youngest messmate, Gordon, shouted the reply: *May they never meet!* This was humorous coming from one so young and untested as Gordon, though he claims intimate knowledge of some nameless London lady.

There were songs and theatricals and the skits of Mr. Bazeley, who did a merciless impression of the assistant surgeon, his rump in the air as he goes searching for a tear in the shipside only to expose a tear in the seat of his trousers. To achieve the assistant surgeon's anemic pallor, Bazeley used mess flour to powder his face. Cook was displeased.

As much as I enjoy the fresh beef and bread—a relief from ship's biscuit—I cannot hear flute music without thinking of William Lowden. By the way Samuel Lowden stands at the fringe, wiping his eyes with his thumb, I know he is thinking the same.

21 October 1802.—It is customary that a sailor crossing the line for the first time must receive a haircut from the assistant surgeon. On our voyage, that sailor is Abbas.

Unfortunately it seems the assistant surgeon is still miffed about yesterday's theatricals and has vented his frustrations on poor Abbas and his head of once-thick black hair. ("Standard cut?" Abbas had asked him, to which the assistant surgeon replied that it would be just the standard he deserved.) Since we are without mirrors, Abbas asked me to honestly tell him how he looked. I told him the truth, that his hair had been subject to an uneven harvesting. Abbas is now morose.

In all honesty I believe he looks tougher than before and a bit desperate, which is a good thing, for he now looks more like the rest of us.

28 October 1802.—Today a stranger appeared to the NE. We gave our secret signal—two tiers of lights—to which the stranger made all sail away. Our suspicions roused, we went after her. Captain ordered the *Peppercorn* cleared for action. I was powder monkey for which I have luckily been practicing all last week with blank cartridges. At one a.m. the stranger hove to and showed one tier of lights, then two, then three—the proper signal it should have given in the first place . . . The stranger was revealed to be H.M. frigate *Egyptienne,* commanded by the Honourable Captain Bowser.

Captain Bowser informed us that the Peace at Amiens was over. War had been declared between England and France on 19th May. ("That was quick," I heard Bunn say.) In fact, Captain Bowser alleged that he had more French prisoners on board than all his ship's company. He was therefore obliged to press several of our seamen into naval service.

Captain Bowser and Captain Northcote walked round the decks. We stayed at our quarters, heads high and breaths held, hoping not to be picked. Abbas stood ramrod straight by Mr. Grimmer. I'd once told Abbas that since his race has such a poor reputation he is unlikely to be impressed into service. As Captain Bowser walked past him, I prayed I would be proven right. Only now, writing these words, do I realize how much his friendship has meant to me.

In the end Captain Bowser pressed eight of our men into service on board the *Egyptienne.* One was Gordon, poor fellow. He looked most miserable boarding the *Egyptienne,* clutching his sea-chest like the boy he still is in some ways.

With the *Egyptienne* gone and England once again at war, Captain Northcote ordered us to check the guns and prepare for defense.

· · ·

30 October 1802.—Night watch with Abbas. He asked me a surprising question: why Samuel Lowden hates him so. "How do you know he hates you?" I asked.

"Does he cuff me out of love?" came the reply.

Abbas cited several other incidents of ill-use, mostly of a verbal or casual nature, always beyond the notice of others. Sometimes he would block Abbas's way, forbidding him to pass. Another time Abbas found a rat tail in his gruel and later was asked by Samuel Lowden whether he liked meat for breakfast.

I told Abbas something an old shipmate had told me, when I'd complained of harsh treatment on my first voyage from Deptford. "There are only two things on board a ship: duty and mutiny. All that you are ordered to do is duty. All that you refuse to do is mutiny. And the punishment for mutiny is the yard-arm."

We fell quiet then. I had never seen a man swing and hoped I never would.

These trials would pass, I assured Abbas. In a few months we would be in London and—the idea occurred to me as I spoke—I promised to take him personally to my father's banker friend, the teaman on the Strand, to secure us both a better position on the next ship that would have us. I have always wanted to see China and Ceylon, the Sooloo Bay and Straits of Bally &c. Some of the ships going to those parts are over 1,000 tons with canvas berths and servants for the mids, every possible comfort. I reminded him of my goal to become a ship's captain, which is not an impossible dream, for Captain Northcote is a ropemaker's son. He carefully collected a lifetime of savings through hard work and shrewd investment, then put it all toward the *Peppercorn.* With so much cargo on board, the captain's investment will surely double, triple, if and when we make it safely home.

And, I said, if God were to so bless me with a similar trajectory, I would bring Abbas along as my Chief Mate, for a captain needs officers he can trust . . .

I asked for Abbas's thoughts on the matter but he was in the grip of his own concerns. Most men of his background would be grateful for the opportunity but out of sympathy for my friend I let him be.

. . .

14 November 1802.—By God's grace we have rounded the tip of Africa. We follow the same route as the first European to test these waters, a man who named it the Cape of Torments. His own greatest torment, I believe, was in not reaching India. Still his master, King John II, wanted a more inspiring term—that is, inspiring to potential seamen—and so named it the Cape of Good Hope.

As our convoy turned N by E, the ocean swelled and a squall set in. Captain Northcote elected to rush the weather head-on and helm down, in order to evade the French frigates in our wake. The sea was breaking over the *Peppercorn* but she performed beautifully, racing at 12 knots per hour, foaming at the bow, masts bending back.

This morning we have bent on new sails and resumed our course. There is an atmosphere of joy and relief now that we are out of danger. My leg troubles me—I may have injured myself from running into something during the storm, though I do not remember doing so. Along the inside of my left ankle, there is a bruise like a deep red thumbprint pressed beneath my skin.

20 November 1802.—The bruise has spread up my leg, though not in hues that a bruise would usually take on. The pain is a nuisance but tolerable.

I showed my leg to the surgeon, Dr. Goodwin, who thinned his lips at the sight. "That is no bruise," he said. "Have you been taking your lemon juice?"

I said that I had taken my daily dose of the scorbutic, as had been required since our fifth week on board. Dr. Goodwin did not seem convinced. He gave me a dose of malt wort, which he'd said had worked for Captain Cook. "But Cook is dead," I said.

"Not of the sickness," Dr. Goodwin said sharply, as if I were a fool not to remember the murderous savages of Owyhee.

That is what we call it—the sickness. A disease too foul and shameful to name. I recall a handful of sailors who fell from it during our first voyage. Their mouths stank like the breath of the walking dead. Their insides rattled when they walked, if they could walk at all. The worst was when a deckhand named Hugh sat on the poop deck and sobbed for reasons he would not explain, and was taken down below, where he died an hour later.

Dr. Goodwin, seeing my upset, told me to come back every day for the malt wort, which would prevent the spread. And too he mentioned that we will soon make landfall at the island of St. Helena, where I may pack my legs in earth. The sickness, he told me, was the body's way of mourning the land. As much as we might lust for the sea, the land is our home.

I am taking his words to heart. I shall not trouble any others with my sufferings.

25th—Caught the SE trade wind. Pleasant weather.
26th—Light morning winds from the N. Abbas was first to point toward the sky. A pigeon was winging past, perhaps taking note of our ragged party and wondering why we were cheering so.
27th—Saw the island of St. Helena NW by W.
28th—Came to anchor off St. James Valley on St. Helena. I drew the earthy smell into my lungs until they could hold no more. Praise God in Heaven.

29 November 1802.—I know not how to describe this day, one that began full of hope and ended in such vexation.

St. Helena is an island of two volcanoes, Jamestown wedged in between. English colors fly from the towers of a handsome stone fort. I stood on the shore and sifted black sand through my fingers, having never before seen the like.

During the day we replenished our water casks and victuals. Afterwards, with some leisurely hours to ourselves, we explored the island. Marks and Bunn preferred to stay in Jamestown and test their manhoods with the Saints—so they are calling the local whores. (Rightly so, for anyone who would sleep with those two should be canonized.)

At night Captain Northcote allowed us a bonfire on the beach while he and his officers were received as company by H.M. frigate *Earl Howe.*

It was a fine time at first, filled with music and tales and arrack, a harsh liquor tapped from these lush green trees. I persuaded Abbas to take a sip, which he did reluctantly at first and then with increasing interest. Soon he was teary-eyed and brimming with feeling. He spoke of how he had always labored alone or almost alone. He had never felt part of so great a thing as a ship. A body with so many organs. How he would miss us! Grimmer, with his bowlegged stride and complaints of lumbago. The chaplain, with his quivering prayers. I told Abbas he would not be missing us in the morning, for a hangover would surely take up all the room in his head.

Abbas grasped my forearm. "You, Thomas, you I shall miss the most."

These words sobered me, as did the rest of his confession, which he had thus far been keeping to himself.

He told me he intends to break his contract with the Honourable East India Company and desert us as soon as we arrive in Deptford.

That he intends to make his way to France.

That he has never desired to be a mariner, that he means to study with a clockmaker in the town of Rouen and become some kind of inventor.

Stunned I said, "But you have four-plus years on your contract."

"I will break it," he said with a shrug.

"But what of China and Ceylon? Our next voyage? We talked of getting us a midshipman's berth with a cabin, a servant—every comfort . . ."

I trailed off for he was squinting at me, or, rather, at my mouth.

"Thomas, your breath smells like the grave."

Before I could reply, he clapped my shoulder and staggered off in search of more arrack.

. . .

The moon was high. I sat on the black sand. The tide washed over my legs, unfirming the earth beneath me when it ebbed. No one saw I was gone. Nor did they see the whale, huge and white, some ways from the shore. Strange that she should come so close to land. I thought to call out to my mates but no: the whale was meant for me, a sign that I was not alone.

12 December 1802—Weighed and made sail.
13th—Extensive drilling practice with great guns and small arms.
15th—Shared night watch duty with Abbas. A long and quiet night. Ever since the bonfire at St. Helena, we have lost our ease. I misjudged him, I know this now. That a Hindustani, given the honor of an Englishman's post on one of her Company's ships, should now repay us through deception and desertion—it would make any mariner grit his teeth.

But I have no intention of disclosing his schemes. If I did the captain would have him hanging from the yard-arm before breakfast.

20 December 1802.—Today Mahmud Abbas was punished with a dozen for insolence to the boatswain.

I am hard pressed to imagine what Abbas might have said to deserve such a punishment, given that he is the least insolent person on the ship. He looked to me while his thumbs were triced up, as though I should explain or intervene. But who am I to command the boatswain? Who is Abbas to object? Sailors are not made of porcelain and even if Abbas does not wish to be one of us, he must play the part. He must do his duty before the mast, as we all have or will do. A bucket of saltwater over the back and life carries on.

But the cry that escaped him when the salt dashed his wounds. God help him.

There is something else that troubles the mind. Throughout the flogging, Samuel Lowden wore a strange expression. Not cold and hard as he used to look while cracking the cat-o'-nine. This time he looked at ease, as if his arm were not connected to his mind. And he was humming to himself. Humming as he shook a bit of flesh free from the barbs.

22 December 1802.—At night I hold a handful of black sand to my nose. Dr. Goodwin advised me to take a pocketful from St. Helena, though I have not found the scent restorative.

23rd—Persistent dewfalls throughout the night. Dangerous for those of us who were sleeping bare-chested in our hammocks. I have been coughing all day.
24th—Several casks of salt pork gone rotten. Thrown overboard.
25th—Christmas Day. A bowl of my mother's potato and leek soup. I fill my mouth with a spoonful and spit out black sand. That is when I awake to find no soup, no sand, only a flat black sky and soon someone, maybe Marks, is telling me for the love of God to stop sniveling.

27 December 1802.—I fell while carrying cordage this morning. The quartermaster sent me down to the hold, without asking me what was wrong or looking at my leg. I reckon that somehow he knows, as must the others, though they keep their distance. I can hardly stand my own breath.

In the hold, I found Bunn slumped against the wall, the lantern light swinging dimly over his face. "Warm greetings from hell," he said. Dr. Goodwin spooned malt wort into his mouth. Bunn grimaced, then asked whether he could have his lemon juice cold. This was how he'd taken the scorbutic while on the *Lady Jane* and no one on that ship had fallen sick. Dr. Goodwin retorted that the water had to be boiled in order to destroy contaminants and told Bunn to leave medicine to the educated.

Dr. Goodwin proceeded to his next patient, who was slouched in shadow. The man's shirt was open at the chest, his ribs covered in spongy red sores.

It was Samuel Lowden. I had never seen him so slovenly, yet his eyes were devoid of surprise or shame. "Good heavens, Thomas," he said, "you look a mess."

29 December 1802.—Today Abbas approached me after Sunday dinner. I tend to sit apart from the others and eat quickly so my presence will not trouble anyone. He found me on the poop, where I was finishing my biscuit.

I asked how he was. The stiffness of his posture said enough.

"Are you taking the lemon juice?" he asked.

I turned away and nodded. We stood at the taffrail, looking out over the waves.

"Thomas, did I tell you I was a woodcarver for Tipu Sultan?"

I said that he had. He hovered between silence and speaking, as if trying to decide which would be wiser.

Then he told me, in a kind of unblinking spell, how he'd also served in Tipu's army during the final siege, assigned to carry the wounded and the dead. He managed to carry no one. "Goats are slaughtered with greater care," he said.

He told me of how, on the battlefield, he had fallen beneath the weight of a dead man, and how he lay face-down beneath that corpse for three nights. He had visions. In one, Tipu Sultan was bending over him, reaching out a hand. Abbas nearly reached up, which would've betrayed his position to the sepoys. To see the ghostly Tipu Sultan dissolve before his eyes—he had never felt so abandoned or alone.

(And yet he was reporting all these hardships in a tone so detached, I did not know whether to believe him.)

Finally he turned to me and said, "Thomas, I am sorry to disappoint you and am grateful for your friendship. But you must understand, I did not come through such misery in order to serve others. Now I serve myself."

And then he left me by the rail, speechless.

How long I stood there, I cannot remember. I only recall that all at once, I was besieged by pain. I put my head in my hands while a battering ram swung from one side of my skull to the other. I thought my time had come. That my insides were coming unglued. My muscles from my bones from my skin. Unraveling.

But then by some miracle: I forced myself to look up.

There she was, in the distance, her back breaking through the water. The whale, my own, white and cool.

Her tail thrashed, gold coins leaping off the waves. There, there was my salvation.

I see her whenever I close my eyes.

30 December 1802.—This day, my messmate A. Bunn died of the sickness and was buried at sea. I cannot sleep. Marks, who previously silenced me, is weeping quietly in his hammock.

2 January 1803.—Constant rain. The night past Mr. Forrest, quarter-master, died.
5th—Edward Gammage, cooper's mate, died at ten p.m.

10th—Stormy weather. Every day men are laid down by the sickness. Abbas is the only man to walk tall, untouched. Strange to think that one of his race should prove hardier than the rest of us. It was Samuel Lowden who first called my attention to this peculiarity as we were down in the hold. He was prating away, no longer caring whether anyone saw his gums, which are now black as mine. "Striding about like a rajah," said Samuel Lowden, with more bemusement than bitterness. "As he will be, soon enough."

Samuel Lowden is still in the hold, I believe. When I left him he had moved onto the topic of comets.

·   ·   ·

11th—Our ship is in shambles with such a feeble-bodied crew as ours. Sad to see the *Peppercorn* in this condition, having kept her always in crack order. I have hardly the vigor to hold my pencil but I wish to record that Captain Northcote offered the toast today though doing so is beneath his station. He raised his cup, faltering before he said:

"For absent friends and those at sea."

Another called out: "Absent friends."

13th—Yesterday, Samuel Lowden, boatswain, died an hour past midnight.

I have heard that his suffering was worsened by his desperation to talk, to tell anyone listening that we had been cursed, that the Hindustani had cursed us all, that we should throw him overboard or expect to meet our own ends at the bottom of the sea.

May God rest his soul alongside that of his beloved brother, William.

I have not seen the Hindustani in days.

20th—Mother, I have such dreams. Here you are breaching the water in the form of a whale, falling back with a great and happy splash. We are both whales, swimming side by side, mining the deep. These dreams feel more vivid than my very own life. Last night I reached for the moon. It was solid in my palm. I took a bite and my mouth filled with warm baked potato. Look at me, Mother, stepping into the dark and I am no longer afraid.

25 January 1803.—Mother, you were right about the *Confiance*. She is exactly as you described. Square topsails and gallant sails, all yellow and black. She lies low and sleek on the water, deadly, beautiful.

· · ·

I do not like to burden you, Mother, but there is a chance I may not come home. In the event of my death I have asked Dr. Goodwin to send you my Diary so that you may read my testimony and beg mercy for my Soul.

The *Confiance* came on us at night, under cover of sea-fog. By the time we realized we were under attack, we found ourselves unable to maneuver. The *Confiance* had wedged our rudder. There was no time to clear the ship for action, not even to hoist our colors.

The *Confiance* gave us a broadside, which we returned. Action continued for an hour or so during which our men were cut down by the dozens. Our sails were shot to netting, our rigging cut, our masts ruined. Captain Northcote took the helm until a ball knocked the hat off his head.

"Stand down," called Captain Maquet, commander of the *Confiance,* "or next time I shall not miss."

And so Captain Northcote surrendered. He has sunk his life's fortune into the *Peppercorn* and her cargo. There are no words for our sense of defeat.

Captain Maquet boarded us along with a lieutenant and a handful of overguzzled Frenchmen who relieved the officers of their sidearms. Maquet cut a striking figure in his gold-buttoned coat and silver-tipped cane.

. . .

"I only ask," said Captain Northcote, watching the enemy descend the ladder into the cargo hold, "that private property not be tampered with."

Maquet's lieutenant replied in English: "That depends on the good behavior of your crew and their willingness to serve."

Maquet gestured at us with his silver-tipped cane. "Are there any French speakers on board?"

He said this in French. I hesitated in a way that must have suggested comprehension, for Maquet was soon in my face. His hat was pulled low on one side yet failed to conceal his disfigured ear, which looked something like a chanterelle.

"Ah, how droll!" he said in French. "You look just like a mid we took off the Brunswick in September of last year. Is your name Dickorie, by any chance?"

He was testing me. I made my face blank as a wall.

"Poor Dickorie has lost his hearing," said Maquet and whacked the side of my head with his cane.

I fell. My ears rang. A part of me, some inexpressible part, felt far from all that was happening. Another part of me—the part that did not wish to die—was yelling that I did not speak French but *he* did—*him*, take *him*.

·   ·   ·

I was pointing to Abbas. His head was slightly cocked, his face as soft with innocence as in the moments before he was flogged. If I could have, in that moment, I would have killed him.

The enemy made off with their plunder: crates of pepper and tea and rice, rattan, cotton, casks of wine. They also took ten of our healthiest members: four mids, the sailmaker, the ship's cook, the master carpenter, and of course Abbas, *le prisonnier indienne.* I was spared by Maquet, who said of me: "Just look at him—he won't last the week."

This morning at seven a.m. the *Confiance* quit our presence and sailed southward, carrying our men and our cargo.

I have been sent down to the hold with my bedding. Once crammed cheek to jowl with prizes. Now it holds me. I wish for a view of the water. All I have is the small wooden whale. *I want to make a thing that will last,* he told me. What a thing that will be. I hear the tread of men walking above. The creak of the ship sides. I put the whale to my nostrils and up wafts the smell of what might be linden or birch or oak, sweet Jesus, let it bear me home.

ROUEN, FRANCE

1805

I

Early one morning in May, Jehanne Du Leze drapes a black cloth over a lectern. This she sets outside the door of her half-timbered home on Rue Bertaux. Atop the lectern she places a clothbound guest book, inkwell, and pen, then returns inside, leaving the door unlocked. She takes a seat beside the dining table. The other chairs have been removed, the table laid out with the body of Lucien Du Leze, or Père Du Leze, as he has come to be known.

She has been keeping vigil since the day before, watching his eyes sink ever so slightly in their sockets. Cotton keeps the nostrils from foaming. Incense burns from the mantelpiece to cover other smells.

People stream in and out, murmuring their respects, bringing loaves of bread, jars of rillette, slices of cold meat and cheese. She thanks each visitor for coming. Most of the visitors she already knows, yet every face is newly strange. Attached to a body that will go on bathing, eating, sneezing, sleeping. She watches these anonymous bodies in black bombazine, milling about the corpse, and wonders if they, too, have ever considered not being.

Lucien's sister, Isabelle, takes her hand and says that the hearse has arrived. The body is lifted into the wooden coffin, the lid drawn shut, the bolts screwed into place. Isabelle warned her that this would be the worst part, yet it seems no better or worse to Jehanne than any other part. She and Isabelle ride in the cabriolet behind the horse-drawn hearse, the other mourners walking ahead. Jehanne imagines that the procession, passing beneath the Gros Horloge, looks from above like a spill of black ink.

Jehanne keeps her veil lowered throughout the ride, the only way to endure an hour in closed quarters with Isabelle. Her aunt keens and sways, shaking her head as if arguing with Lucien's soul. No service, Lucien had insisted, just put me in the ground. Until his last breath, Isabelle had remained ironclad in her faith that he would have a change of heart.

They arrive at the cemetery. A former pupil has come all the way from Normanville to deliver a eulogy in the form of a sonnet, setting Lucien's life to a dubious rhyme scheme:

> . . . *He learned from the masters of Paris*
> *Astounding the king with his prowess.*
> *So was he sent to the Orient—*
> *Adventure turned to banishment!*

"There's more?" Isabelle whispers tearfully as the poet turns the page.

> *Yet God looked kindly on Père Du Leze,*
> *Sparing him from maritime sickness,*
> *And endowed him with orphaned child,*
> *Mademoiselle Jehanne, pious and mild.*

At the sound of her name, Jehanne shrinks into her bonnet.

"O son of Rouen, now take thy rest," says the poet, closing his eyes, "knowing thy name be ever blest."

A single encouraging clap is hushed.

Down into the earth the coffin goes, dappled by a soft rain.

. . .

Even in mourning, Isabelle is imperious. After the funeral, she uses all her powers to try to persuade Jehanne to come stay at Isabelle's country house in Banneville. "A woman, alone in this squalor?" Isabelle says, looking around Jehanne's parlor.

"You have lived alone all these years." Jehanne unfastens the buttons of her pelisse, which she tosses onto the back of a sofa.

Isabelle picks up the coat and folds it over her arm. "I am old. It's a given." But Jehanne refuses the offer, and keeps refusing until Isabelle goes away in her little cabriolet, the hood drawn up.

Peace at last. Jehanne brings the soggy guest book into the house, along with the lectern, pen, and inkwell. She builds a fire and hangs her stockings over the grate, steam wisping off the wool.

She ventures into Lucien's room. There is the narrow bed, the table with its basin and ewer. A dish with soap worn to a pit by Lucien's palms. She opens the doors of his enormous wardrobe, releasing odors of stale smoke and rosemary. She draws aside a panel in the back. The hidden compartment holds two things: a cask of Rioja, which he was saving for a special occasion, and a velvet box containing an agate ring.

She slides the ring on her finger—a perfect egg of agate, with a hole clean through the middle—a gift from Tipu Sultan to Lucien for a job well done. The surface is smooth, rippled with cream and coffee striations. Lucien once pulled it off his own thumb, with mock majesty, and dropped it into her palm on the occasion of her nineteenth birthday. Then he closed her hand and kissed her knuckles. She can almost feel the brush of his whiskers, still.

She returns the ring to the compartment and brings the Rioja to the living room, where she slumps into a caned armchair and watches the fire chew the wood. If Isabelle were here, she would tell Jehanne to pin her knees together. If Lucien were here, he would tell Jehanne to ignore Isabelle and sit however she wanted. But no one is here, and for the second time in her life, Jehanne feels both very adult and very alone.

·   ·   ·

For the first fourteen years of her life, Jehanne was raised by the women of her family, sometimes at her grandmother's house, or those of her aunts, always caught up in some happy, barefoot scrum of children. Occasionally her father would visit with bananas or sweets and take her to a church and test her French. She had no idea why he decided she should go back with him to France. To become a lady? To be his caretaker in old age? She battered her grandmother with questions until her grandmother threatened to lop off her tongue. Plenty of times Jehanne had been threatened with a tongue-lopping, but not with the words that followed: "You are their daughter. They owe you no explanation."

"They" being Jacques Martine, whom her grandmother never called by any name, referring to him only from a formal distance. She had never approved of the moony Frenchman who claimed to have been struck by the arrow of love or some such mortifying nonsense upon glimpsing Jehanne's mother at a wedding. Yet he was smart enough to know that he had only to prevail on Jehanne's grandfather with elegant rifles and delicate sets of china, over games of pachisi and false promises of conversion, until, at last, the old man said *Oh well, why not,* and the match was made.

Jehanne had heard her mother was beautiful, with a heart-shaped face and full lips. You have her smile, her aunts used to say. Consequently Jehanne went through a phase of smiling into every reflection—mirrors, ponds, the flat sides of knives—in search of the mother she'd never seen with her own eyes. Not that she wanted her mother's beauty. Being beautiful meant that a man could take you away from your kin and deposit a baby in your belly, only for a demon to slither up your birth tunnel as soon as the baby was born and kill you. At least this was the story Jehanne was told by a cousin, regarding her own birth. "The only demon," said her father, when Jehanne asked him to verify the story, "was that witless mop of a midwife."

For the journey from Mysore to Pondicherry, Jehanne wore a stiff white frock and black shoes tight as fists around her feet. Along the rim of each eye she wore a stroke of her grandmother's kohl and a dot on her cheek meant to mar what was otherwise lovely, to ward off the Evil Eye.

When she stood hand in hand with her father at the port in Pondicherry, she could only think of her grandmother's hand, callused and firm, and how it hurt to be touched by her, no matter how gently, and how that hurt was love, a hard leathery love, a far cry from her father's languid clasp.

The voyage was dull, but the one person who gave shape to her days was Lucien Du Leze. Sometimes she found the old man sitting in silence, his eyes closed, his face turned up to the sea breeze. He had a reserved manner but softened in her presence, possibly out of pity. He came up with games to play with the yellow spinning top she'd brought with her, Double-Flip and Hit the Target. "Remember, there are no losers in this game," he liked to say at the start, "unless of course I am the winner." If her father happened by, he would draw Lucien away for a walk—sometimes right in the middle of a game! She hated her father most at such moments. *Rantallion,* she'd mouth at his back, *rantallion* being a curse word she'd picked up from the sailors and which she assumed to mean *rascal.*

It was soon after the stop in Isle de France that her father started coughing. The next morning he failed to rise from bed. Lucien helped him to the sick hold, along with several other invalids. Days or weeks later, she cannot recall, the chaplain was swinging a little pot of smoking incense over the bodies, which were shrouded in sailcloth, ankles tethered to leg irons. She was convinced that her hatred was at least partly responsible, that her resentment had weakened him in some way, allowing a demon to enter through some orifice—as it had with her mother—and stop his heart.

She remembers little from the rest of the journey. A good thing, Lucien said, for she was sickly and silent the entire time, always staying close to walls. He worried she, too, would be buried at sea.

One thing that helped to bring her out of the gloom was the toy that Lucien had brought with him. It was a tiger atop a prone English soldier, his head turned to one side as the tiger fed on his neck. The wood held a mysterious smell, still fragrant beneath the lacquer.

Minutes on end, she spent staring at the toy, painted in juvenile colors yet mature in subject, such that she felt herself maturing as she pondered the agony of the man, fated to lie forever between death and life, betwixt platform and predator, a predator that was both frightening and alluring. She wished to intervene, but the carving was all of a piece and denied intervention.

Abbas had made the toy, Lucien said. "The same one that made your spinning top. You remember?"

What a question. Of course she remembered.

Lucien fell silent, brooding as he thumbed the little carved ear. Then he handed the toy to her and told her to keep it under her cot, which he'd had installed in his own berth. It seemed that some sort of arrangement had been made between her father and Lucien, placing her in Lucien's care for the foreseeable future, which, unforeseeably to Jehanne, turned into the rest of Lucien's life.

Two months after the funeral, Jehanne leaves her home dressed in Lucien's oilcloth coat and crosses the street to open the shop. She draws the black drapes from the mirrors and windows, aware that she is flaunting the conventions of bereavement. Women are meant to mourn for seven years; it's been sixty days. Yet she cannot stand for another minute the yawning emptiness of her house.

Not that she wishes for more visitors, more colorless words of comfort. No, she much prefers the dense dusty hush of the curiosity shop, every piece of eccentric inventory chosen by her own hand, obtained on biannual trips to surrounding towns. There is the globe made of cowrie shells and the shark jaws mounted upon a large mirror. There are Lucien's clocks, glowing on curved stems of brass. There are hats and brooches of her own design, butterflies in bell jars, scarabs in resin pendants. And of course the taxidermied marmot that Lucien so hated. "Either it goes or I go," he said, two days before he fell unconscious off his wooden stool. By the time the doctor arrived, she'd managed to fold his arms over his chest.

Most of the revenue came from Lucien's business in watches and clocks. His final repair sits on the table at the rear of the shop, a pendulum clock with the head of Socrates, its back exposed, Lucien's empty pipe beside it.

In a drawer she discovers a small screwdriver. She sits on his stool and stares into the intricate lacework of gears. In her youth, she often watched him work, the pipe clamped between his side teeth, until the gears rolled against one another as if of their own magical accord. How badly she'd wanted to learn, how she'd begged him to teach her. Instead Lucien sent her to the convent for lessons with Sister Marie Angele.

If so much as a scrap of Kannada escaped her mouth, Sister Marie Angele's ruler would strike the nearest surface with frightful strength. The mere mouthing of Arabic, and the ruler striped her palm a livid red. By twenty, Jehanne was accomplished in catechism, Danish, English, lacemaking, and needlepoint, and resigned to a lifetime of learning little else.

And now here she is, a hunched monkey with a tool in her hand, staring at the clock as if it might instruct her.

More than once, Isabelle has said: "Why must you make everything so difficult, Jehanne? Simply move in with me for a time and then we will settle you."

"But what of the shop?" Jehanne said. "The house?"

"That will be for your husband to decide, my dear. If we can find you one. Being a half-breed will count against you. Oh, don't look so oppressed, Jehanne. My mother used to say I was slim as a knitting needle but I never let that stop me from finding a husband."

Jehanne stabs the point of the screwdriver into the surface of the table. This leaves a small, satisfying nick. She stabs the table twice more, which is less satisfying, puerile in fact. She sets the tool aside and puts her head in her arms.

When the shop door opens, she sits upright.

A bearded man hovers in the threshold, cap in hand. His black hair is combed back, his skin brown, a foreigner in local clothes: black overcoat, buff-colored breeches, buckled shoes.

They stare at one another. It seems to her that the man does not move, does not even breathe, before he asks: "Is this—" He swallows visibly. "I am looking for Lucien Du Leze."

She has given the news to countless people over the past months, so often that the fact feels drained of emotion. Yet this man—with his worn face, his eyes that could bore a hole through a door— makes her hesitate.

Slowly she says, "Lucien died two months past."

"I do not understand."

"He collapsed. The doctor thought it was his heart," she adds, watching the man's cap fall to the floor. He makes no motion to pick it up. "Monsieur?"

He sways, catches hold of the counter. "Forgive me . . ."

Taking him by the elbow, she guides the stranger to the little table and plants him in a hard-backed chair. He stares blankly ahead.

Abruptly he begins to speak, though she cannot tell who is the audience. He says the innkeeper told him about Du Leze, but he'd had to come see for himself. He says he was hit on the head by two falling acorns this morning and, though he knows he should not take this personally, it did seem a bad sign, and yet he has always been bad at reading signs, he has always made the wrong decisions, signs or no signs—

"Here: drink this." She sets a pewter cup before him, hoping the wine hasn't turned. One gulp and he grimaces. "What is your name?"

"Abbas," he says heavily. "Some call me Mahmud Abbas."

"Abbas? Abbas, the one who made the Musical Tiger?"

He looks over at her, unseeing. The beard is misleading, and yet.

She fetches the spinning top from its shelf and sets it on the table in front of him. "The same one who made this?" He blinks at the top, his hands hanging empty by his sides. "I played with it every day on the ship from Pondicherry. It was the only thing that brought me joy. Lucien and this."

"May I have more wine?"

She pours. "Do you remember me? My father was Jacques Martine, though now I go by Jehanne Du Leze. We met in your workshop? And then at the festival?"

He seems not to hear her at first. Then, after a few more gulps, he looks at her with the faintest light of recognition. "Jehan," he says, switching to Kannada, "Jehan who loves jokes."

The sound of her mother tongue passes through her like the first rays of spring, softening the ice of the past six years.

"*Haudu,*" she says, and it's almost as if their mouths have decided for them: they will never speak to each other in any language but their own.

Abbas is too despondent to say much more. She offers her lunch of bread and hard cheese and the last of the duck rillette, then watches, worried, as he forgoes the food for heavy pours of wine.

Eventually he begins to answer her questions. She gets him to say how long he has been in Rouen (a few nights), and where he came from (Saint-Malo).

"Why Saint-Malo?" she asks.

"That's where our captain lives. The captain of the *Confiance.*"

"The pirate ship? You became a pirate?"

"My plan had been to come here and study with Lucien Sahab."

"Yes, that was Lucien's great wish."

"Bad timing," says Abbas, swallowing the wine as if he no longer tastes it.

When she asks him how long he will be staying in Rouen, he shrugs at the cup in his hand. Then he wobbles to his feet and says he is going for a walk.

"In this state?" she says. "You'll wind up at the bottom of a well." She watches him turn a slow circle, his brow furrowed. "What are you doing?"

"Looking for my hat."

She snatches it up from the spot where he dropped it, holding it away from him.

"That's my hat," he says plaintively.

She prevails on him to lie down on the cot in the back of the shop, a ticking mattress where Lucien used to rest his swollen knees. Just an hour or two, she insists, until the wine has burned off. Once

Abbas is lying down, she surrenders the cap, which he places over his face. In a muffled voice, he says: "You are much changed, Jehan. But also the same."

She hovers, wishing for specifics. But soon he is snoring.

Abbas awakens in the night but keeps his eyes closed. He does not want to see the velvety shapes of clocks and curtains and cabinets, does not want to be reminded that he is farther from home than he has ever been.

Sleep is no refuge. Wine gives him vivid dreams, and because the wine was bad, tonight's were a mela of terrible memories. Stepping on dead men's faces. Baring his back and facing the sea, shards of light clawing at his eyes. And Thomas, his only friend, pointing an accusatory finger as if hacking the air between them to pieces.

Afterwards, on the *Confiance*, Abbas held himself apart from his shipmates, new and old. He sat alone at every meal, kept silent through night watch. Some took his quiet for a deep flickering intelligence. Mr. Grimmer, the master carpenter who had hired him, took offense. "We are surrounded by depravity and disorder," he confided in Abbas. "We have only each other to lean on now."

Abbas did not see depravity and disorder on the *Confiance*. He saw a crew that decided most matters by vote—one to each man. He saw Captain Maquet—Citizen Maquet, as he dubbed himself—strolling the quarterdeck with the barber, as if all hierarchies had been dissolved. Through others, Abbas learned that Maquet was once a slave trader, as courteous to his crew as he was cruel to those he called his *chiens negres*.

In the end, it was a vote that decided Grimmer's fate, when he stood accused of desertion. "Will none of you speak for me?" he shouted at his trial, wrists bound. Abbas felt the scorch of his glare and turned away, just as everyone, including Grimmer, had turned away when Abbas was accused of insolence to the boatswain.

Then Grimmer was marched onto a tiny island, uninhabited except for the bones of what might have been other deserters. They left him sitting cross-legged on the bank, wrists unbound. In his lap was a pistol with a single bullet in the chamber. As the *Confiance* weighed anchor, Grimmer lifted his head from his hands and wished Citizen Maquet a quick passage to the bottom of the sea. He said this in a calm, almost cordial voice, as if they would all see each other soon enough.

As the night wears on, Abbas's back begins to itch. He turns onto his side, reaching for the scars, those tangled tracks beneath the skin.

Finally, in a fit of boredom and disgust, he goes to the window and parts the heavy black curtain. The moon is large and bright, flat as a nailhead holding up the sky.

He is reminded of the hottest nights when he and his brothers slept outside and the stars were bright with life. Somewhere, perhaps, his mother is staring up at the same moon, wondering what has become of her youngest son. He can see her very clearly at day's end, unwinding the thinned rope of her hair and settling onto her side, an arm folded under her cheek, her other arm draped over the space where once he'd been small enough to fit.

Yet he knows there is no space for him beside her now. His face, touched by death, would frighten her. *What happened to you?* she would ask, and he would not have the language to answer.

II

The next morning, Jehanne hurries across the street, terrified to find the shop curtains open. She had drawn them shut before leaving yesterday, to prevent word from getting to Isabelle that her niece was housing a brown man. Isabelle, slim as a knitting needle, piercing in her judgment. Also Jehanne's last source of financial support.

Another step into the shop and Jehanne halts. The cot is empty. The Socrates clock rests on the little table, in perfect ticking health.

Fear swings through her: Abbas is gone. So much she had wanted to say to him, the words dancing in her mouth, as French never would.

"You've come," he says from behind her.

"Ah!" She wheels around to find him standing with an open pocket watch in hand.

"*Pardon*. I am feeling much better. And I fixed the clock with the head on it."

"I thought you hadn't completed your studies."

"Simple repairs I can do. And if you would allow it . . ."

He looks down. She feels him summoning his nerve. Ask me, she thinks. Just ask.

"Would you let me stay here if I worked to earn my keep?
Until—"

"Of course!" she says, then more reservedly: "Until you find a better situation. We must help one another, being countrymen and all."

He thanks her and retreats to his worktable, though she encour-
ages him to first eat breakfast, or what was left of the cheese and
bread she brought yesterday.

As she wipes down the windows, she notes his reflection in the
glass. He eats slowly and vacantly, his jaws working hard at the crust.
Where is the boy who proudly presented her with the yellow spinning top? In his place is a heavy-eyed man, so hopelessly still a fly
could cross his forehead without him noticing.

She has an idea of what will cheer him. Off she goes, hunting
through Lucien's notebooks and blueprints until, at last, she finds
the page, soft with age, neatly cut from a newspaper.

"Look," she says, laying the piece of paper on the table, a column
no taller than her hand. "It is your tiger."

He squints, scanning the lines of tiny English text until he
reaches the illustration. Here his chewing stops. The illustration cap-
tivates him.

It occurs to her that he may not read English or any language at all, so she explains that the clipping is from an English newspaper, a review of a London exhibition marking the fifth anniversary of the fall of Seringapatam and featuring a collection of Tipu-related items belonging to a Lady Selwyn, wife of the late Colonel Horace Selwyn of Twickenham, "including but not limited to: Tipoo's footstool, the Musical Tyger, some curious arms, and the war turban and dress that Tipoo wore during the Adoni campaigns." The Musical Tyger is said to have been the main attraction. Dozens of visitors lined up for the exhibition, in order to have a chance at turning the Tyger's hand crank. This would "produce a moan which may be interpreted as either the low growl of the tiger, or the half-suppressed agony of the sufferer." The author speculates on the "tyrant's nightly ritual" of playing the Tyger, "with no other view than to excite in his imagination those acute agonies in which it was his common practice to indulge."

She pauses, unsure if Abbas is listening. His gaze has not strayed from the illustration.

"How did you come by this?" he asks softly.

"An old friend in London sent the clipping. He said he went to see the tiger himself at the Selwyn house—it is called Cloverpoint Castle. The lady has a great collection of Oriental curiosities, and a particular obsession for anything related to Tipu Sultan. This friend, Mr. Pike, is a farmer and a gentleman, but not of noble blood or lineage. He simply arrived at the house and asked for a tour, and she kindly gave it. Although there was one bit of bad news. Mr. Pike said the automaton had fallen into disrepair. Mostly it lives under a sheet. Lucien's greatest wish was to go and see it himself, perhaps even offer to repair it . . ." She breaks off, unable to finish, and waits for Abbas to give some sign of having heard her. She also notes his scent, which is good and strong and a little embarrassing, or unnerving, for it reminds her that she has welcomed a near-stranger into her life, a man she only met once or twice, and who does have about him a whiff of instability.

Finally, with effort, he slides the paper toward her.

"You keep it," she says, and the light in his face brings the boy of him back.

From the Red Hen, Abbas carries very few possessions: a toothbrush, a bar of blue soap, a comb, and a folding knife. The rest of his clothes he keeps in a small leather case he calls his "sea-chest" tucked under the cot. By the time she arrives in the morning, the cot is always perfectly made, as taut and impersonal as he is. Still, the mere sight of him, sitting on Lucien's stool, dismembering a piece with tiny tools, lifts her spirit.

During his first two weeks of employment, Abbas does what he can with a handful of pocket watches and clocks whose ailments are not beyond his powers to cure. Cleaning gears and stripping movements, he can do. But the cuckoo clock is another matter. Behind its little doors lie two little Dutch girls who should be rolling out of their houses on the hour and coming to meet in the middle, where they tap foreheads before rolling back on their tracks. Instead the little Dutch girls are locked in a mutual silence.

He looks to Lucien's blueprints for guidance, but the penciled writing is cramped and fading, impossible to decipher.

Defeated, he asks Jehanne to return the cuckoo clock to its owner. Same with several other pendulum clocks whose owners will, in all likelihood, go across town and seek help from a rival clockmaker by the name of Godin.

To make himself useful, Abbas chops wood, tends the small vegetable garden, and replaces the roof slates when a storm blows them off. Every few days, he visits the grave of Du Leze to weed the flowering thyme and keep it from creeping into neighboring plots. Once, on his way to the gravesite, he catches sight of a blade-thin woman in black, bending to put flowers on the headstone. He turns on his heel, hoping the woman—who can only be Isabelle—hasn't seen him.

. . .

For Jehanne, these are weeks of promise as she makes two sales of her own. One woman buys a hat of Jehanne's design: yolk-yellow satin, swirled on the crown, with a little tail dangling off the side. An engraving of a turbaned Mughal from one of Lucien's books had served as inspiration. In a complimentary tone, the customer says it reminds her of a palmier biscuit, so Jehanne says, yes, that was the very inspiration: palmiers. The customer leaves with hatbox in hand. Two days later, her sister arrives, asking for another in blue.

Jehanne is in disbelief. Her designs have always tended toward the eccentric (scarab earrings and matching brooch, a belt woven of peacock plumes). She sees each as a minor mark of defiance, an acknowledgment that her taste will never align with every other woman's, nor does she want it to. What surprises her is the joy she derives from the sister who says, "I wager all the ladies will be wearing your hats at the Feast of Saint Josephine."

The only awkwardness is when a customer catches sight of Abbas, working at the little table in the back of the shop. "Ah!" they might say, or: "I didn't realize . . ." leaving Jehanne to quickly explain that Père Du Leze's former pupil has come all the way from Mysore to help with the business.

"Does Godin know?" asks Madame Boldt.

"What does it matter?" Jehanne says curtly, while pulling a needle through the wool of a torn stocking. Madame Boldt leans closer, filling Jehanne's nose with her cloying floral smell.

"Godin is a guild member, dear." Madame Boldt flicks a glance at Abbas, who is pretending not to listen. "And the guild doesn't take kindly to outsiders."

After Madame Boldt leaves, along with her catatonic cuckoo clock, Abbas asks Jehanne to say more of Godin. "Is he a good clockmaker? Does he have an apprentice?"

"Steer clear of that man," she says. "A real *rantallion,* that one."

"Jehan," he says, with a grimace.

"What? He is."

"You do know a *rantallion* is—"

"A rascal." She hesitates. "Isn't it?"

He regards her with growing bemusement. "A *rantallion* is a man with a poker of insufficient length—"

"No!"

"—and oversized plums."

Jehanne claps her hands over her ears, but her umbrage gives way to a memory of the butcher's boy whom she once called a *rantallion* because of his faulty scale, and how, ever since, he has avoided looking her in the eye . . .

"Oh my," she says, her hands falling to her lap, but Abbas is laughing, and both of them have forgotten, for now, the subject of Godin.

Fashions take time, Jehanne tells herself, on those days when no one passes through the shop. Meanwhile she takes measures of austerity—rarely lighting a fire, wearing two pairs of stockings and padding her mourning clothes with wool, subsisting mostly on a twelve-pound loaf. Occasionally she is light-headed.

A neighbor invites her for a dinner of boeuf bourguignon, just the thing on a cold day, but then Jehanne finds herself in the awkward position of having to return the invitation. And so, a few days later, she pushes a pram—one that she took from the shop display—through a park far from home where no one knows her, and catches two pigeons with her bare hands. Shudder of wing, snap of neck, then she places them in the pram, under the blanket, hoping no one has seen. What's the difference? she thinks to herself, on the fast walk home and later as she plucks them in her kitchen, badly severs their heads from their necks (bloody mess), and roasts them to a golden hue with sprigs of rosemary, hoping they will pass as quail. The neighbor pronounces the meal delicious, though Jehanne herself declines a portion.

No longer does she crave meat of any kind, just the taste of normalcy again, the sense that calamity is not always at the door. She convinces herself the present is just a phase, and that someday she will light the hearth again, someday she will not have to deal with the ferrety little utility man, to ask him for one more month's worth of oil on credit, which makes two months' credit, to which he is happy to oblige because it means she will allow him to reach down her dress and repeatedly squeeze her right breast as if juicing it. (This happened only once, but the breast in question is still haunted by his fingernails.) Someday a squeeze will no longer suffice, someday the Ferret will require full payment plus interest, the kind of interest in which she is wholly uninterested.

That day arrives sooner than she expected, on the first Monday in June. It's the sound of him knocking at the shop next door that has her rushing about, looking for a place to hide. When Abbas asks what she is doing, she commands him from under the counter: "Say I am out! No—I am in mourning!"

"But you are here."

Quickly, in so many words, she explains what happened last time with the Ferret. Abbas listens in dead silence, and then, when she is finished, he sets down his tools.

"Just do as I say!" she hisses after him, but it's too late: she can hear the Ferret's footsteps approaching the door. He has barely stepped into the shop before Abbas is backing him out onto the step, politely insisting that he, Abbas, will see to the payment just there, in the alley beside the shop. The Ferret, congenial as ever, is bewildered by this brown-skinned stranger but allows himself to be steered away, out of Jehanne's view.

"He is giving you an extension," says Abbas, upon returning alone, five minutes later. He will say no more on the subject, only massages his knuckles and takes up his tools.

The next time she glimpses the Ferret, he is using his left hand to knock on a door across the street, his right hand so bandaged he cannot so much as cup an apple.

What if is a question that has begun to plague Abbas with every swipe of his rag and swish of his feather duster. What if the next customer who enters with a faulty clock is the last customer he will ever encounter? What if old Dumonde returns, saying his pocket watch is now moving slower than before? What if the mysterious guild runs Abbas out of town? What then?

On a Wednesday, Abbas tells Jehanne he is going for his afternoon walk with no destination in particular, a lie she seems to accept.

He passes beneath the Gros Horloge and approaches the bridge that will take him across town. Beneath the bridge, a black sow nudges through a mound of rubbish, two piglets at her legs. When he reaches the other side, he asks a man for directions to the shop of Monsieur Godin.

He is told to walk along the Robec, a rancid stream only so wide as his wingspan, with planks laid across for pedestrians to access the shops on the other side. As astounding as the smell is the color, purple in some places, indigo in others, a thing of stink and beauty.

As he veers away from the stream, the smell lessens, yet his nausea remains. Finally he reaches the shop with window boxes of welcoming pink hydrangea. His entire future seems to rest on whatever will happen beyond that door.

The shop, when he enters, carries the faint waft of mildew. All around him, on every shelf, are round clocks in square wooden housings, Roman numerals clear and firm. Not a hint of gold leaf or Grecian myth. These are clocks that detest trends. These clocks are symmetrical and dour, marking the day, reminding people of what little work has been accomplished and all else that remains to be done.

At the far end is Godin, sitting at a worktable laid out with wooden gears. He is stirring a teacup with a screwdriver, glowering as he sips.

Abbas steps forward, cap in hand. "Good day to you, Monsieur Godin."

"Yes," says Godin, "it was."

"Forgive me for interrupting, monsieur."

"Well, what is it? Have you run out of business to steal?" Godin sets the cup aside and stands. Though he is equal in height to Abbas, his head is imposing in its rectangularity, stacked on the broad plinth of his shoulders. He inspects the wooden gears spread like freshly baked biscuits over his work surface, lifting and lowering them as if he can't decide which to eat.

"I had no intention of stealing anything," Abbas goes on. "I was simply continuing with the clients who had been loyal to my former master, Lucien Du Leze. Whom you may have known."

"Of course I knew him," says Godin, selecting an unfinished gear. He sits, shoulders hunched, and begins to hone the teeth with a tiny file. "An old dandy who made dandified things. And now here you are in his place, untrained, practically thumbing your nose at the Kindly Company of Clockmakers." Godin blows at the tooth. "That's the name of our guild and, to be candid, I hate it. One would think that after four hundred years we could vote on a new name, but there is such a thing as rules."

"Monsieur, I apologize for causing offense. Mademoiselle Jehanne, my master's daughter—"

"Oh, please. Men like him don't have daughters."

Abbas pauses to suppress his anger. "Mademoiselle Jehanne is alone. I was trying to help her."

"How platonic of you." Godin sets down the gear and interlocks his fingers. "Why have you come here, then? Absolution—is that all?"

"I came to ask if you would take me as an apprentice. I was learning clockmaking under Monsieur Du Leze, but he left for France before my training was complete." Abbas steps forward—Godin leaning away—and spreads the newspaper clipping of Tipu's Tiger on the corner of the table. "We made this automaton, Monsieur Du Leze and I, many years ago."

Godin has yet to look down at the clipping; instead he is squinting at Abbas with a mixture of distaste and bemusement. "You wish me to complete your training so you can go on to be my competitor."

"No, monsieur, I wish to make automata, like this one." Abbas taps on the illustration. "And at the end of the training, if you wish, I shall take my skills elsewhere. I have no one in Rouen. Nothing is keeping me here."

Godin regards the clipping at a skeptical angle. He asks several questions about the size of the automaton, its internal mechanics and movements, to which Abbas can offer only incomplete replies.

At last Godin slides the clipping away from himself. "You're saying you made this?"

"Yes—Du Leze and myself."

"How do I know you aren't lying?"

"Because I told you how it works. And my name is on it, on the bellows within."

"And if I told you my name were on the Gros Horloge, would you believe that, too?"

Abbas stares in disbelief. "But it is me, it is mine, mine and his . . ."

"Listen here: the guild will never accept a savage. But I, being of a more liberal cast of mind, might be persuaded if the automaton were here in the window of my shop."

Godin gestures toward the window, which bears his name backward, in gold lettering.

"How would I bring you the automaton, monsieur? It's as big as I am!"

"Bring me the bellows, then. With your name on it, proving you are who you say." Godin picks up the clipping between two of his fingers and drops it into Abbas's open hand. "You seem an inventive fellow. Invent a way."

Into the rotten waters of the Robec, Abbas stands staring for a very long time. He hears a cart clattering over stones, a bleating goat. Someone murmuring, "What's wrong with that fellow?"

The bells are ringing for Vespers. The same bells he used to hear day after day from the churches of Pondicherry, where he crouched on the wharves as people passed, his hand a curled claw. *Prove you are who you say.* But who he is no longer matters. Only what he has to his name. Empty-handed, he is nothing.

A fat drop of water falls on his head. He looks up to see so many blue ghosts waving from high windows. He squints and they become skeins of cotton, drying from poles. And yet there is something to their blue undulations that conjures the begum's verse:

> *Were an artist to choose me for his model—*
> *How could he draw the form of a sigh?*

He sighs along with the skeins. To make something as indestructible as those two lines. To have that small power over the grave.

III

Jehanne sells only four of her palmier hats before the sales dry up. Ah, well. She has another idea: to ask Isabelle for a loan and turn the shop into a café. She will auction all the curiosities, plus a good many of Lucien's pocket watches and clocks. The sales plus the loan will get her through the first three months. On a large piece of paper, she maps out the location of the tables and the serving counter, shelving to hold tins of tea and coffee. Convincing Isabelle will take some doing, yet for once, Jehanne feels certain and strong, for she has repaired the broken hasp on her bedroom window and trapped the kitchen mouse and juggled the bills as they came.

And then comes a letter from Isabelle, derailing all such plans.

Jehanne reads the letter twice, then tosses it onto the hearth, though the words are already seared in her mind. Her aunt, scolding her for taking "a Moorish paramour," a rumor that has seeped across town and which Isabelle confirmed with her own eyes by taking her little cabriolet down Rue Bertaux early one morning. *I was wondering why I had not heard from you in weeks or why I had not seen you at church. I had thought maybe you were too aggrieved to attend or that you had sought out another parish. How wrong I was. Until you put an end to this affair, I will not cross your threshold, nor will you be invited to cross mine. You may consider my support, financial and otherwise, revoked.*

Standing in the parlor, Jehanne sips from the cask of special-occasion Rioja until her lips go numb. Light fades from the panes. She stares at the chandelier—not the first time she's measured the distance with her eyes. The year she arrived. Her darkest year. From that time she recalls not sorrow or even sadness, but an absence of feeling altogether, and no one to whom she could describe the lack.

Curled in the cane armchair she sleeps, and in the perfect moments before she awakes, she hears the *tink-tink* of a pestle grinding spices, a rooster crowing, her grandmother calling her by name to wake up already and face the day.

In the morning, Jehanne still has her key in the door when Abbas opens it for her, stepping aside with a sweep of his arm. He has spread a cotton tablecloth over his worktable, where a little almond cake lies on a napkin, alongside a cup of violets.

"I picked the flowers on my walk this morning. And the cake is fresh from the bakery. May I?" He pulls out a chair. Slowly she sits, bewildered. He compliments the tablecloth, a scalloped cotton embroidered with linen thread, bordered in morning glories. "I found the tablecloth in that cabinet. I hope you don't mind. Is that your needlework?"

She nods.

"Good," he says, seemingly to himself. "That will be of use."

Having skipped breakfast—and supper, come to think of it—she sets her confusion aside for cake. The first bite is warm and buttery, yet she cannot fully enjoy it, for she is also aware of him, staring.

"I have a proposal," he says. "A way to secure your future and my own."

The floor of her stomach falls. A proposal? She sets down the cake and brushes the crumbs from her fingers. She does not know how she'll respond, but she will not be proposed to with crumb-coated fingers.

"It is to do with the Musical Tiger. The automaton."

The bite goes down like a ball of cotton. "The automaton?" she says. "Tipu's Tiger?"

"All these years I thought it had been destroyed in the siege. Until you showed me otherwise."

"Yes, well. I thought it would bring you some comfort."

"It did. I mean, it will, once we get it back." Abbas takes the seat opposite hers. "Here is my proposal: just listen before you reject it. We can make this Lady Selwyn a bargain. Three items in exchange for the Musical Tiger, two of them forgeries, one of them true."

"What items are you referring to?"

"Those that would suit her taste for all things Oriental. Something like a garment belonging to Tipu. Not his actual garment, of course, we would have to make one . . . but you still have Tipu's agate ring, I assume?"

"Of course I have it. I plan to have it for the rest of my life."

"*Or* we trade our items for the automaton, and bring it back to Rouen. We charge visitors, just like this Lady Selwyn. As you know, the French would pay well to see an Englishman being eaten on a daily basis. And just like Lady Selwyn, you go on tour with the tiger, displaying it in the same galleries that housed Vaucanson's Flutist and the Chess Player of Maelzel, in London at Spring Gardens, in Paris, Milan, Geneva, cities you would never see otherwise."

Bridges and clock towers rise in the skies of her mind. "What about you—what do you stand to gain?"

"The automaton would serve as proof of my potential. With any luck, it would convince Godin to apprentice me. And you, Jehanne, you would be free from financial worry."

"Or jailed for larceny. Or left dead by the roadside. Do you know what highwaymen are? They will slit your throat for a jar of herring."

"Then we won't take herring." When she frowns, he reaches his hands across the table. "I would not let anything happen to you, Jehanne. I regard you as a sister."

"I never had a brother." She nudges the cake away. "They seem very annoying."

"You don't want the cake?"

"I've never been so interested in sweets."

"That's not how I remember you."

"And how do you remember me?"

"The second time I met you, you were eating sweets like you were in a sweet-eating contest. Licking your fingertips and all."

Jehanne folds her arms. "That doesn't sound like me."

"I also remember the handkerchief you gave me. The blue flowers were very fine, but your skills have only grown." He runs a finger across the embroidery of the tablecloth, unaware that she is staring at his bowed head, noting the grassy thickness of his hair, wondering what it would be like to sink her fingers into it. "Sewing a cushion should be easy for you, no?"

"No," she says. His face falls.

"Don't pout," she says. "I was saying no to the ease of it, not no to the whole plan, though I do have some practical objections . . ."

But he is already shaking her hand as if they are in perfect agreement.

Two months later, in September, Jehanne is riding a diligence out of Rouen, headed for the port at Calais. This is the first phase of a two-week journey to Cloverpoint Castle.

She has ridden the diligence before, accompanied by Lucien for the yearly trip to Paris, where they used to acquire new merchandise from flea markets and clock parts from the Marais. This time she feels his absence keenly. The inside of the coach is more clogged than before; she has been unable to secure one of the corner seats, by the window, and is packed into the middle of the back for a fare of thirty sous. A sour smell coats the air. Overhead a net has been strung from the ceiling, sagging with hatboxes, cloaks, and one ominous sword that no one thought to sheathe.

The general mood seems to lift once they set off, tinny bells jingling from the wheelhorses' reins. She wishes Abbas were sitting beside her, or at least within view. But he is riding on top, in the imperial, among the other servants, to maintain his pretense as her valet.

Her own pretense is that she, Jehanne Du Leze, is white, as lily white as a lady sitting for a portrait, not a smudge in her bloodline. The woman in the corner seat seems to see through the ruse, scowling like the schoolgirls who used to call her Brioche in summertime, for the way she browned. But then the scowl becomes a sneeze, and the woman mutters an apology out her coveted window.

Jehanne glances up at the sword and whispers a swift *Bismillah ir-Rahman ir-Rahim,* a prayer she has not uttered in six years.

There was so much to do in the weeks leading up to the journey that Jehanne had barely entertained all the worst possible scenarios.

The work began with a letter to Lady Selwyn, which Abbas had Jehanne transcribe seven times, on the grounds that an *f* too closely resembled an *s,* or the numerals were too skinny, the letters lacking confidence. He offered only a grunt of approval at the end result.

> *To her collection, Lady Selwyn may like to add several items that were once in the possession of Tipu Sultan. I acquired these items through my Father, Monsieur Lucien Du Leze, a French clockmaker who attended the court of Tipu Sultan, and made for him a number of pocket-watches and clocks. So pleased was Tipu Sultan with my Father's work that he bestowed on us the following items:*
>
> *Two Howdah Cushions*
> *One Royal Robe worn by Tipu Sultan*
> *One Agate Ring worn on the littlest finger of Tipu Sultan*
>
> *If Lady Selwyn should wish to enhance her collection, and the Wealth of England, with these items, I would be happy to visit and make terms.*

For materials, they plundered Lucien's cupboard, which contained folded shawls and fabrics from his time in Mysore. Of these they selected a simple off-white muslin for Tipu's robe. (She'd suggested silk or something more royal, but Abbas shook his head. Any other king, but not Tipu.) Two velvety crimson shawls would make the cushions. Jehanne bought several spools of gold thread with the money Abbas supplied, rustling each note from his fold as if these were his last.

Her days took on a pleasant tedium, consumed by stitching. Abbas had sketched the exact shape and proportion of each item, the royal insignia on the velvet, the tiny gold blazes scattering the stripes. She was astonished by his drawings and wished that she could finesse her needle as gracefully as he did his pen. When at last she presented him with the first of the finished cushions, a lightness filled his face. She watched his gaze trace the intricate golden path of the thread, as if he'd forgotten about their schemes, as if her embroidery was truly worthy of a king.

A day later, it was his turn to be evaluated, after he returned from the barber.

"What?" he said, unhappily scratching his shaven cheeks. "Does it look bad?"

"Not bad. Boyish."

He shook his head. "I have no faith in barbers."

"Oh, I don't know," she said, turning away, putting a palm to her warming neck as she reminded him that vanity was beside the point: valets do not have beards.

Jehanne is relieved when the dilly stops to bait the horses. All the passengers pour into the nearest café, aside from Abbas, who stands watching the horses—their heads hanging, their legs wet and muddied up to the knee—while the postillion unhitches them from the harness.

"Did you know," asks Abbas, head tilted in study, "that when a horse gallops, each hoof meets the ground at a different moment?"

"Yes," she says. He looks at her doubtfully. "I did."

He turns back to the horses. He is not the easiest conversational partner, yet he is her only partner, so she lingers, staring with him at the horses.

She wishes Abbas would say something reassuring, to divert her from her fears. She still fears highwaymen. She fears the sky, its constant promise of storms. She fears for what she is leaving behind: her shop, her home. She fears Lady Selwyn never received her letter. She fears Lady Selwyn will accuse her of quackery and set about in some unpredictable way to ruin her as only the powerful can do. But none of these fears register as sharply as the fear of staying home and waiting for the future to take her, a fear that feels akin to a kick in the backside.

"I wonder what Lucien would think of all this," she says, hoping to draw Abbas into conversation. "I am certain he would be horrified."

"Or perhaps he would have come along."

"Lucien? I never knew him to be so adventurous. Did you?"

"I only knew him as a teacher. A great teacher."

When she asks what made Lucien great, Abbas looks beyond the horses, as if trying to summon a profound answer. Then, with a shrug: "He had faith in me."

Jehanne touches her waist, at the precise fold where she'd stitched the agate ring inside her skirt. She can feel the comforting shape through the fabric, can still hear him say: *You are worth a roomful of these.*

"A lady should not be weeping in front of her valet," says Abbas.

"I am not weeping," she snaps, wiping the corner of her eye. "And anyway, you are not really my valet."

And here is yet another of her worries—that someone will ask her why she, a lady, is traveling with a manservant. If asked, she will say that the practice is not uncommon in the colonies, all the while hoping that the inquisitor has not been to any of the colonies.

CLOVERPOINT CASTLE

1805

If you come down Clover Lane, the road leading to Cloverpoint Castle, you'll find no clover on either side. The namesake came from Lady Selwyn's obsession with the barbed quatrefoil, which looks like this.

She discovered the shape while on honeymoon in Florence with her husband, Lord Selwyn. They were touring a cathedral when she stopped before Brunelleschi's *Sacrifice of Isaac*. She hardly noticed the bronze figures, fixated instead on the unusual shape that framed them. According to their guide, the quatrefoil had come to Europe from the Orient by way of the Silk Road, printed on luxury items of velvet and silk. But this variation, said the guide, was a European invention, the orientation of the barbs alluding to the crucifix.

Throughout this presentation, Lady Selwyn kept tracing the shape with her eye. Her husband had just inherited from his uncle a country house in Twickenham, two hours' drive from London. A lath-and-plaster house, rough as a pumpkin. At twenty-four, she was eager to leave her own mark on the house, and here it was, like a sign from her very ancestors who had fought in the Outremer during the Third Crusade.

Thus began her budding interest in Moorish and Oriental art. The barbed quatrefoil would be found throughout the house, on sky-lights and lanterns and beddings and the backs of chairs. She would even have it added to the family crest, appalling the general popu-lace, who would not soon forget her middle-class origins. Everyone knew she was Lord Selwyn's meal ticket, whom he had married for her coal-mine fortune. Lord Selwyn was the former prime minister's son, and no longer in possession of his father's remittances nor the steady injections of wealth from the sugar plantation in Barbados, which had been sold by an ungenerous uncle.

Now, thirty years after its completion, Cloverpoint Castle sprawls in all its gothic rejuvenation: expanded and encrusted with turrets and pinnacles, washed in white lime. It stands apart from the dowagers' villas that dot the Thames, all with the same serious col-umns, the same Greco-Roman symmetries. On every one of its many facades is at least one window in the shape of a barbed quatrefoil.

One early morning in September, the largest of these windows is attacked by a crow. It happens three times: a barbaric caw and seconds later—the brutal blow of beak against glass.

Rum sits up in bed, shocked out of sleep. He'd thought he heard a gunshot. He'd thought himself back on the battlefield, a sepoy in search of the nearest exit, which of course there never was. He hears the butler running down the hall, clapping his hands and bellowing, "Shoo! Shoo, I say!"

Another caw, another blow against the glass. Fellowes can han-dle the bird, Rum decides. Dealing with belligerent fowl is a butler's territory. Rum is personal secretary and land agent to Lady Selwyn; tending to her business is his.

"My lady," says Rum, upon entering the Yellow Parlor.

Lady Selwyn is sitting in one of the two chairs by the fireplace, her face turned to the crackling flames. At seventy-two years old, she is sharp, vigorous, and given to dressing in her own designs, which sometimes gives the impression that she has dressed herself in the dark. Today it is some sort of voluminous cape made of pale pink crepe de chine, floating about her shoulders like a pair of flying lungs.

"Rum," she says, "did you hear that demonic bird? Fellowes said it scratched the glass."

"I do believe it was a crow."

"What did it want, do you think?"

"I suspect it saw its own reflection and mistook it for a challenger."

"I do hope it is not an omen." Her eyes shine, as though some part of her is attracted to the idea. "The hunt is in three days. Anything could happen."

"Nothing will happen, my lady, so long as you do not take the jumps."

She turns her face to the fire. "But I am so good at them."

"Aggie," he says quietly. "We discussed this."

She exhales and sits back, her cape making a noise as it crinkles.

He goes to turn a log in the grate. The sight of the flames lapping at the wood makes him pensive. Blinking, he turns his back on the fire, determined to remain sharp in the presence of the guest.

Her name is Jehanne Du Leze. She sent them a letter one month ago, expressing admiration for Lady Selwyn's collection of curiosities from the Orient, including the famous automaton Tipu's Tiger: *If Lady Selwyn should wish to enhance her collection, and the Wealth of England, with these items, I would be happy to visit and make terms.*

Several years ago, Rum accompanied Lady Selwyn to London for the two-year anniversary of the Siege at Seringapatam. Ladies sported little round hats, each with a long Mughal-style plume nodding from the front. Servants wore tunics cinched with tiger-striped sashes. For a shilling, crowds gathered beneath a mural on the ceiling, which slowly cycled through the various stages of the siege. Here were the English forces massing around the ramparts of the fort (no sign of sepoys, Rum noticed); here was Tipu shooting a rifle into the crowds; Wellesley holding a lantern over the dying body of Tipu (confoundingly shirtless, a sword cut in his muscular torso); the palace burning; big-bottomed native women carried off like sacks of grain; the flag of the East India Company flapping from the ramparts.

For two more shillings, the crowds formed a line that snaked around the block for the chance to see, up close, the automaton billed as Tipu's Tiger. Most approached it with reverence and awe, half crouching to get a look at where the tiger's tooth sank into the soldier's neck. Some of the ladies paled, and had to be escorted away. Of course, there was the occasional ape who plunked his hands on the organ keys and sang "God Save the Queen" as if he had invented irony itself.

Throughout the festivities, Rum remained by Lady Selwyn's side. She attained something of a celebrity status as the owner of the automaton, and as such she attracted the Tipu fanatics. One zealot tried to sell her a tiny bundle of hair in a clear case, swearing the hair had been clipped from Tipu's mustache. The gall! Even more galling: Lady Selwyn actually squinted at the hairball and asked Rum to go looking for a magnifying glass.

Lady Selwyn has always been a dreamy type, easily taken in by auras and imaginings. It is, in part, what he admires about her.

Rum wishes only to protect her from those who would take advantage. (Such grifters are everywhere, and take all forms, even quite possibly that of a Frenchwoman with admirable handwriting, laced with persuasive little flourishes.) And even if the Frenchwoman is right, and these are indeed the possessions of Tipu Sultan, what would anyone want with a cushion into which the tyrant had farted away his final days?

Were it up to Rum, the Frenchwoman would be given a quick

tour of the house and sent packing. But Lady Selwyn insists on taking a peek at the fabled objects. "If they're fake, I'll know within minutes," she has said.

At half past ten, Fellowes appears in the doorway and announces the arrival of Miss Jehanne Du Leze. Fellowes does not look at Rum, and knows better than to look twice at Lady Selwyn's cape. Instead he addresses the window and steps aside.

In she comes: a woman with dark hair and streaks of pink in her cheeks, as if she'd run all the way to the house. She wears a yellow dress, open at the neck, and on her head is perched a bizarre little turban of bright yellow.

"My lady," she says with a curtsy. *"Enchantée."*

"Welcome." Lady Selwyn gestures to the open seat. "Please, join me by the fire. I trust the coach was smooth?"

"So smooth I was able to read my newspaper, madame. Your English coach is far superior to ours."

"And what is the news from France?" says Lady Selwyn. "Aside from whatever the Little Corporal is stirring up."

"Indeed these are precarious times, madame." The Frenchwoman gives a little shrug, then offers: "Though you would not know it from the weather."

Suavely played, thinks Rum, waiting by the fireplace to be introduced. The ladies compare last year's summer with this one. Rum notes the satin purse in her lap. Not silk. Not a woman of means. He catches her eye.

"This is Mr. Rum," says Lady Selwyn, "my land agent and advisor."

"Enchantée," says the Frenchwoman, dipping her head so that the tail of her hat flops over her shoulder. Rum finds the hat ridiculous, even repellent.

"I must say, that is a splendid hat," says Lady Selwyn.

"Merci, madame." The Frenchwoman touches the fringe. "I made it myself, in the Mughal fashion."

"Did you?" Lady Selwyn touches the clasp of her cape. "I made this clasp from a tieback on my curtains."

"How very clever, madame!"

"I design many of my clothes and all of my hunting outfits. But I have never endeavored to make a hat." Lady Selwyn's eyes gleam with inspiration.

"Would you like to try mine, madame? Is it wrong to ask?"

Lady Selwyn accepts with delight.

"Does it suit?" she asks, cocking her head at Rum, who cannot even voice a word of tactful disagreement before the Frenchwoman cuts in:

"Madame looks like a world traveler."

"Oh, how I wish to travel. I used to, with Lord Selwyn. But I am getting on in years."

"And the house requires Lady Selwyn's constant attention," says Rum.

"Yes." Lady Selwyn nods at Rum. "That, too."

"But what is there to see when you live in one of the most beautiful country houses in Europe?" Miss Jehanne smooths the risen brown strands of her hair. "French country houses hardly come close. Much to our envy."

She smiles eagerly around the room, until her smile comes to rest on Rum, who is not smiling at all.

"I wonder," says Rum, "if we shouldn't see to the matter in your letter."

"Of course. Monsieur?" she calls to Fellowes, who is standing by the doorway. "Would you be so kind as to call my valet?"

Valet? Rum is astonished. No maid?

Even more astonishing: the valet who enters is a young man with brown skin and black hair and a severe side part. In his arms he carries a leather trunk. Rum stares. He has not seen another Indian in six years. He has seen Africans in London. Even made the mistake of asking a Turkish fellow if he was from India, much to the Turk's offense. But this one is Indian, he is sure of it. And not just Indian. That nose, that fleshy, flaring nose. That nose is Malabar or Madras. That nose is his own.

"Rum," says Lady Selwyn, a bit sharply. "Would you please bring the little table?"

Jerking into action, Rum retrieves a corner table and sets it before the guests. The valet places the trunk on top and unlatches the lid.

Miss Jehanne reaches out her hand. "The cushion, Abbas."

Rum, having resumed his place by the mantel, now freezes. *Abbas.* A Muslim, then. Hyderabadi, perhaps . . .

"*Rum,*" says Lady Selwyn, holding up the cushion. "What do you think?"

"Hmmm," he says neutrally, peering down at the cushion and its tangle of gold embroidery.

"Indeed it is Tipu's emblem," Lady Selwyn says. "The tiger devouring the two-headed bird of the Wodeyar dynasty."

"Which dynasty?" asks Miss Jehanne.

"The *Woe-dee-yars.* Just one of Tipu's many sworn enemies. Well, before he was killed. Now we've installed one of their children in his place."

"A ten-year-old, I believe," says Rum, trying to detect some response from the valet, annoyance or allegiance. The valet maintains the same reserved look, even as he brings forth from the bag a folded garment.

"And this," says Miss Jehanne, unfurling the garment so that it drapes across her own lap, "is called a *jama.* It is Tipu Sultan's robe, which my father saw him wear on occasion."

The fabric is a faded white muslin woven with translucent stripes and patterned with blazes of gold foil.

"I dare say." Lady Selwyn examines the reverse side of the fabric. "This pattern is typical Tipu. No one else would've been allowed to use it."

Finally the valet presents Miss Jehanne with a small velvet box held in both his hands. Just as Rum was taught, when presenting a gift. Give and take with both hands.

"May I?" asks Miss Jehanne, and slips the ring on Lady Selwyn's pointer finger.

Lady Selwyn raises her hand, regarding the ring with a dreamy expression. "This one has an aura, does it not?"

At the mention of auras—a dangerous turn—Rum decides it is time to intervene. "From where did you obtain these things, miss?"

There follows the same old story about her father the clock-maker, Tipu his patron. Rum listens for inconsistencies, of which there are none. "My father was a favorite of Tipu Sultan and received these gifts before returning to France. I have no use for them, but I would prefer to leave them to a patron who would preserve them."

"For a price," Rum adds.

"To be negotiated," says Miss Jehanne.

Lady Selwyn strokes the robe. "Look at the workmanship, Rum."

He pinches the fabric. "Looks a bit worn."

"Perhaps because he wore it," says Miss Jehanne.

The ladies discuss the howdah cushion, Miss Jehanne claiming that it is from Tipu's own battle elephant, perhaps the very elephant, they speculate together, on which he rode into the Battle of Pollilur . . .

Meanwhile Rum is holding the ring up to the window. The agate is thick and smoothly hewn, rippling with hues of caramel and cream. It is not the agate itself that holds his interest so much as the hole that once fitted the tyrant's weakest finger.

"Try it on, monsieur."

Miss Jehanne's voice seems to reach him from far away, and he realizes that the two women are staring at him.

He sets the ring on top of the table. "I doubt it would fit. They say he was very fat." He returns to Lady Selwyn's side and awaits a change of subject.

"Well," says Lady Selwyn, "this is all very interesting. How long will you be staying in the village?"

"A few nights only, madame."

Lady Selwyn says she will have to consult with her advisors (of whom Rum knows himself to be the only one), and possibly bring someone from London to appraise the ring. "As you wish, madame." Miss Jehanne submits a regretful smile as if aware that the answer, eventually, will be no. "I shall not take up more of your time. But I do wish to know . . ." She winces a little. "Is it possible to tour the house? We have come from so far—"

"My dear, it goes without saying. I used to guide the tours myself." Lady Selwyn rises, continuing to speak as she leads the way to the entrance hall. "But then someone broke the bill of my Roman eagle. First century AD, that statue. And to conceal their mischief, they pocketed the piece! That is why I've shut my house to the general public and only receive select guests." Lady Selwyn shakes her head, as if confounded by human nature. "The problem with people is that they look with their hands."

She stops at the foot of the staircase, beneath the gloomy glow of a wrought-iron lantern. "Perhaps you recognize the design of these stairs. I based them on the library staircase at Rouen Cathedral."

"Ah, yes! I did find them familiar. You have been to Rouen, madame?"

"No, but I saw the staircase in a book and liked it very much. I desired a sort of stylish melancholy." She points out the tapered columns, the vaulted and arched windows, drawing their gazes up to the suit of armor, which once belonged to Francis I, and now glows quietly from a niche on the second landing. "Stairs give me trouble so, alas, this is where my part of the tour ends. Rum will see you the rest of the way."

Miss Jehanne thanks her again. "I promise we will see with our eyes only."

"We?" asks Rum.

The Frenchwoman pauses, glancing at the valet, who is standing with his hand on the newel post, as if he were expecting to join the tour. "I, we," she says, and gives a little laugh. "My English is sometimes confused."

She nods at the valet, who shows the slightest hesitation before stepping back into the shadows.

Unlike most visitors, Miss Jehanne asks very few questions while on the tour. She simply nods at everything he says with a sort of perfunctory glance, her enthusiasm dimmed without the presence of Lady Selwyn.

In the library, he points out the pierced Gothic arches of the bookcases. "These were based on a side door of the choir illustrated in Dugdale's *History of Saint Paul's Cathedral.*"

"Mm," she says, her head turned up to the ceiling.

"The ceiling is copied from the Queen's Dressing Room at Windsor Castle."

"And those heads?" She points to the painted profile of a brown face on the ceiling, wearing a pointy red hat. "Who are they?"

"Saracens. Muslims. It is a motif to signify Lady Selwyn's ancestral connections to the Crusades."

"They are everywhere, these heads."

He points out the two knights on horseback—each a Selwyn family forebear—but she turns away, reaching out a hand to steady herself against the mantel.

"Miss?"

With her hand still on the mantel, she presses her other hand to her brow. "Oof, I am a bit dizzy. Too much looking up, I suppose."

He offers her the crook of his arm, which she takes. "Travel can be tiring," he says.

"True. I am not used to it."

"Shall I bring you back down, miss?"

"No, please. Not until I've seen the tiger."

Slowly he leads her down the hall, past several busts and curios, and into the Peacock Room. It happens to be his favorite, with the flocked wallpaper in peacock blue, the circular ceiling and its golden fractals and radials. On the opposite side, the stained-glass window throws a quilt of colored light onto the only object in the room.

"This is Tipu's Tiger," he says.

The automaton rests on a long table, the tail of the tiger extending off the edge. To Rum's eye, it has the air of a neglected old hulk. There is the hole where the crank was broken off by some vandal at the London exhibition. There is the cloak of dust, lit up in patches of red and blue from the painted panes. The soldier's face is turned toward the window, so that the tiger's profile is first to greet them.

Most visitors walk right up, slack-jawed and staring, but Miss Jehanne seems to hang back for a moment, as if held in place. Rum fills the silence with facts. "It was discovered by British troops during the Siege of Seringapatam in 1799. Colonel Selwyn was awarded the piece by the prize committee, for his outstanding service during the wars." He watches her approach the automaton slowly, removing one of her lace gloves. She places a bare hand on its back, then traces the shape of one of the hollowed blazes. Though he cannot see her face, he can read the reverence in her touch. "Tragically, Colonel Selwyn died of dysentery some two weeks after the war's end."

Rum waits as she takes her time, circling the automaton, crouching here and there to examine the soldier's face or to close her hand around the wind stops.

"It is believed that the mechanisms are French," he continues, "but the exterior is so crude it could only be the work of artisans local to Mysore."

"Crude?" she says. "How is it crude?"

"The stripes look nothing like tiger stripes. Neither figure has the appearance of reality—"

"Is that the purpose of art? To copy what is?"

His jaw tightens. What is the Frenchwoman playing at? "Shall we go downstairs, miss?"

"Perhaps that is best. I do feel rather tired."

She takes his arm as they move down the hall. At the top of the stairs, she stops. "Ah, I left my glove in the Peacock Room. Monsieur, would you mind . . ."

He leaves her holding on to the top of the banister and goes to retrieve the glove, which he finds on the floor between the window and the automaton. The lace is delicate, still warm from her touch.

He is on his way out of the room when he hears it—a shocking series of thuds. He bolts down the hall.

Miss Jehanne lies motionless at the foot of the steps, her cheek against the floorboards, her eyes shut. The valet is crouched by her side, pressing her throat for a pulse, his fingers dark against the pale of her skin. He looks up at Rum, alarmed. "She has fainted," the valet says. "Is there a bed where I may place her?"

By this point, Fellowes has come running; it is more running in one day than he has done in a month. "What happened?"

"The lady fainted," says Rum. "Let's get her to the Holbein Room."

Slight though he seems, the valet lifts her without strain and climbs the stairs, every so often adjusting his arm to brace the back of her neck. Fellowes goes to inform Lady Selwyn and bring water at once.

The valet waits until Rum has peeled back the blankets, then eases her beneath the sheets, quickly covering her stockinged calves.

As the valet steps away, Lady Selwyn enters, demanding explanations. "But how did it happen?" she asks Rum. "You were with her, weren't you?"

"I'd left her to retrieve her glove from the Peacock Room," says Rum. "I had no idea she would . . ."

"Look, she's trying to speak," says Lady Selwyn, leaning over the Frenchwoman. "Miss Jehanne?" She takes the hand, pale and limp, in both of her own. "Miss Jehanne, can you hear me?"

Miss Jehanne blinks once, slowly. "Oui."

"Her lips are a bit bluish. Do they seem so to you, Rum?"

He squints, but sees no bluishness.

In comes Fellowes with a jug of water and a glass, which sloshes as Lady Selwyn takes hold of it. "You must drink something, Miss Jehanne. Come, help her sit up, Rum."

Miss Jehanne allows him to prop her against the pillows. The effort seems to revive her a bit. Between small sips, she shakes her head. "I feel so silly, madame. Arriving as your guest and leaving as an invalid."

"Leaving? In this state?"

"I will trouble you no further, madame. In ten minutes, I shall be rested and able to take the coach back to town." Here, Miss Jehanne pauses and places a hand to her breast, concentrating on her breathing for a moment.

"Absolutely not," says Lady Selwyn, watching her. "You are too frail. And the journey would be bumpy."

"She did say the coach rode smoothly," Rum offers, before Lady Selwyn mutes him with a look.

"I insist that you stay," says Lady Selwyn. "Cloverpoint will put you on your feet."

"I have none of my clothes," says Miss Jehanne.

"*I* can supply you with clothes. Or your valet can bring them. We can find him a room down in the Cloisters, with the other servants."

After much couldn't and shouldn't, it is settled. Miss Jehanne and her valet will stay for several days. She will take sweet walks in the gardens and rest as much as possible.

Rum knows better than to question Lady Selwyn's decision in the presence of others. He also knows that she is lonely for the friendship of women sometimes, that he cannot supply her with the feminine whimsy and gossip exclusive to her sex. And yet. There is something about the two of them, their sudden and mutual ease, that unsettles him. This he chalks up to his usual aversion to houseguests.

Long after Mrs. Chapman has left for the evening and Fellowes has gone to bed, Rum retires to his bedchamber. His is the Blackstone Room, with walls of silk damask and matching chairs, as well as a glass cabinet that contains one of her favorite curios: a black stone from which an Elizabethan necromancer used to summon ghosts. ("There's no one I trust more than you to guard it," she said to Rum, who could not imagine the person who would choose to thieve a round slab of rock.) He would have preferred a humbler room, but there are no humble rooms in Cloverpoint, except for the vaulted basement where Fellowes and seven other servants live. Lady Selwyn has dubbed this "the Cloisters."

Traditionally, only the mistress keeps a room upstairs. Yet it is hard to dispute the fact that Rum doesn't exactly belong in the Cloisters, either. He is neither gentry nor servant but something in between, an offensive characteristic to the English, who pride themselves on putting a man in his proper place.

Yet Rum is of the opinion that his place is wherever Lady Selwyn says it is. Which is why, in the middle of the night, he goes to her room.

Their meetings take place on Mondays and Fridays. If Lady Selwyn hasn't slept well, or is feeling otherwise disinclined, she skips dessert. This is a code only Rum can read, meaning *I need my sleep tonight, dear.*

But this happens very rarely, in times of excessive fatigue. For a woman of advanced age, she has appetites.

On the night in question, Rum enters Lady Selwyn's room without knocking. At the far end of the room is a high canopy bed, framed by a pair of ornate screens. The room is dark; a guttering candle by the bed throws an inviting light. With every step, he can make out a bit more: the dark arches of her eyebrows, the silver plait of her hair, falling down her shoulder. She is wearing a cream kaftan with gold stitching, her knees drawn up behind an open book. She is reading; he loves the lost expression on her face when she reads.

A floorboard creaks beneath his foot, prompting her look.

"My dear," she says, closing the book. "What kept you?"

He climbs into his side of the bed, which was at one time Colonel Selwyn's side of the bed. The first time Rum claimed this space for himself, five years ago, he was curious to find that he felt almost no guilt at all.

She blows out the candle on her nightstand.

"But I want to look at you," he says.

"Look with your hands."

The sex is lively, in spite of the dark. He loves the sag and splay of her breasts, the sweat beneath them, her soft belly, her dappled thighs, her throat. He buries his face in her hair. Camphor and lavender and some other aged scent. She has ruined camphor for him; he can't smell it without finding himself aroused. But what is wrong with that? What could be more right and fortunate than two people finding one another in the twilight of their lives, their bodies too old to be anything but honest? A shudder rolls through her and then she melts into laughter.

"Hush," he says, though he is pleased with himself. The pattern on the canopy seems to be writhing with his every breath.

"The servants can't hear us from the Cloisters," she says.

"I've run into Fellowes before, wandering around. Said he heard a noise."

"'Tis a wonder he can hear through all that ear shrubbery."

He chuckles. Her fingers idle in the field of his chest hair.

Eventually she rolls away and opens the drawer by her bed. "Deary, have you seen my meerschaum? Oh, there it is."

The meerschaum was her father's pipe, a long and rustic-looking thing with the profile of a scowling bearded man on the front. It is the one thing Rum dislikes about Lady Selwyn—this nasty, mannish habit of puffing after sex.

She exhales into the dark. "I know what you are thinking."

"What am I thinking?"

"That snuff would be more ladylike, but snuff—"

"—makes you sneeze."

"And the meerschaum brings me close to my father." She puffs contemplatively. "I can almost feel his presence in the room."

"Likewise," Rum says dryly.

A sweetish smoke fills the air. He grows drowsy with it, nearly dozing off until she taps the bowl empty into an ashtray.

"Tell me something," she says, shifting her weight in the bed. "Are you certain the cushions aren't genuine?"

"It's the lady I find ingenuine. And the Musulman."

"Who? Oh, the valet—how do you know he's a Muslim?"

"It's their names, always sounding like an elephant stomping on something. Mah-*fuz*. Mu-*stafa*."

"His name is Mahfuz Mustafa?"

"No, I am simply making a point. And what kind of woman travels with a manservant? A lady should travel with a maid."

"A bad lady." Her hand moves downward, taking hold of him. "Very bad."

But it is too soon for Rum to resurrect himself. He shivers and pulls her hand to his chest. Eventually she drifts off; he can tell by the gentle hiss of her snore. He eases out of bed, and, as noiselessly as possible, ties his robe and leaves before he can be discovered by one of the morning maids.

II

Rum is up early the next morning, long before breakfast. He stands at a window in the Long Gallery, gazing out over the meadow, his hand pressed against his neck. Must have strained a muscle sometime last night. (Is it possible he can no longer make love without sustaining an injury? Humiliating thought.) The morning chill gives no comfort, nor does the general gray gloom.

It is September already. The summer was too short, albeit warmer than the year before, when the snows of February turned into summer storms, one frigid wet month passing into the next and the next, all runny noses and drafty rooms, the sun concealed behind a wall of cloud.

But what was a sodden hem compared to the sufferings of Lady Selwyn's tenant farmers, their crops washed away by floods? Such was the case all across the country, so that for the first time in memory, grain had to be imported into Liverpool. Imported! The price of bread shot up. One of Lady Selwyn's tenant farmers committed suicide, hanging himself in the barn where once he'd hung wheat to dry. Terrible years. On one of their trips into town, Rum and Lady Selwyn had been astonished and horrified by the number of beggars along the road, like some army of the damned. Reaching through her window, Lady Selwyn dropped as many coins into palms as she could, as did Rum. Afterwards, they refrained from these monthly trips, preferring to send for their supplies.

Perhaps it was this period of isolation that piqued the villagers.

The weather had been cold and rainy, so that was the main reason. Another reason, shared only between Rum and Lady Selwyn, was the sense of some brewing ill will among the villagers. Rumors of reform and agitation. Oh, but that was Scotland's problem, Lady Selwyn had said, Scotland and maybe Northumbria. Such unrest would never touch their lives.

And yet there has come a change in the air, as hard to identify as it is to deny.

Hopefully the sun will break through the clouds by late morning, when he and Lady Selwyn leave for town. They have revived the twice-monthly tradition, for it is crucial that Lady Selwyn see and be seen. He sighs, not thrilled about himself being seen. But he feels dutybound to accompany her.

His breath has marked the glass. He wipes the window with his kerchief, leaving a smudge.

Below the smudge, he catches sight of two figures making their way across the lawn: Miss Jehanne and her valet. Miss Jehanne limps along, as to be expected after yesterday's fall. A green shawl covers her shoulders, a wide-brimmed bonnet surrounds her face.

They pause beneath an old pin oak. She places her hand on the trunk and looks up into the branches. She is speaking, presumably to the valet, who stands some paces behind her, though Rum cannot make out the shape of her words.

Then she turns to face the valet, allowing Rum a good look at her. Straight back, sober face, quite different from the chirpy version on offer the day before. He cannot blame the Frenchwoman for posturing. Lady Selwyn has that effect on people. One badly wants her approval and never goes to bed with the feeling of having fully obtained it. There is always the sense that she is looking past one, out yonder, to the possibility of something more exciting on the horizon.

Rum wonders if the valet is a little bit in love with the French-woman. He doesn't seem so. In fact, he seems only vaguely engaged by whatever she is saying and even—to Rum's utter shock—turns away from her to face the river!

When Rum first joined the Selwyn household, he read twelve times cover to cover *The Gentlemen's Book of Etiquette and Manual of Politeness; Being a Complete Guide for a Gentleman's Conduct in All His Relations Towards Society.* He read it so many times that the spine broke, loosening the pages like old leaves. Now Rum can summon up the authoritative voice of Cecil B. Hartley at will. *Remember, however, "once a gentleman, always a gentleman."* Nowhere in the book did Cecil B. Hartley permit the valet to turn away from his master in the midst of the master's speech. A valet is meant to wait on his master—or, in this bizarre case, his mistress—and to present the master with his undivided attention.

Rum is still stewing over this breach of etiquette when Miss Jehanne glances back toward the house. He retreats behind the curtain, nearly certain he hasn't been seen. He takes another peek to find her looking in the same direction as her valet—toward the river, framed by trees—as if keeping the company of an equal.

"He is watching us," says Jehanne, turning to face the river.

"Who?"

"Don't look. The Indian fellow."

"Why?" Abbas asks. "Did I do something wrong?"

"I don't know, I never had a valet. That was your idea."

They look rigidly at the river.

She would have thought a fellow Indian would make her feel at home in this place, having spent most of her life searching for the faces she'd known in her youth. Not this Indian. His courtesy is superficial, his scrutiny runs deep. Though she is equally curious. At their first meeting, she'd glanced at him whenever possible, wondering *Are you . . . ?* while he was glancing at Abbas, clearly wondering *Are you . . . ?* Abbas kept his face cool and incurious.

"Nicely done," says Abbas. "With the falling and everything."

"Thank you. Again, your idea."

"I wasn't certain you would go through with it."

"Neither was I . . ." She recalls the automaton, the faded gold of the blazes, the musty smell that hinted at—or maybe this was simply a trick of the mind—Lucien's favorite tobacco. As she'd walked slowly around the automaton, she'd kept inhaling, trying to hold the fragrance in her chest. She'd released her breath as they left the automaton, but something else had seeped into her, a need. The automaton was within reach, and so was the revival of the shop and a version of life she could live with.

"Now what?" she says.

"Now you charm your way into her favor. Win her trust."

"You make it sound as simple as winding a toy."

"She is alone, growing old. You are beautiful and charming. How complicated can it be?"

A strong blush rises up her throat. She feels him staring.

"Are you all right?" he says.

"Why?"

"You have a rash on your neck."

She places a palm at the side of her throat. "It's not a rash."

Abbas narrows his eyes. "It appears to be spreading to your face."

"Shall we go inside?"

He turns to go.

"Abbas."

"What?"

"Your arm. Offer me your arm."

Awkwardly he angles his elbow, stiff as a coat hanger. She takes it. Like so they walk toward the house, their shoes lightly squelching in the grass.

Halfway to the house, Abbas slows, forcing her to take note of what has drawn his attention: a young man of less than twenty, whetting a scythe with a smaller knife. The man has pockmarked cheeks and light blue eyes, his brows so golden they seem almost nonexistent. Between passes, he nods a greeting, each *zzzing* grating her nerves.

"I do miss that sound," Abbas says quietly.

Jehanne says nothing, only looks back over her shoulder at the man, who is still watching them.

Rum greets the guests with a nod that sharpens the pain in his neck. The Frenchwoman asks him if he is quite all right, her face suddenly alight with enthusiasm and innocence. Yes, thank you, he says, giving no explanation, and says that Lady Selwyn is waiting to take breakfast with Miss Jehanne in the Yellow Parlor.

"Then I shall not keep her waiting," says Miss Jehanne with a superfluous curtsy. She moves past him, followed by her valet.

"I thought your man and I might have breakfast together," says Rum. "Down here. In the Servants Hall."

The Frenchwoman looks back at the valet, determined to conceal her unease as best she can, which, in the presence of Rum, is not quite enough.

After delivering Jehanne to Lady Selwyn, Rum returns to the portico, struck by the way Abbas is standing, looking dreamily ahead, his arms clasped behind him, one hand gripping the other elbow. He turns his head. "Mr. Rum."

"Yes, shall we? Do you speak English?"

"Well enough."

As they pass through the French doors into the Cloisters, Rum informs Abbas that the floors are made of expensive Baltic pine. Abbas looks down. Rum points out the long vaulted ceilings, modeled on the ceilings of the side aisle in Westminster Abbey. Abbas looks up. "When Lady Selwyn throws parties," Rum goes on, eager to evoke some sort of reaction from the young man, "which we call *festivos,* we bring musicians into the Cloisters so that their song can flow up through the ceiling and into the Long Gallery, where there is much dancing and revelry."

"We?" says a voice. It is the surliest of footmen, Mr. Flood, eating toast at one of the tables. Rum makes a terse introduction. He and Flood have been on unfriendly terms ever since a bottle of wine was discovered in the footman's empty boot. At least this was the rumor. By the time Rum confronted both the footman and the butler, the two had formed a sort of partnership, and the firm of Flood & Fellowes denied any knowledge of the theft.

Flood wipes his hands on a napkin. "You and Lady Selwyn throwing parties together now, Mr. Rum?"

"No, but if we do, Mr. Flood, perhaps you can provide the wine."

Rum goes to the kitchen to retrieve a tray of tea and biscuits. When he returns, he finds to his relief that Flood is gone.

"His bell was ringing," says Abbas.

"What a shame," Rum says, pouring the tea with a conspiratorial smile. He means to make the boy feel at ease in his presence. Two chums taking tea. "Would you like milk and sugar?"

"Neither, sir." Abbas places a hand over the mouth of his cup. "I dislike tea."

"Coffee, then?"

Abbas consents to black coffee.

Beverages arranged, Rum settles onto the bench. "I learned to appreciate tea while in the army, even without milk and sugar."

"Which army, may I ask?"

"The Honourable East India Company. Madras Native Infantry. I was aide-de-camp to Colonel Selwyn during the Mysorean Wars, which ended, as you know, in Seringapatam."

"Srirangapatna," Abbas says softly. "That was my home."

They blink at one another, mutually disarmed.

Abbas breaks the silence with a loud slurp of coffee. Rum wonders whether he shouldn't take the boy aside and give him some tips for future success as a valet: no slurping, no turning your back on a superior, *et cetera*. "And you, Mr. Rum? Where are you from?"

"Hindustan."

"Yes, but where in Hindustan?"

Rum takes a moment to answer. "Bednur."

"Bednur?" Abbas raises his eyebrows. "Is that Haidarnagar?"

"According to Haidar it was." Rum takes a quiet sip of tea. "But who can keep track. These days an Indian city changes names as frequently as a lady changes dress."

"At least the lady has a choice of dress."

Rum shrugs, takes a bite of biscuit. "I left at age twelve. Hardly remember it. Did several different things, wound up in the army. You were not at the siege, I presume?"

Abbas shakes his head.

"Well, victory was swift," says Rum. "Necessary for deposing a tyrant of such inhumane proportions."

"By tyrant you mean Tipu Sultan."

"That is indeed who I mean. I know your people used to call him all sorts of grandiose things—God-Given Overseer of the Heavens and the Earth and Everything in Between—"

"I have no people, Mr. Rum."

Rum stares, strangely irked by this declaration. "That cannot be true. Every man belongs to a people, even if it's the people he serves."

Abbas tilts his head. "You consider yourself an Englishman, then?"

"In a way, yes, having left home at so young an age."

"Why did you leave?"

The question, so bluntly uttered, startles Rum, such that he finds himself telling the truth: "Because there was no home for me to go back to."

"After the annexation, you mean?"

At first Rum thinks Abbas must be joking. *After the annexation:* how architectural the term, how bloodless! But Abbas, perfectly serious, is waiting for an answer.

"Before Haidar Ali *annexed* us," Rum says, "my father was chief minister to the queen. She was prepared to fight for us, but the situation turned hopeless and so she went into hiding. At that point, Haidar believed he had everything under control. He even thought he would move the capital to Bednur, so fair was our city, our climate." Rum's voice grows distant with the telling. "One night my father took me deep into the forest. He told me if he was not back by morning, I should walk to the next village. That was the last time I saw him."

A sound rises from the forests of his mind—the sizzling hiss of crickets, sawing at the air as he listened for his father's footfalls, listened and listened.

Abbas is listening, too, with the eager attentiveness of a child wishing for a just ending to the tale. "Later," Rum says, "I learned my father and mother were executed for plotting to poison Haidar Ali. Hanged along with hundreds of others."

Abbas drops his gaze. Rum says nothing more. He has already said too much, has exposed the festering wound of himself.

"I should not have asked," Abbas says quietly. "Forgive me."

Rum rises and clears the table, departing before the sweat that beads his brow becomes noticeable.

After summoning the coach, Rum goes to collect Lady Selwyn from the Yellow Parlor. He halts in the threshold. The two women are seated by the window in the Bergère chairs, where she and Rum were sitting the day before. The chairs have been pulled closer today, within arm's length, a little claw-foot table chaperoning the space between.

At first the women take no notice of his presence. Lady Selwyn is shuffling cards on the table, the Frenchwoman making a noise of appreciation as the cards flutter in a little arch. "My father taught me that one," Lady Selwyn is saying. "Horace never approved—he said card tricks were for taverns."

"Mmm," says Miss Jehanne, clever girl, careful not to disagree with the dead husband. "Is it the thumbs you are using?"

"Yes, it's all in the thumbs."

As they chatter on, Rum remains still, frozen as a figure in a portrait, like those that fill the gilded frames on these walls, each man striking a pose of casual authority. One has his arm on a writing table, a quill in his meaty hand. Another carries a rifle. Yet another carries a paunch. All are the sort of men who would not hesitate before entering a room.

"Oh, Rum! Good morning."

He bows. "My lady. Miss Du Leze."

"We are playing cards," Lady Selwyn declares, beaming at his approach. "I'm going to teach Miss Jehanne how to shuffle, and she's going to teach me a French dance—what is it called, my dear?"

"La gavotte."

Rum turns toward the Frenchwoman. "I am surprised you are capable of dancing, miss, what with your recent injury."

"I am feeling better with every hour of madame's presence," says Miss Jehanne.

"How miraculous," says Rum. "Unfortunately, Lady Selwyn has made plans to go into town today."

"Have I?" says Lady Selwyn.

Rum nods. "The coach is ready."

Lady Selwyn taps a card against the tabletop. "Well, why don't you go without me, Rum?"

"But tomorrow is the fox hunt, and my lady requires a new hat." Rum adds, "So you said yourself."

"Oh, the hunt!" Lady Selwyn gazes up at Rum, her lips parted in a way that makes her look senile. "I completely forgot."

Rum refrains from asking how she could've forgotten; one glance at the Frenchwoman and he has an idea. To her credit, Miss Jehanne is looking lovely this morning, the green in her shawl complimenting the gray of her eyes.

"Maybe," says Lady Selwyn, "I shall wear one of my usual hats. Or Miss Jehanne can help me make a new one."

"I can already imagine the possibilities," says Miss Jehanne.

"As can I," says Rum.

"Good." Lady Selwyn gives a decisive nod. "Rum, you shall go into town and get what we need."

"If that is your wish, my lady."

Rum looks expressively at Lady Selwyn, waiting for her to revise her wish.

While the ladies play cards, Abbas wanders the grounds, looking for a fallen piece of wood to whittle. An unsettled feeling clouds his mind. He should not have asked after Mr. Rum's past, should not have broken his own cardinal rule: Do not look back. Forward, ever forward.

He places his hand on a thick old trunk and looks up into the whispering leaves. He remembers Du Leze, reaching out and fondly running his fingers through a cluster of downy catkins. Abbas had found the gesture endearing, had thought maybe one day he, too, would move through the world with a natural ease. Only now does he know how much harder it is to cultivate ease in a world that is wary of you.

His thoughts are interrupted by a *snip-snip* sound on the other side of the tree. There he finds a young man on a ladder trimming dead branches with a pair of pruning shears. Abbas recognizes him: the man who was whetting the scythe earlier in the day. They wish each other a curt good morning. Abbas asks him what the tree is called.

"Chestnut," says the man, reaching up to yank a tangled branch. "Are there no chestnut trees where you come from?"

"No."

"What kind, then?"

Abbas pauses, searching his mind for the English words for palm or banyan or fig. "I cannot say."

The man is hardly listening, his attention taken up by the stubborn branch. "Oh, to hell with it," he says, releasing the tree. "Not about to break my neck for her."

Abbas helps him gather the fallen branches. For a time they work in silence, depositing the cuttings into a sack, until the man asks: "What brings you to Cloverpoint?"

"My lady wishes to sell some items of interest to Lady Selwyn."

The man looks up sharply. "What sort of things?"

"Several objects that were once in the possession of Tipu Sultan, ruler of Mysore."

"More gewgaws for her collection? She already has that tiger toy, what more does she need?"

"It is not my place to say."

Nor yours, is what Abbas means, which the man seems to absorb with a snort. He withdraws a flat bottle from inside his trouser pocket and takes a wincing sip, then exhales at the wilderness, becalmed for a spell. "Do you think she will buy any of it?" the man asks.

"She has expressed interest."

"She should be taking an interest in her farmers. She has a duty toward us."

"I thought you were a gardener."

"My father's farm is a quarter of an hour from here—my farm now, since he died. I only do these odd jobs in a pinch." The man pockets the bottle and wipes his brow with a familiar air of resignation.

Do not look back. Forward, ever forward. And yet Abbas finds himself saying: "You remind me of someone I once sailed with."

"You were a sailor?"

"I have been a number of things."

"By God, I wish I could say the same," the man says. He shifts the ladder to another side of the tree. Abbas bids him good luck with his work.

"Do me one favor," the man calls to his back. "If you see Mr. Rum, tell him Middle John would like a word." He pats his pocket. "But don't mention this."

The man—Middle John—nods before getting an answer, as if they are already compatriots of a kind, the very assumption Abbas made about Thomas Beddicker, and which he will not make again.

For a change in ambience, Lady Selwyn moves the card game to the Red Salon, her favorite room in Cloverpoint Castle. The walls, paneled in red watered silk, give the sense of being seated inside a great pulsing heart.

But Miss Jehanne knows none of the games that Lady Selwyn plays, not Whist or Bridge or Gin. The only game they know in common—and which Lady Selwyn recalls from her life long ago—is Strip Jack Naked, or, as Lady Selwyn used to call it in her youth, Loot.

The rules are these: Both players begin with no cards, the stack sitting between them. Then each player takes a turn flipping the top card on the stack. If two successive cards are a match, whoever is first to slap the stack claims the pile of cards beneath. The one with all the cards—or loot—wins.

They play in pleasant silence. Lady Selwyn's gaze wanders to the painting of Horace and herself, hanging on the wall behind Miss Jehanne. In the room he had so hated. "Who wants to sit inside a heart?" he said. Well, Horace had no eye for art. No Lord Byron, he. Practically born with his father's jowls. The jowls she grew to accept, but his tragic lack of romance, his disinterest in nature, his intense phobia of bees: these were harder to digest. Not to mention the fact that their carnal relations were as silent as the grave . . .

Lady Selwyn exhales through her nose, dismissing the memory.

"Madame?" says Miss Jehanne.

"What? Oh, nothing, I was simply . . . I was thinking about your cushion. I consulted my books last night and found the exact same insignia."

"So your instincts were correct, madame."

"Indeed they were. Have you put a price on each of these items?"

"Ah, no," says Miss Jehanne. "Madame would know best. *Mon dieu,* how this pile is growing!"

They continue laying card after card until Lady Selwyn pulls the queen of hearts, which matches the queen of spades beneath. At that point, Miss Jehanne does an extraordinary thing: instead of slapping the stack, she reaches across and slaps the back of Lady Selwyn's hand.

Lady Selwyn is shocked. She cannot remember the last time she was slapped so boldly. Maybe as a schoolgirl, rapped across the knuckles. Miss Jehanne seems to have shocked herself, her hand over her mouth.

"*Vraiment désolée,* madame. It was an accident. I was taught to slap hands, you see."

"That hard? Even the ladies?"

"Yes, madame, in the convent school."

"What little barbarians," Lady Selwyn teases.

"But we can do your way."

Lady Selwyn rubs her hand, her skin all abuzz. "I think I like your way. It's much more . . . invigorating."

And so they stack and slap and laugh, their mirthful sounds carrying down the hall. By the end of the game, at Lady Selwyn's insistence, they have come to call each other by their Christian names—Agnes and Jehanne.

After lunch, they move to the Peacock Room, where Lady Selwyn reads aloud from Byron's *Poetics*. She sits in one of her specially designed chairs, with the quatrefoil carved into its rigid back. Jehanne has received permission to recline in the window seat, her legs raised. She tilts her head against the glass, using the light to her advantage.

Lady Selwyn reads from a book as big as a Roman missal, drawing her finger across the page. Jehanne wears a dreamy squint, as if lost in the contours of the tiger, when in fact she is looking beyond the automaton, to the top of the stained-glass window. A hook hangs down from the shutter. She wonders whether the shutters are closed and locked at night. If not, one might be able to steal the automaton, piece by piece, lowering each by rope and pulley through the window, carrying them to a boat hidden among the reeds, on the banks of the Thames.

"You are distracted, my dear. You don't like Byron?"

Jehanne turns her head. "No, I was quite transported."

Lady Selwyn gives her skeptical look.

"You see through me, madame." Sheepish, Jehanne plucks at her skirt. "I have no head for poetry. To be honest, I prefer stories."

"By whom? I may have someone you like."

"Crebillon, Laclos . . ."

"Laclos." Lady Selwyn raises her eyebrows. "I hear he is quite racy, even for the French."

"At the convent, we had one copy of *Liaisons* among seven girls."

"Were you discovered?"

"No, but the book disappeared. Even nuns need entertainment, yes?"

Lady Selwyn laughs with a snort, in spite of herself. Snortling, she called it as a little girl, doubled over and wheezing with her brothers. Long before she entered the world of elegant curtsies and gloved insults. And yet it seems fine, even comfortable, snortling before Jehanne.

"You know," says Lady Selwyn, sitting up. "I don't have Laclos, but I have something else you might like."

Lady Selwyn refuses to explain, only offers Jehanne her arm and leads the way down the hall.

They come to a plain narrow door, which Lady Selwyn unlocks with a key from her skirt pocket. "Only I have the key to this room," says Lady Selwyn, stepping aside to let Jehanne pass first. "You'll know why in a moment."

Jehanne wonders if the maids should be granted access, for the air is musty and close, almost suffocating. She moves toward the single object that occupies the space: a pedestal holding up a large hardcover book. The cover is the brown-red of drying rose petals. The spine is loose, barely holding the pages together.

"I have a secret, Jehanne." Lady Selwyn rests her hand on top of the book, her voice but a murmur. "I am a novelist."

Jehanne raises her eyebrows, awaiting the juicy part of the secret.

"And this is my novel. Would you like to read it?"

"I . . ." Jehanne looks down at the novel, which has the thickness of two stacked Bibles. "I can think of no greater honor."

"Are you trying to fluff me up, Jehanne?"

"No, madame—"

"Because I want your honest opinion."

"Which you shall have." In a year, Jehanne thinks, or however long it will take to read the behemoth.

"I call it *The Saracen's Lamp.* One day I hope to publish it under a pen name. If the contents were associated with myself, all would come to ruin."

"*Pardon,* what would come to ruin?"

"Why, my name, Jehanne! One's name is all one has."

It seems to Jehanne that Lady Selwyn has a few more things besides, but she murmurs her agreement.

"And yet I feel that you are someone I can entrust with this." Lady Selwyn pauses. "Can I?"

Lady Selwyn's face is so clear with yearning, so simple with hope, Jehanne can only say yes and receive the book into her arms, promising to return it directly to Lady Selwyn—Agnes—upon reading the final page.

The wheel goes over a rut, causing the coach to jump. Rum clutches the bag of sundries in his lap. The apothecary shop had everything Lady Selwyn needed—French rouge, almond oil, powder bags, and masks—but no more of Rum's eau de cologne. After double-checking the shelves, the druggist came back with a homemade concoction in a little vial; it fairly reeked of Catholic priest. Rum bought it anyway, charging the total to Lady Selwyn's account.

Rum is attentive to smell. He can suss out what cook is serving for dinner simply by raising his nose. Which is why it pains him, even now, to remember the time outside Porto Novo when Colonel Selwyn grimaced, sniffed the air, and said, "What *is* that odor?" only to look to his left, where Rum was standing, and utter sheepishly: "Oh." All the same, Rum was grateful to be informed of his odor at a time when he could still do something about it, which was more than could have been said for Colonel Selwyn, whose morning breath could have dropped a horse.

The apothecary shop was only the beginning of an unpleasant afternoon in the village. He'd stopped for lunch at the Bell, only to feel himself probed by every eye as he made his way to the corner booth. The barmaid brought him roast instead of chicken pie, an honest mistake, though she seemed only vaguely apologetic. Fine, he said, he would eat the roast. And though he'd eaten roast before, this time, as he tugged his knife across the beef, he was reminded of the first time he watched a piece of meat being cooked, how it turned from pink to brown. Having been raised a Brahmin, he'd never known that flesh changed color in the fire.

Rum has never been one to dwell on the past. How to account, then, for all these regurgitated memories?

The countryside idles by. He opens a newspaper and gets through half an article about some Tory politician before feeling motion-sick. Something is agitating him, some pinballing feeling in the pit of his stomach, preventing him from sitting still.

That damned valet. Where did he get off, asking where Rum is from? A personal question such as that. They are not intimates. They are not in Hindustan. Rum's father used to ask the same of every passing traveler—*Where is your home?*—drawing the person into a dialogue about this or that village which was near this or that town on the bank of this or that river. Why did his father need to know? How did it help him to make these mental maps? Rum stares out the window, wondering about a man whose face he has nearly forgotten, though he can still feel the brush of that beard against his forehead, deep in the forest, when Rum was still his son.

To relax himself, Rum tries a breathing technique he learned from a Madrasi clerk long ago. (Press the right nostril with thumb and inhale; then press the left nostril with pinky and exhale.) What was his name—Chandran? Balan? Odd fellow. Although everyone had seemed odd during his first few weeks in the Seat Customs Department. And yet how proud Rum had been to copy important documents for the British East India Company, how excited to collect his monthly six-rupee salary at only fourteen years old, how certain he would someday rise to the rank of dubash.

But over the years, he watched others rise all around him, from writer to dubash to chief dubash, men who lined their pockets with the difference between a low-priced buy and a high-priced sale. The Holland brothers were then in charge, corruption their signature style. With no promotion in sight, Rum leapt at the chance to join the military. Enough hunching over desks. He would be a cavalryman; he would learn to ride a horse!

So he learned to ride, so he rose in rank. Sometimes he feels a touch of pride for the life he has crafted, with Lady Selwyn's help. She may have abandoned him today, but he has much else to be grateful for. She gave him a home.

His nerves have eased a bit by the time they turn onto Clover Lane, lined with yews. And there is beloved Cloverpoint. He opens the curtain and peers out. He never misses a glimpse when they go riding back, becalmed by the sight of the house growing in the distance, its uneven shape giving it the appearance of something alive yet asleep.

He is almost himself again as he steps out of the coach—that is, until he hears someone barking his name.

It is Middle John, ambling over with his hands in his vest pockets, his head tipped back as if to look down his nose at Rum, who is taller. "Mr. Rum, a word if you please."

Rum experiences a guilty pang, and braces himself.

A week ago, Middle John came to Rum, claiming his seed drill had been smashed by a fallen elm and needed replacement before the next planting season. Rum agreed to visit the farm and assess the damage himself, and then promptly forgot. He so rarely forgets, yet with all his other responsibilities, it has been known to happen.

"John," Rum says, greeting him with a nod.

"Mr. Rum—"

"I know, John. The seed drill."

"You told us you'd come this week."

"It is on my agenda, I promise you that."

"Promises don't plant clover, Mr. Rum. I need a new seed drill to arrive *before* planting season."

Rum studies the young man's reddish squint, the telltale scent of gin hovering around him. "As I said, you shall have one if the old one cannot be repaired."

"I think I'd know better than you the answer to that question! It's the same damned drill my father used his entire life. There's new ones on the market now with all manner of improvements."

"I said I will come next week, Mr. Townshend. Today I am needed here at the house."

Middle John sways slightly. "Because of the French guest?"

Rum does not reply.

"I hear she's selling a whole new round of gewgaws for Lady Selwyn's collection. Does you think that's right, Mr. Rum, at a time like this? Farmers barely on their feet after these last two seasons?"

Rum can feel it bubbling within him, the old and incomprehensible wrath, suppressed on most days. This is not most days.

"John Townshend." He takes a step forward, drops his voice low. "Lady Selwyn has no use for your advice or for you. As such, you are dismissed from service."

"Because I dared to ask a simple question?"

"No, because you are a drunk."

Rum regrets the indefinite article—*a drunk* having a vastly different effect than *drunk*—the latter a fact, the former a slap.

And yet, surprisingly, Middle John wears a bored expression, as if the accusation is meaningless to him.

"Well, at least I have some integrity," he says, then tilts his head to one side. "At least I'm not a schemer with two fingers in Lady Selwyn's coin purse."

Middle John takes a step forward and waits, both of them knowing there can only be one kind of reply.

For a period of time unknown to him—eleven minutes, to be precise—Abbas has been standing in the entryway, staring at the mounted display of the wooden cravat. The very same one whose purchase Lord Selwyn had bemoaned, asking what anyone would want with a wooden cravat. Want, to Abbas, is beside the point. He has never seen anything like it, aside from an actual cravat, so thin is the pleated lace, so delicate the perforations, so airy and starched the bow that holds it up—all of wood. Wood! He dares to graze a fingertip around the knot—the thrill shoots straight to his marrow.

Enraptured, he fails to hear the front door open.

"Oh," says Rum. Abbas retracts his hand. "Hello."

Abbas waits to be scolded for touching the art. Tensed, he realizes Rum is tense, too, his one hand tightly holding the other.

"I see you've met our wooden cravat," says Rum.

"It is incredible."

"Lady Selwyn wore it once, as a jape." Rum nods, makes to leave. "Well, enjoy—"

"Mr. Rum, do you know what tool the carver used?"

"Tool?"

"He cannot have used a mallet. Maybe a chisel? Or a gouge?"

"The man who might tell us has been dead some centuries. Grinling Gibbons. Born 1648, died 1721."

"I wonder what kind of wood is so soft and pale as this . . ."

"I don't recall," says Rum.

Abbas notes the strange way Rum is holding his own hand, bracing it against himself. Abruptly Rum clasps both hands behind his back.

"Limewood," Rum says. "I just remembered the cravat is made of limewood. So light, it trembles whenever someone goes up the stairs. Let me show you."

Rum hurries up the stairs, and, true enough, the cravat trembles gently. Delighted, Abbas nearly calls to Rum—*As light as lace itself!*—before realizing that he is gone.

III

Rum sits up—chilled and sweaty—surprised to find that night has fallen, and outside his window the sky is dark, but not nearly as dark as the night he'd been dreaming of, when his father made him swear never to go home . . .

He has slept through dinner, something he has not done in all his six years of service.

He winces at the pain in his hand, the knuckles tender to touch. What came over him? Countless times he has been called this or that, and simply smiled and bobbled his head at the abuse. What was it about this time that made him curl his fist and send Middle John clutching his bloodied nose? Rum held out a hand to help him up, but Middle John only spat into the gravel and staggered off on his own, muttering of consequences.

Which is now what worries Rum.

Middle John is of a lower class, but race is the final ranking. Here in this land, a brown man is a nobody, even if he is a son of Bednur, that jewel of a city nestled so deep in the forest it managed to escape the eye of conquerors for years, a kingdom of elegant houses and paved walkways, of foundries that forged swords of the lightest, strongest steel, a city enriched by sandal and spices and guarded by the fort of Shivappa Nayaka, fronted by so many stairs that climbing them was akin to ascending into sky.

A city he can no longer see in his mind's eye, not exactly. Even his house is a pinkish blur.

He puts his head in his hands. His stomach grumbles, but he does not need food. He needs her.

Grazing a palm against the wall, he blindly makes his way to her door, listening before nudging it open. She is asleep. He crawls into bed beside her. The mattress has a loamy softness that makes him feel held.

She stirs, turning to him. "Rum?"

"Yes. It's me."

Her voice is slurry with sleep. "Where were you at dinner?"

"Forgive me, I . . . I was occupied with some property matters."

"Not to worry. Jehanne kept me company."

Rum is silent. Jehanne? When did she become *Jehanne*?

"I'm a bit tired for an escapade, Rum."

"Of course." He is embarrassed. "I simply thought I might check in on you."

"At midnight? Really, you are too transparent." Her teasing tone annoys him, so much so that he blurts the truth:

"I punched someone today."

She rises up on one elbow. "You? Punched someone?"

His eyes are closed when he nods.

He hears her fearful question: "Who?"

"Mr. Townshend."

"No! Townshend? But he's so old, Rum, and so gentle. A true salt-of-the-earth sort of fellow."

"Not that Townshend. That one is dead."

"He died?"

"Yes."

Her face goes foggy for a moment. "Oh, yes. He did die, you are right. Who is the Townshend you punched?"

"His son. Middle John."

"Middle John, of course. Well, that makes sense. He seems the sort of person who gets punched on a weekly basis. Why did you, though?"

"He insulted me. He used a vulgarity."

"Because you are an Oriental," she concludes, shaking her head. "The small-minded fool. Not that I am surprised. There are so few people of vision in the world."

He is about to explain the seed drill situation when Lady Selwyn adds lightly: "Jehanne has vision."

A silence goes by before he asks what Jehanne has to do with his punching Middle John.

"Nothing," she says, addressing the canopy. "But I suppose I have a confession to make as well—I asked Jehanne to read my novel."

"*The Genie of Al Sha'am?*"

"That's not the title anymore, and you know that."

He sits up to look her fully in the face. For a moment, he glimpses in her expression a rare flash of guilt. "How could you, Aggie?"

"I feel I can trust her. And I want someone to read it, to give me an opinion."

"*I* read it. Some of it."

Rum hesitates; this is a sore spot between them. For it is true, he has been unable to bring himself to read the chapters that clearly feature himself, or his avatar, an aging genie of "immense sexual appetites." In the novel, the genie is called forth from an antique lamp in the possession of one Lady Alexandria Van Den Bosch, mistress of Slyborn Keep. A romance ensues. Of the novel's forty chapters, thirty-one feature the genie.

"This is dangerous, Aggie. She will read it and make assumptions."

"As I've told you many times, the genie is not you."

"His name is Rajma Allabad—"

"I told you I was open to suggestions."

"—and you describe his nose as being *beakish*." Rum points to his own somewhat beakish nose.

"Rum, darling, listen to me . . ."

She lays a hand on his arm, but he is already clambering out of bed.

"No. You must get it back. In whatever way. If she were to tell someone about it, we—you—" He stops short, met with her pinched expression.

"You punch a man, and I give you my support. I confide in a friend, and you scold me as if you were my own husband."

Rum does not reply.

She takes a dignifying breath. "I think we have said enough. The hunt is tomorrow. We should get our rest while we can, so good night."

She scoots under the covers and turns away from him.

On his way down the hall, Rum conducts an internal monologue with no one to serve as his audience aside from the sculpted busts and statues along the walls. *You see how agitated you make me!* he says to the bust of Molière. *I am leaving, I have had enough,* he announces to the statue of Mrs. Richard West, and pauses, feeling sorry for lashing out at Mrs. Richard West. Hers is one of the finest statues in the house, a beautiful young woman, draped in Grecian robes, stepping forward as if to stride off her plinth. The actual Mrs. West died in childbirth, leading the grief-stricken Mr. West to commission numerous statues in her image, her face smoothed of pain. The longer Rum studies the face of the wife, the more it seems to him that there is a small sneer in the corner of her mouth, a coldness to her blank brow.

From somewhere behind him, a creaking pierces the silence.

Rum freezes, pressing himself against the pedestal. Is it Fellowes? What the devil is he doing, doddering around at this hour?

Holding his breath, Rum waits until he hears an unmistakable *clunk,* heavier than a footstep. A thief, perhaps. They've never had a thief before, aside from Flood and his boot. Rum feels roiling within him all the fury of one whose own estate is being pillaged. He steps down the hall toward the muffled noises, which seem to be coming from the Peacock Room. The double doors are ajar. He peers through the gap, his attention drawn to the flickering light of a candle on the far windowsill.

In the darkness, the automaton looks strange in shape. It takes a moment for Rum to make out that the top half has been removed. His heart quickens. He searches the room for the culprit.

A shadowy figure rises from behind the halved automaton. It is the Frenchwoman's valet! Rum watches as the valet places his hands on the edge of the hull, looking the insides up and down. He touches a finger to one of the battered brass pipes, a lost expression on his face.

Abbas reaches into the head cavity with both hands and dislodges . . .

What was it called?

Yes: the grunt pipe.

"Mashallah," he says under his breath.

Gently he handles the grunt pipe, tipping it over to examine the bottom, bracing it against his chest so he can run a finger down the accordion-folded hide. And while he knows he shouldn't, he presses the bellows. But oh what a rumble, and there is Lucien Sahab shouting in French, blood freckling the floor and him saying *I shall have to sew you.* The needle going in and out of his own skin with frightening ease.

There is the tiniest rut, where his chisel went skidding. And there are the blazes behind the ears, painted too close together. Behind each imperfection is a story only he would know, a story interwoven with his own. He has made other things, admired his own creations, but nothing has so altered him, nothing has led him to the thought that dawns on him now: *This is all that I am. This is all I have to give.*

And if he should go back to Godin empty-handed? Then he will be nothing. The past nine years will have been a waste.

A rustling from the doorway. Abbas drops into a crouch.

He waits a full minute before replacing the grunt pipe and the lid of the automaton. He slips out of the Peacock Room and pauses in the hallway, so that the spy whose slipper is poking out from behind a pedestal will see that Abbas is empty-handed. To prove it, Abbas runs his hands through his hair and smooths down his jacket. And yet he knows, as he retreats down the stairs, the damage has been done, and tomorrow he will have to contend with it.

IV

At dawn, a group of servants comb the grounds for foxholes. These they stopper with rocks, so that when the hounds give chase later that day, the foxes will have no way of going home.

While the foxes wander unawares, Rum is pacing the perimeter of his room, trying to figure out what to do about Abbas. He cannot stop thinking of the valet's face, the reverence with which he touched the insides of the automaton. (And was he wiping away tears, at one point?) Maybe the valet had trespassed out of curiosity, eager to see the thing for himself, having been denied the opportunity upon arrival. Why bother Lady Selwyn about this minor transgression? She might jump to conclusions, might even have him arrested. Is curiosity reason enough to ruin a young man's life—a young man so far from home?

By the time Rum has donned his riding clothes, he has taken a decision. He will bring the matter to Miss Jehanne. He is to accompany her that day, during the hunt, which will give him ample opportunity to question her. Perhaps she will betray some ulterior motive, if one is lurking behind that sweetly simple facade.

Feeling confident about his course of action, he descends the grand staircase. Halfway down, he halts.

There is Middle John, holding his cap in both hands, being escorted by Fellowes through the vestibule. His nose is well bandaged, his brow knitted as if parsing some confusion in his mind. In passing, he spots Rum on the stairs.

Middle John lingers a moment, still looking confused, as if he expects Rum to provide him with a solution.

Fellowes opens the door, prompting Middle John to fix his cap on his head before hurrying out.

Upon closing the door, Fellowes gives Rum a withering look. "Lady Selwyn is in the Yellow Room," he says, striding away before Rum can pose a question.

Strange to find her standing in the middle of the room, wearing such a cold look. "You didn't say anything about a broken seed drill," she says.

He is taken aback by her tone. "I was going to, but you wanted to talk about Miss Jehanne and your—" He glances back at the doorway. "Story."

"My novel, Rum."

"He should not have come to you with his grievances. I told him I would see to it."

"Now you don't have to."

He asks for an explanation, but Lady Selwyn refuses to say more on the subject. She has a very elaborate outfit to wear and Jehanne is waiting to help her put it on.

Meanwhile Middle John is standing outside the house, uncertain, his nose tolling with pain. He had come here not only to report on Mr. Rum and the seed drill, but to impress on Lady Selwyn that her farmers need subsidies of a kind, to bring them back from the brink where the last three harvests have left them. But she only let him get as far as the seed drill before palavering on about the dignity of the farmer, surely the most perfect of human beings, and then eulogizing his own father as "the gentlest and kindest of all creatures," and finally summoning her butler to press a few notes into Middle

John's hand, urging him to follow in his father's dignified footsteps. "You wouldn't want to go to your grave having done so little that dying is your greatest achievement, would you?" (To which, most infuriatingly, he had mumbled, "No, Mum.") "Good. I take it this matter is finished. Do send my regards to your mother." Cowed and confused, off he went.

Oh, how she roped him in words, such that he only remembered what he'd wanted to say once those great doors had closed behind him.

Now he looks back up at the tower, where, he has been told, the largest of Lady Selwyn's gewgaws is kept. The Musical Tiger. A thing he will never be invited to see.

And why not? he thinks, staring up at the clover-shaped window, genuinely bewildered. Why shouldn't he see? Why do some people get invitations and other people get so much less?

Either it should be shown to all or shown to none. His belief gains solidity with every throb of his nose. All or none.

Later in the day, the drive is aswirl with harriers and terriers and horses, along with a flotilla of young men in red coats. Among them is Lady Selwyn's only son, Richard.

How to describe Richard Selwyn? Rum would call him an amateur archaeologist and expert irritant, always criticizing one thing or another about Cloverpoint, from the fox droppings in the yard to the existence of the pin oak that blocks the view from his bedroom window. Legally speaking, the house and land belong to Richard, but he disdains the idea of living in the country, even if it is only two hours' drive from London. Instead he lives in his own London apartment, when he isn't panning for bones along the banks of the Euphrates.

Rum dreads the day when Richard will retire to the country and claim Cloverpoint as his final home. All Rum can do in the meantime is rely on Lady Selwyn's protection and Richard's commitment to bachelordom.

As they wait for Lady Selwyn to arrive, Richard and his London friends sit easily on their all-white horses, white being the fashion for their status. Their red jackets glow in the early-morning sun. A few of them shoot curious looks at Rum but none approach, and no introductions are made.

Rum stands beside his own roan-colored horse, holding the reins of the piebald pony that Miss Jehanne will be riding. He rubs at his temple. The squire's hat he wears is too small for his head. Already he can feel a brewing headache.

A great peal of laughter comes from the men, in response to something Richard has said. He has gained a bit of weight in the face. It is an improvement, Rum thinks, one that draws a likeness to his father. How affectionately Lord Selwyn used to speak of young Richard, predicting for him a life in politics, a prime ministership, even. "You should see how he argues," Colonel Selwyn said. "A little lawyer in the making."

Richard sighs at the house, and looks over to Rum. "What's keeping her?" he demands.

How Rum would know her arrival time is beside the point; he reassures Richard that Lady Selwyn will be arriving in ten minutes.

One minute later, Lady Selwyn descends the steps in full fig, wearing a massive galleon of a hat, a dark blue jacket, a flouncy bustle, trousers, and riding boots.

"What a hat," says Richard, dismounting. He approaches to deliver a kiss on her cheek, stalled as she fights her way through the veil. "Is it a hat? Never mind. Mother, you look radiant."

Nearly everyone agrees that Lady Selwyn looks radiant; those that don't keep their mouths shut. In Rum's opinion, the outfit radiates eccentricity, but the last time a guest used that word to describe her style, the guest was not invited back to Cloverpoint.

Rum hangs back, watching the young men massing around Lady Selwyn, their flattery so thick they fail to notice Miss Jehanne until she has come down the steps.

"And this," says Lady Selwyn, gesturing behind her, "is my guest from France, Miss Jehanne Du Leze."

The men bow their heads and utter greetings. The Frenchwoman curtsies. The outfit that looks so eccentric on Lady Selwyn looks bold and artful on Miss Jehanne. It is not her youth so much as the natural confidence with which she carries the garments, in contrast to Lady Selwyn, who keeps touching her headdress as if to reassure herself that it hasn't floated away.

"We designed the hats this morning," says Lady Selwyn. "Miss Jehanne and I."

"Quite a collaboration," says Richard.

"It has a French feel, don't you think?"

Richard squints through his smile. "How did you meet, again?"

"Details later, Richard dear." Lady Selwyn summons Rum with a wave. He walks the piebald pony to the group of three.

Lady Selwyn scans the pony with a disappointed look, as Rum knew she would. "It's a colored, Rum."

"Yes, my lady."

"Miss Jehanne isn't pulling an onion cart, is she?"

"No, my lady."

"Then?"

"Mother, don't blame Rum," says Richard. "He can't be expected to remember all our customs."

Rum ignores the swipe. "Mr. Dickens was unable to locate a white pony on short notice."

"Is that true, Mr. Dickens?"

Lady Selwyn's words fall on Mr. Dickens's deaf left ear. Eighty-five years old, he is hunched in his saddle as if taxidermied in place. Before Lady Selwyn can appeal to his hearing ear, Miss Jehanne speaks up. "Any horse belonging to Lady Selwyn is one I would be pleased to ride. May I, madame?"

"Yes, I suppose we shouldn't waste any more time." Lady Selwyn manages a final frown at the offensive pony before going off with Richard to mount her horse.

"It's been some time since I've been hunting," says Miss Jehanne, once Rum has fixed her in the side saddle. "Thank you," she adds, as he hands her the thong and lash.

"Thong end up," Rum says.

"Hm?"

"You are holding it upside down."

As she hastily rights the thong and lash, he mounts his horse.

"Will you be taking the jumps, miss?"

"Must I?" Jehanne looks stricken.

"Usually the ladies do not. Sidesaddles lack a leaping horn."

"Ah." She glances at his saddle, trying to identify the leaping horn. "It has been a while since I rode. It must be like swimming, no?—one never forgets."

"That we shall find out."

The horn sounds. Master Dickens sets off down the road, trailing the dogs, their little tails bobbing skyward, followed by the huntsman and hunting party. Rum and Jehanne bring up the rear, riding slowly, side by side.

"I hear Lady Selwyn is an excellent horsewoman," says Miss Jehanne.

"Indeed she is."

"She wishes me to see her jump, but at her speed, I am not sure if—"

"She told you that?" Rum says sharply. "That she will be taking the jumps?"

"Why, is there something wrong?"

"What exactly did she say?"

"That she could pilot her horse over fence and fen as smoothly as the gentlemen. I remember that part because it rhymed."

"Oh no." Indeed, this is one of Lady Selwyn's favorite self-descriptions.

"And she said she wanted very badly that I should see her riding in like Artemis at the death of the fox."

Rum cranes his neck but can see no sign of Lady Selwyn among the stragglers in the hunting party. He wishes to ride ahead to wherever she is and ask for—nay, demand—well, probably not demand but certainly *insist* upon a word in private. Or perhaps make some sideways reference to Richard about her myopia. No doubt she will hate him for it, but at least Richard will demand that she refrain from jumping. Unfortunately, none of these options are available to Rum, for he is tethered to a Frenchwoman with all the equestrian skills of a coatrack.

Then Rum has an idea. He reaches over to grab her reins, halting both their horses.

"Monsieur . . . ?"

"You should go home," he says. "I will tell Lady Selwyn you are unwell and unable to continue."

A daft smile hangs on her face. "But Lady Selwyn wishes me to see her jump."

"She is not fit to take any jumps. She simply wishes to impress you." He pauses, wondering if he has said too much. "If you go home, she will not be inclined to take such a risk."

"Is it not her decision which risks to take?" says Jehanne, with a quizzical tilt of her head.

Rum looks desperately to the last of the hunting party, now far away, white horse tails swishing back and forth.

"Shall we?" says Miss Jehanne.

"No."

"No?"

"I would prefer to have a word with you. About your valet."

"I realize it is strange," she says, "a lady with a valet. But you see, in the colonies . . ."

"Last night I saw him snooping in the Peacock Room. The room next to yours."

She blinks several times. "When?"

"In the middle of the night."

"Do you always take midnight walks, monsieur?"

"That is not your concern. Your valet was taking apart the automaton, piece by piece."

"Perhaps he was simply interested in its workings."

"I am interested in the Crown Jewels, but there would be consequences for my pawing at them in the middle of the night."

"Well, he didn't take anything, did he?" Miss Jehanne says hotly. "It's just as it was. Isn't it?"

"You are angry," says Rum.

"But of course I am angry, you are accusing my valet of stealing, which he would never—"

"No, you are angry with him for getting caught. What have you put him up to?"

"Me? How ridiculous."

"I insist that you tell me now, Jehanne Du Leze, if that is even your name."

Her lips thin with contempt. "You are threatening me?"

"Tell me what you are plotting, or I shall go to Lady Selwyn."

To his amazement, she widens her eyes and says: *"Ooo-OOO-ooo."*

"What do you mean *Ooo-OOO-ooo*?"

"It means that I find the threat minimal. In fact, I think Agnes will be alarmed at the way you are addressing me now." Jehanne sits up straighter in her saddle. "I demand that you take me to her." She makes a clicking sound with the side of her tongue, as if to prompt him or the pony, perhaps both.

The distant baying of dogs splits the air. The hounds have flushed a fox from its hole.

"Best find your way back," Rum says to Miss Jehanne.

"Wait—how?"

"You know how, don't you? One never forgets."

And off he rides without her.

Rum gallops tall and able on his colored horse, the wind rushing in his ears. Normally he loves riding. He revels in the sense of abandon, the danger, the release, the freedom, the feeling that he is just another man among the scarlet coats, all of them moving too fast over hill and dale to distinguish his face.

Yet these are not normal circumstances. Behind him is a sneaky young woman, plotting God knows what. Ahead of him is his beloved, half blind to the young woman's machinations and whatever jumps lie ahead. Maybe it was wrong to leave Jehanne stranded. He makes a plan: a quick word with Lady Selwyn (or two emphatic words: *No jumps*), then ride back to Jehanne and lead her home. He is almost positive that the pony will still be munching on the same patch of grass by the time he returns.

Catching up to the party, he is overcome with terror.

There is Lady Selwyn, galloping toward a fence, hat flapping like a pennant against the back of her head, and she is not slowing her horse as she should, she is going full throttle, as if the fence were imaginary, and before he can think better of it, he bellows: "Damn you, Aggie, *jump!*"

At the final moment, she pulls the reins and then flies—gliding over and landing lightly on the other side of the fence.

In the seconds after her landing, his first feeling is relief: she is safe.

His second thought: he is not.

Did he actually yell *Damn you, Aggie, jump*? He did. Whether the rest of the party heard him remains to be seen.

Rum joins the rear of the party, hanging slightly back, careful not to draw attention to his presence. For the time being, everyone is fixated on a fox. Chased by the harriers, it managed to scramble inside its hole, though not very far, for its tunnel is blocked by a stone.

A terrier goes to ground and drags the fox out by the leg. The fox is panting and mangy, scrabbling at the dirt with its front paws. The dog releases its leg; they snap at one another, equally matched in size. Then the dog is joined by dozens of others, crowding round the fox, which shrinks yet holds its ground, growling until the first pounce.

From inside the mob comes the final sounds of the fox: a series of ragged squeals. The dogs are crowded like suckling pups, gnawing leg and tail, the back of neck, bits of gristle and teeth and orange fur. Eventually the huntsman waves off the dogs and cuts the fox tail with his knife. This he hands over to Lady Selwyn.

Her adrenaline glow subsides to a grimace. The tail is skinny and unremarkable without the fox attached. The horses shift, some bending to partake of the grass.

Lady Selwyn brightens suddenly, looking around, holding the tail slightly away from her body. "Rum? Where is Miss Jehanne? She might like to see this."

Rum trots forward. "Miss Jehanne returned to the house, my lady. She was feeling unwell."

"Oh, so now my mother is *my lady*?" Richard's voice is cutting. "A few minutes ago, she was Damn-You-Aggie."

"Richard!" cries Lady Selwyn.

"Did you not hear him, Mother?"

"I . . . I may have heard something along those lines."

"*Damn you, Aggie, jump.* Those were his very words."

Lady Selwyn turns to Rum. For once, she looks flustered, and this frightens him. "Did you, Rum?" she says, trying to marshal her authority, even with her hat hanging off the back of her head, a raggedy fox tail in her hand. "Did you use my Christian name?"

The dogs are panting. Rum can hear his own heart. It is as though he and she are enacting a play for the benefit of the men, their hard looks pressing in from all sides, meaning to eat him alive.

He thinks to give a reason or explanation but stops himself, knowing this will not quell their appetites.

"I did, my lady."

"And?"

"And," he says, "I apologize."

"You don't sound apologetic," says Richard.

Rum holds her gaze. He knows exactly what the rest of them want, for him to dismount and drop to his knees and simper behind his folded hands. All he cares to know is what she wants.

Lady Selwyn addresses him in a firm tone, though her eyes never rise any higher than his collar.

"You shall return to the house, Rum. See to Miss Jehanne."

"Yes, mum."

He catches her flinch; if there is one word she hates being called, it is *mum*.

"And take this with you," she says, handing him the fox tail, still warm.

. . .

At first Jehanne panicked, watching Mr. Rum gallop away from her. Now she is bored. It has become clear that the pony has no interest in moving away from its grassy buffet, no matter how many times Jehanne tugs at the reins.

"This must be the caviar of country grass," she says.

The horse continues to nibble.

A mistake to click her tongue at Mr. Rum; she could see he was offended. Yet he had caught her off guard. She had no idea Abbas would go sneaking into the Peacock Room at night and sabotage the whole plan. And now what? Now they must revise their strategy or abandon it altogether and go home.

She presses her heels into the pony's sides, to no avail. She shifts her hips and looks down at the hard earth. Why does this mission require her to keep falling from various heights?

"Wait," someone calls from a distance.

She looks around until she spots Abbas, jogging across the grass. She should be angry with him, and yet the sight of him lightens her somehow.

"Let me help you," he says, stepping forward. He raises his arms. She reaches down to put her hands on his shoulders, nervous, though not about the horse. His hands are firm on her waist. She catches a whiff of his scalp.

He steps back, looking surprised for some reason. "There."

"Thank you," she says.

He puts a hand on the pony's side; its tail twitches in reply. "You didn't get very far."

"Mr. Rum and I had a spat. He abandoned me."

"Yes, I noticed. What did he say?"

"He saw you with the automaton last night. He thinks I put you up to it. He says if I don't confess all, he will report back to her." She watches Abbas stroke the pony's side. "What were you doing?"

He opens his mouth, hesitates. "I was simply making sure it was all there."

"You may have ruined our chances."

"Not all of them." He turns to her. "Why don't you ask her directly?"

"What—for the tiger?"

"Say it's your only connection to your dead father. Say you would trade the robe, the cushions, the ring—all three things in exchange for what is merely a big broken toy. But make sure you say it when Mr. Rum is not present."

"That mongoose is always present."

"You shouldn't call him a mongoose."

"He called me a liar!" She pauses, thoughtful. "I am not a liar. I simply find the truth to be negotiable sometimes."

(Her face reminds him, suddenly, of the time she said to him, with that same exact angle of the head, the same pensive frown: *Papa says only a fool would be a toymaker.*)

"What?" says Jehanne.

"What?" says Abbas.

"You were smiling a little."

He shakes his head. "Listen, you must appeal to her on an emotional level. Women succumb easily to sentiment."

"Has that been your experience with all the women you've known?"

"Be serious, Jehanne. Clearly she favors you."

"That is true," Jehanne admits. "We have grown rather . . . intimate."

Abbas raises his eyebrows. "*Intimate* intimate?"

"Close."

"You do not find her repulsive?"

"I find her very handsome. And charming, at times."

"But she is a woman."

"You are a nuisance and still I love you."

The sentiment trots out of her mouth before she can grab it by the tail. She stares at the ground, hoping desperately that he did not hear, though the silence—lengthening, excruciating—says otherwise.

"This must be the caviar of country grass," she says finally, putting a hand to her throat. Quietly she adds: "It's not a rash."

"I know," says Abbas, also fixated on the grass. "Shall we turn back?"

"What about the pony? Oh."

The pony is simultaneously eating his lunch and voiding his bowels. They decide to leave him in this carefree state.

Across the meadow they walk, an awkward distance between them. Jehanne steadies the sides of her hat with her hands, but soon gives up and takes the whole thing off.

"Do I look ridiculous?" she asks him, trying to smooth the risen strands.

"You could never." Abbas pauses. "Well, you could. But it would take effort."

V

There is a lull in the day, between the hunt and the festivo, where the guests take their naps and the servants make preparations. Abbas flees the house before Fellowes can draft him into polishing the silver. He needs to walk, to clear the forest of his thoughts.

Beneath a silver birch, he finds a feather, foot-long and glossy, gray flecked with white. The kind of feather Jehanne might like to use in one of her hats. She excels at making hats. He secretly enjoyed watching her in her father's shop, turning a creation in her hands, lips pursed in concentration. "Peacock or pheasant?" she asked him once, testing one feather, then the other. "Pheasant," he said. She nodded, tucking the feather behind grosgrain, then stood back and cocked her head in dissatisfaction. And she kept working, kept trying in a way that felt familiar.

Jehanne Du Leze, Jehan of the frizzy hair and ferocious honesty, the blush that always betrays her. She has loosened something in him. Some trace of his boy self.

He taps the feather against his palm. A thought comes to him, unbidden, of a little boy picking his front teeth with the shaft of a feather, the mother saying *Chee! Leave it.* That was weeks before the siege. He has not thought of that mother and child in years, cannot even summon their faces, but her gentle hand cupping the back of the boy's head—that gesture he remembers acutely.

A breeze picks up, flustering the boughs. He recites a soft surah to rest their souls.

His mother was right: he has not a sliver of Junaid's piety. He has shirked his prayers, he has stepped on faces, he has neglected to pilgrimage, he has drunk to excess, and yet the worst offense he can think of would be to waste his God-given gift. The burning thing within him. The burning that brought him this far and that he must go to any length to make visible—not only to himself but to the unkind world, a world that is no place for the forming of attachments, not for one such as him.

His scars tingle. He rubs his back against a craggy trunk.

You are a nuisance and still I love you.

His heart skips mutinously.

Upon returning to Cloverpoint, Jehanne leaves a message with the butler, that she is regretfully too exhausted to attend the *festivo*. Fellowes repeats her message in a tone of disbelief, leading her to wonder if she is making a mistake.

No mistake, she decides later that evening, as she eases into a tub of warm bathwater. Rear-sore and relieved, she exhales, gripping the sides of the ceramic tub.

She can still feel the clasp of Abbas's hands on her waist.

You are a nuisance—

She shudders, though a part of her wishes she'd insisted on a response to her declaration. What would be on the other side of his reticence?

She slides under the surface of the water to stop herself from thinking.

Later, she finds it impossible to sleep through the opulence of flute music and the clopping of feet. She pulls Lady Selwyn's novel from its hiding place inside her valise. In bed with the book, she expects to fall asleep within the first ten pages.

Before she knows it, the party sounds have dimmed. By the end of chapter two, she learns that the heroine, Lady Alexandria, has spurned the suitor introduced by her mother. The final lines of the chapter draw her into the next: . . . *and in the dead of night, she shouldered her bow and went off into the forest, too furious to realize what dangers lay ahead.* Dangers? Jehanne must know about the dangers. So she gallops on, and like that, chapter two becomes three, four, and six, with Lady Alexandria having acquired a magical lamp from a passing peddler, who claims the lamp to be a relic from the Outremer, dating back to the First Crusade. *Guinevere wiped the side of the lamp with her kerchief, and thought she saw glimmering in its surface not her own reflection but the dusky features of a Saracen! Another wipe of her cloth, and he was gone, yet a haunted feeling had taken up permanent residence in every corner of her being—*

A knock at the door. Jehanne startles, wrenched from her waking dream. Another knock. "Yes, one moment!" She sets the novel aside and ties her robe before opening the door.

It is the young maid, giving a little curtsy. "Miss, Lady Selwyn wishes to know if you will be attending the duck race."

"Duck race? What is a duck race?"

"A race with ducks, ma'am."

Jehanne waits for the maid to explain why ducks, of all creatures. The maid, it seems, is simply waiting for an answer.

"No," says Jehanne, "I am feeling a bit tired from the hunt."

"Yes, my lady." The maid curtsies, turning away, when Jehanne stops her. "One moment. I should like to put my regrets in writing."

Jehanne retrieves the robe from her trunk, folding it so that the arms cross over the chest. The maid returns with paper and a fountain pen.

"No inkpot?" Jehanne says, studying the nib.

"It's all inside, miss."

"How sneaky." Jehanne writes a quick note and blows it dry.

She slides the envelope between the crossed sleeves, along with the little velvet box containing Tipu's ring. "Would you leave this on Lady Selwyn's bed?" she asks the maid, who whisks the bundle away. Watching her go, Jehanne lingers by the door, brushing off the thought that Lady Selwyn could be capable of stealing.

VI

Although she remembers little from the night before, Lady Selwyn wakes up with the distinct sensation that she made an utter fool of herself.

She should not have had so much to drink, but the unhappy business with Rum had ruined the hunt, and then there was the absence of Jehanne. All this had put Lady Selwyn in a mighty sulk, liquor the quickest cure.

She recalls smoking her meerschaum and drinking hot whiskeys and eating excessive amounts of oysters. She may have pontificated on their aphrodisiacal qualities. She may even have danced excessively with one of Richard's friends, the one with swirls of copper in his wavy hair—yes, *he* was the one to whom she'd held forth on oysters, a lecture that ended with her coyly saying she liked to shuck them herself.

The thought makes her writhe in her bed.

In the afternoon she takes black coffee and rye bread in her room. Via the maid she sends a message to her guests: She is resting and regrets that she cannot bid them goodbye in person. Peering from behind her drapes, she watches them ride away. Now, at last, she can sleep.

She rises in the late afternoon, feeling slightly repaired. In fact, she is looking forward to dinner with Jehanne. Unless Jehanne disliked *The Saracen's Lamp*. The note suggests otherwise. It sits tucked within the arms of Tipu's robe, which is folded on her writing desk.

I thought you might like to spend a night with Tipu's robe and ring. It is the least I can offer you for allowing me to spend the night with your novel, which I am so greatly enjoying.
   J.

Lady Selwyn has read the note twenty-seven times and still doesn't know how to interpret the phrase *so greatly enjoying*. False flattery? Hyperbole? Honesty? And what if the end disappoints? People are so opinionated about endings.

Fed up with her own musings, Lady Selwyn turns to the business of selecting a dress for dinner. She wants to look a certain way: confident, above criticism. None of her dresses seem to impart the right feeling. One by one she slides them along the rack. Silks and taffetas. No and more no until she comes to the final dress on the rack: the Spitalfields silk, painted florals on a field of canary yellow. Lord Selwyn danced her around the Bellavia ballroom in that dress. She'd felt like an affirmation in yellow. She draws it from the shadows just as he drew her away from the wallflowers, snobbish London types, dripping in pedigree. They looked down their noses at her, for she was not of their kind. Glanced at her hands as if she might have soot beneath her nails. She had twice their money, but without a title it would never be enough. Lord Selwyn asked her to dance. Asked her to marry him. Did *not* ask when, on their wedding night, he turned her over and took her like a farm animal. Terrible! She wept. He was sorry, yet made her to feel as though she were the one woman on earth who did not like being taken like a farm animal. Well, they had been young, and unused to one another. They found their ease, eventually, though it was never quite right, never more, for her, than a chore.

So passed the lonely years: so went Lord Selwyn to India, to fight in one uprising after another. (He promised not to fall in love with one of the leathery bags that passed for English ladies in that land.) Distance allowed her to see his flaws with crystal clarity, and sometimes, when she was feeling particularly abandoned and annoyed, she kept a running list of his deficiencies. Remote, unfeeling, uninspiring, hard of hearing, and then suddenly: dead. Dead! It took years, many days and nights and days made nights by doses of laudanum, to comprehend the loss.

But there was Rum to make sure she did not take too much, did not stray too far. He was patient. He was firm with visitors. He waited for her to see how vivid and green was the world after a terrible rain. It was difficult to remember how exactly they happened upon their romance of, what, five years at least. There was that one night, where they talked until dawn. She did more of the talking, of her childhood, of things she'd never told anyone, not even Lord Selwyn. Such as the time at age five when the staymaker came to bind her waist. How she stood on the window seat with arms outstretched like a bird, bound for flight, for travel, for sights unseen. How the first day in the stays was hell itself, ambitions grounded, wings clipped. "Be still," her mother had counseled, "breathe and be still."

Though Rum did not like speaking about himself, he was a very good listener. In bed, he took command, and perhaps it was his military training, but he was good at giving orders, and what was more surprising: she liked taking them! Even liked being taken like a farm animal, under the right circumstances.

It was all so gloriously confusing, love in the twilight of life.

But now, what would she call her feeling for Rum? Affection, surely. Love, of a kind. But does she well up with excitement at the sound of him coming down the hall, as she used to? No, they have grown too familiar, too rote in their routines, marching toward the unspoken arrangement of man and wife and all its proprietary notions.

She returns the Spitalfields silk to the wardrobe—it is too old-fashioned after all, with its panniers and hoops, not to mention too small. An idea occurs to her.

Ever so gently, she unfolds the sleeves of Tipu's robe. It feels as though she is welcoming a ghost, inviting it to dance. After removing her own robe, she draws her arms into the bell-like sleeves, fastens each silver hook and eye down the front, then cinches the tasseled robe at her waist. Lastly, she slides the agate ring onto her pointer finger, where it fits best. Her entire body tingles at the audacity of it all—she, a coal baron's daughter, wearing the robe and ring of Tipu Sultan! That is, if Jehanne is to be believed . . .

Before the mirror, Lady Selwyn catches her breath.

Forget the Spitalfields silk. Forget bindings and earrings. Here is the person she always wanted, as a girl, to be. Unbound and destined for elsewhere. Feet set apart, fist propped on her hip. Lady Magellan. Flat-chested adventuress. One who could move sylphlike from one foreign land to the next, shifting shape and tongue and custom as it suited her, a citizen of the world.

On a whim, she closes her eyes and kisses the ring, cool and smooth against her lips.

She gestures with the hand wearing the agate ring, pretending to be Tipu himself, making pronouncements. *Bring me my slippers. Bring me his head.* She has a vision of throwing a lavish ball, like the one at the Bellavia ballroom. (Orientalia!) Hers would be a masquerade, and the dress code would demand fashions inspired by the Orient, though none would rival the authenticity of what she wears now. A gut feeling tells her these objects are as true as any in her collection, including the automaton.

She cannot wait to discuss Orientalia with Jehanne. But it is only four o'clock, too early. A stroll through the Pleasure Garden, then. She goes to the window, hoping the head gardener is gone for the day, as she should not like to suffer small talk from old Hill.

And there is Jehanne in the Flower Garden, as if the sheer thought of her had brought her into being! Oh, but the valet is with her, standing a respectful distance apart. An odd bird, that one. Not very well trained, judging by the way his hands are wedged in his pockets. Lady Selwyn thinks to ring for Sally; her hair needs tending. Yet something about the sight of these two through the window makes Lady Selwyn linger.

VII

In the Flower Garden, Abbas reviews the original plan. At dinner this evening, Jehanne will try to persuade Lady Selwyn to trade the automaton for the robe, the ring, and the howdah cushions.

In case Lady Selwyn should reject the offer, Abbas introduces a backup plan. At an hour past midnight, he and Jehanne will sneak into the Peacock Room and remove from the automaton both the organ and the grunt pipe. These can be detached and carried back to Rouen, where Abbas will carve the automaton anew, fitting the grunt pipe and organ inside, and none but the two of them will know the difference.

"Luckily your room is next to the Peacock Room, which will make it easy to transfer—" Abbas stops. "Are you yawning?"

"Sorry." Jehanne shakes off her fatigue. "I was up all night."

"Doing what?"

"Reading *The Saracen's Lamp*. It was wonderful."

"You do not have to rehearse your flatteries on me."

"I am not! It was transporting and tragic, and the end . . ." She meets his skeptical eye. "What? Only you can recognize a work of art?"

"I wish to know what you think of my plans."

"I agree to the first plan and reject the second. Why thieve anything at all? Why not build the whole thing over again?"

"Because I've never built an organ or a grunt pipe. I would have learned those skills if I'd completed my education . . . had I the chance to."

Jehanne studies him. He seems agitated, tense. "Abbas, we agreed that if Lady Selwyn rejected our offer, we would give up and go home."

"That is no longer an option for me."

"Come now, there is always another option."

"You do not understand."

"Hear me out," she says. "You and I could go home. We could go back to the old way."

"And live off what?"

"We will figure something out. You know I am very resourceful, even when the resources are thin."

And to her own surprise, she steps closer to him, searching his face, which looks down at her with either concern or fear. "We are both alone, aren't we?" she says. "We may as well be alone together."

Before she knows it, she has placed a hand on his cheek. His skin is surprisingly soft, as if made of a clay that could be smoothed over, unstrained, if he would allow it.

"What are you doing?" he says and removes her hand.

"Thinking aloud," she says, attempting lightness. His face is tight with anger.

"I gave up everything—my home, my life. My family. And for what, to spend the rest of my days on a cot in the back of your shop, living on stale bread and *love*? Is that your idea?"

He looks away from her, exasperated, his tongue probing the inside of his cheek. She stares at a bed of snowdrops, and only at the snowdrops, as he tells her he cannot return her feelings. The little white blooms nod in the breeze.

Quietly she says, "All right, then."

"All right what?"

"All right to the original plan, what we agreed on. Not the thieving."

She waits for him to wring his hands, to turn furious or soothing or beseeching.

"This is not a negotiation," he says. "You need my protection for the way home."

"I do not. I could go myself."

"But you won't."

To the ends of her nerves, she tingles with rage.

"Fine," she says. He begins to speak, but she interrupts him. "Once I am home, you will leave me alone. Find some other place to house your ambitions."

"Jehanne, you are upset, I understand. But when I rebuild the automaton, you will change your mind."

"I would sooner hack it to pieces."

She turns and walks alone to the house.

VIII

To dinner Lady Selwyn wears her favorite set: a pair of earrings and necklace of tigereye, the gemstones winking in the
candlelight.

She has requested a three-course meal of cucumber soup, pork
loins, and potatoes, and a pudding heavy with suet for dessert.
Earthy foods, that one must eat slowly. She wants ample time with
her guest.

Yet Jehanne looks altered this evening, less vivid, a bit sad. Lady
Selwyn wonders if it's something to do with what she witnessed
through her window hours ago. Jehanne and her valet had been
quarreling, or so it seemed. Jehanne cupped the valet's cheek; he
removed her hand. Words were exchanged that caused Jehanne to
stride away.

A lovers' quarrel, or the start of one, Lady Selwyn assumed. The
sight of them together made her own blood quicken.

Jehanne's mood seems to lift when she speaks of *The Saracen's
Lamp*. "I noticed that the initials of the title are the inversion of
Lady Selwyn," she says. "L.S. and S.L. Was it intentional?"

Lady Selwyn pauses, initially confused, then: "Oh, yes, entirely."

Jehanne nods, satisfied to hear her theory borne out. "A secret
for yourself. Since you cannot publish under your own name."

"Now it is our secret."

Jehanne goes on to detail her experience of reading the book throughout the night, how finishing it was like waking from a spell, one from which she hadn't yet awoken entirely. She places a hand on the table and meets Lady Selwyn's eye. "I have restored the book to its room, but truly it deserves a place beside all the other books on your shelves. Whatever name it wears."

Lady Selwyn nods, unable to speak, knowing it can never be so.

"Thank you, my dear." She places her hand over Jehanne's. "Now tell me, what else did you think?"

As much as Jehanne enjoyed *The Saracen's Lamp,* she would like to silence the author, who keeps wanting to know the effect of this or that word, and this or that twist, leaving little room for discussion of anything else.

After dinner they move upstairs to the Peacock Room, for madeira and port. And privacy, Lady Selwyn says, taking the seat closest to the fire.

The ruby spirits glow within beautiful wineglasses, the stem so thin Jehanne could snap it between her fingers. She takes a desperate gulp, as if her nerve might be found in the bottom of the glass. She glances beyond Lady Selwyn's shoulder, at the tiger's head, its wide and focused eye.

Lady Selwyn has just said something about the novel's previous title, how it used be *The Genie of Al Sha'am* when Jehanne says, "Madame—Agnes—I must confess something."

Jehanne sets down the glass with a *thunk* so startling she forgets what she was just about to say . . .

"About Cloverpoint!" Small throat clearing, deep breath. "Agnes, when I first came to Cloverpoint, I had no ambition but to sell you the objects I brought with me and perhaps, if I was lucky, to see the automaton that my father had told me so much about. Never did I imagine it would come to this, that I would come to call you my friend."

Lady Selwyn smiles encouragingly.

"Which is why I feel I can be open with you, Agnes. When I saw the automaton, when I placed my hand upon it, a strange feeling overcame me, as though the spirit of my own father were pulsing from within. Maybe that was what left me speechless, that led me to lose my balance on the stairs. Over the past few days I have felt a sense of purpose blooming within me, such as I have not felt in years." Jehanne fixes Lady Selwyn in her sights. "Agnes, I wish to take the automaton back with me, to Rouen, where it can be refurbished and restored."

Lady Selwyn stares. "And then what?"

"Then I would put it on display. Share it with the public."

"You want me to simply *give* you the automaton?"

"In exchange for the items I have brought."

Lady Selwyn leans back, her brow furrowed with pity or consternation. "Oh, my dear."

"I know I am only a clockmaker's daughter, but he was not just any clockmaker. He was the maker of the automaton. He was—" Here she is surprised by the catch in her voice. "My only friend in the world."

Jehanne stops short. What more she meant to say fades into silence.

"That is not true, Jehanne," says Lady Selwyn. "You have me."

Jehanne looks up, hopefully.

Lady Selwyn is wearing a distant, wistful expression. "It was the East India Company that gave us the automaton. They'd given Horace a choice between a pair of golden pole ends and a silver casket encrusted with gemstones. Any other woman in England would have wanted the pole ends or the casket, you see—they would've torn the gems from their settings and melted the gold. But you know what Horace said to Rum? He said, *Not Aggie.* He said, *It's the story of the thing she cares about.* Which was why he chose an unwieldy automaton, with no inherent value, but stories galore." She trails off, as if having lost track of what she meant to say. "So you see," says Lady Selwyn, collecting herself, "the automaton is one thing to you, and another thing to me."

Jehanne opens her mouth to speak, but Lady Selwyn raises a hand. "Neither of these meanings matter to the object itself," she continues. "What matters is the question of who will care for the object, who will protect it from the wear and tear of time? A French-woman of little means, or me? I have taken the utmost care to ensure the Musical Tiger's long-term preservation."

Termites would have cared for it better, thinks Jehanne, taking a bracing sip of madeira.

"But," says Lady Selwyn, "I believe I may have struck upon a happy compromise."

In a breathless wave, Lady Selwyn describes the masquerade she intends to hold, tentatively titled Orientalia, wherein guests will dress in Oriental masks and costumes (with some creative interpretation, of course), featuring as centerpiece Tipu's Tiger, which will by then be restored to proper working order.

"You must be there, Jehanne." Lady Selwyn's diamond ring tinkles against her glass. "We can plan the whole thing together."

"I shan't make the journey again, Agnes, not so soon—"

"Then don't." Lady Selwyn rises and reseats herself on the chaise, their knees touching. "Stay with me."

"Here? For how long?"

"As long as you wish." Lady Selwyn laughs, hiccups, and covers her mouth. "'Tis true we've only just met, but I've always been led by my heart and I know we would make the very best of companions. And wouldn't you like that, a companion through this difficult time? One who would expect nothing from you, aside from a fine meal now and again, or a sweet walk through the gardens? Your financial struggles would be no more. I would take the utmost care of you."

"Utmost," says Jehanne softly, her gaze straying beyond Lady Selwyn, coming to rest on the curio cabinet standing against the wall, and in whose glass she sees pieces of her own reflection—her hand, her slipper—obscured by other objects.

"You hesitate." Lady Selwyn leans in, lowering her voice. "Is it Rum? You need not worry about him. I would make him understand. But I do have one request for you." Lady Selwyn looks at her intently. "I would expect you to dismiss your valet. I think you find him very . . . distracting."

"Distracting, madame?"

"It's all right, Jehanne. I am a modern woman. But you must understand: I do not like to share."

Jehanne rises abruptly—unwisely, for her head turns light—and goes to stand by the fire, keeping her back to Lady Selwyn. The heat is searing. She struggles to recover her poise, her graciousness.

"No," she says, and turns. "Forgive me, but I will take my limited means over yours."

"Oh, Jehanne, do not be angry with me. If I have insulted you, it was not my intention. Why, I was once like you! I am proof that people can rise from their circumstances—"

"Nothing you say can convince me to stay here."

The force with which Jehanne has uttered this statement causes Lady Selwyn to sit back, stunned.

"Well, then," says Lady Selwyn, her gaze casting about. "I misjudged you, Jehanne. I'd thought you had more vision."

"Your vision is to add me to your collection. Just as you have done with Mr. Rum."

"Stop your mouth! As if you know anything at all about us!"

Lady Selwyn's face is one of pain, betrayal. Jehanne knows she has laid waste to their friendship, but what are friends in this life?

"All this time," Lady Selwyn says, "you have concealed your true nature from me. How heartless you are. I wish you to leave me at once, be gone by morning."

Jehanne leaves without a word or a curtsy. She goes straight to her room, shuts the door, and presses a hand to her mouth.

She hadn't intended to lash out at Lady Selwyn. The true object of her contempt is Abbas, though she doubts she could say anything to wound him.

She hears a creaking down the hall. Though she knows Abbas wouldn't be treading the upper floor at this hour, she braces herself for a knock. She does not want to see anyone, least of all him. Even if she loses her house and the shop, even if she must move in with Isabelle and attend church and wear miles of black bombazine, she wants nothing more to do with him or his plan one or two or twenty. She has had enough.

She presses the pin that locks the door. She imagines him trying the knob, failing to turn it. He will step back, the knowledge dawning on him that she intends to journey home on her own. A minor triumph, yet as the night closes in, even this deserts her.

Upon hearing Jehanne's door fall shut, Lady Selwyn forces herself up from her chair. Her head is woozy with madeira. If Rum were here, he would have taken her arm before she even thought to reach for his. Now the armrest is her Rum. Faithful, unfaltering Rum. She pets the armrest with the back of her hand. She is very drunk.

As such, she surrenders to the familiar gloom of widowhood. Tears fall, the fire blurs. She longs for the company of her meerschaum.

She sends for her pipe and tinderbox, which Sally retrieves from her bedchamber without a glimmer of surprise or judgment. No doubt Sally will tell the others, if they haven't already discovered her habit and added it to the running tally of their mistress's strange ways. Not that Lady Selwyn much cares, once she has given the fire a stir and opened the window and drawn the sweet pipe smoke into her lungs. Out goes the smoke into the crisp evening air; in comes her father's ghost, or what she remembers of him.

Is this what you want, Aggie? her father had asked, on the eve of her wedding. *To be neither one thing nor the other?* He had warned against marrying above her station, had known that to do so would be to make an outcast of herself. But he hadn't understood her, hadn't known she was built of stronger materials than most.

A log softens and snaps. Seated by the window, she leans her head back and closes her eyes, knowing this loneliness will pass, tomorrow or the day after, and rests the meerschaum on her knee, oblivious to the embers that tip from the bowl onto the drapes down below, made of the finest flammable gauze.

A nautch girl in white turns a languid circle. She lowers to the carpet, where Abbas is sitting, watching her slim hands twist at the wrist. Somewhere a fountain murmurs, a bird serenades. He hears a whisper in his ear: *Were an artist to choose me for his model, how could he draw the form of a sigh?* The room is growing hot. The nautch girl is standing over him. She has an ax against her shoulder, her hand light on the handle. She says, "*Khuda hafiz,* Know-It-All," and hoists the ax and hacks him to pieces.

Abbas wakes up in a sweat. No sooner has he relaxed—having found himself whole and unhacked—than a red-faced man in nightclothes flings open the door. The man is clapping and yelling, gesturing wildly toward the hallway, where other servants are rushing past.

Abbas springs out of bed, fully dressed, for he hadn't intended to doze off; he'd meant to stay awake and keep his appointment with Jehanne. All the other servants are in plaits and robes and dressing gowns, the vaulted ceilings of the Cloisters scrambling their shouts.

"Fire! Fire! . . . Get up—no time for that! . . . fill the pump engine first—"

Abbas sprints past them. He leaps up the grand staircase where, if not for the smell of smoke, all would seem tranquil and quiet, nothing at all amiss.

Rum throws a basin of water over the burning curtain. The flames are small but steady, funneling a strong blackish cloud toward the ceiling.

"Rum, here—" Panting, Lady Selwyn gives him her own ewer

of bathwater, retrieved from her room. The smoke thickens. "Go see about the pump engine!"

Coughing, she follows Rum out of the room, leaning her back against the wall. How suddenly the smoke had appeared and from the smallest embers! She'd leapt up, in shock for a moment or two before yanking on the bellpull, rousing Fellowes and Flood from their beds.

Now she presses a kerchief to her mouth and sucks in a breath before running back into the room, to save what she can.

Crossing the threshold, Abbas throws an elbow over his face. A small mane of fire is flapping from the curtain, bright and quiet, but it is the ceiling of smoke that overwhelms him.

He sees Lady Selwyn, swatting objects from the wall shelves into the bowl of her skirt, then running to the adjoining china closet, where she tosses the treasures out an open window. He sees the tiger atop its pedestal, can almost smell the lacquered skin thinning in the heat.

He moves toward the automaton, thinking to lift it, drag it, save it somehow, until he catches a movement from the corner of his eye.

"Jehanne—" he says, but it's only his reflection in a wall mirror.

Beyond that wall is Jehanne's room. But where is she—where is Jehanne? He hadn't seen her on the stairs, had only seen the closed door of her room, perhaps the only closed door in the whole house, all the others flung open by people fleeing . . .

A terrible knowledge settles over him.

He rushes out of the Peacock Room.

Lady Selwyn can hear the men lumbering up the steps with the tub and pump. "Make a chain!" Rum is yelling. "Fill the tub!" She can hear the splash of leather buckets, one after another and another.

But fires, she knows, are impatient beasts. Soon this one will be chewing on the tassels of the rug, then up the pedestal to the automaton, whose lacquered wood will make a pyre of the house.

And so she crouches on the floor, gripping the tassels of the rug on which the tiger rests, pedestal and all. If she can pull the tiger into the china closet and shut the doors, she may buy some time.

The carpet gives only an inch.

Rum yells for three men on each side of the pump to take up the treadles. He will yell himself hoarse, poor man. But a good man. What luck to have known him.

The heat tightens its clasp on her scalp as she wraps the tassels round her fists. *Come,* she thinks, to the tiger, to the heat, to the fumes. Whatever is coming, let it come.

Abbas pounds on Jehanne's door. The knob—scalding—won't turn.

He rams his shoulder into the door, kicks at it. He pummels the wood with his fists, bellowing her name. He looks for help from any-one, anyone—he grabs Fellowes by the elbow, but Fellowes shakes him off and staggers toward the staircase, hacking into a handker-chief. There is no time. Abbas takes one last kick at the door, which shudders but does not give. He begins to understand his own frailty, his uselessness. He races down the staircase, his only thought: to reach her.

Rum grips the long tube attached to the front of the pump engine, and for a moment thinks all is lost; the tube is only the length of his arm. But then: out shoots a miraculous beam of water, arcing across the room, over the flames. He cannot believe the sustained force of so many gallons, rushing through his hands.

Behind him is the steady clunk and splash of the pump engine's handles, punctuated by cries for more buckets, more speed. Rum directs the beam, dazed with smoke and awe.

Abbas runs barefoot over the gravel to the street-facing side of the house. Which window is hers? He will scale the wall. Somehow. He will scale it or die trying. Here is a trellis. He clambers up, wondering how he will set about going sideways, how he will manage to get himself from one window to the next, how he will rap on each window before it's too late.

He stops climbing the trellis when he hears someone from behind calling his name.

"Abbas, what are you doing?"

Jehanne is standing on the gravel below, her arms folded tight across her robe.

He catches a glimpse of her scowling face—oh, that face—before he loses his foothold and falls through space and time, landing on his back with the weight of the sky above him as heavy as the weight of a dead man, pressing the air from his lungs, pressing him into an early grave, and he is gasping for water, for air, for another day, another season, when a hand reaches down to him, a hand he is both desperate and fearful to accept . . .

"Just take my hand!"

Rum watches in disbelief as the column of smoke begins to thin and disperse.

There was a time when he questioned her decision to buy a pump engine; no other country home in Twickenham had such an expensive, newfangled contraption.

You were right, Aggie. He cannot wait to tell her.

But where is she?

And where on earth is the automaton?

Only after running up and down the hall does he find her in the china closet, on her knees, her forehead pressed to the back of her hands, which are resting on the tiger's spine. Her shoulders are heaving. He squints in amazement, his eyes still stinging from the smoke.

As soon as he reaches her, she collapses into his arms.

He lifts her and runs down the staircase, out the door, where the fresh air will surely revive her.

. . .

In reality, Abbas fell only seven feet before landing with a harmless *whump*. Jehanne pulls him to standing.

"Are you all right?" she says, frowning. "What were you doing up there?" She hesitates as he steps toward her. "What's this . . . ?"

She stiffens as his arms go around her waist, as he rests his brow on her shoulder. His head is heavy, his breathing labored. So she yields, she holds him until he calms.

"Jehan," he rasps. "Here you are."

"Of course," she says easily, concealing her own fear, for she knows it could have gone differently. She'd awoken to a riot of shouting outside her door and the smell of smoke. The door knob had scalded her fingers, the little peg that locked the door would not release. She flung open her window and glimpsed the hedges and dove feetfirst, thinking if she had to break something, let it be a leg. But then she staggered away from the fall with a limp and some bruises, thinking next of Abbas. She went around the house, searching for an entrance to the Cloisters. When she discovered him hugging the trellis, she released the breath she hadn't known she'd been holding.

Only now does she feel the weight of what she nearly lost, the life that could have gone up in that pillar of smoke. Her life, small as it is. Still hers.

XI

For the first time in the history of Cloverpoint Castle, the servants have been encouraged to sleep in by an hour, if they can find sleep at all.

The Peacock Room is a disaster—floorboards softened, vulnerable to breakage, curtains in tatters, glass cabinets in shards, and countless curios lost.

Rum attends to the fire chief and his men, ordering Fellowes to see that they are given coffee and water and whatever breakfast can be mustered at the moment. He then sends Palmer to retrieve Richard Selwyn, the police, the coroner, the builder, and Dr. Stanley. Flood has burned his arm; several of the housemaids are badly wheezing. Rum's own lungs feel scorched, his body drained of a stone. He does not care. He does not cry or clutch his head. He goes from face to face, making sounds out of his own. He goes up the stairs and down the stairs and through the past and back to the present, which stuns him again and again, like a bird against glass.

At one point, Rum finds himself standing beside Lady Selwyn's body. She lies in the middle of her bed, looking very small and alone. Her eyelids have an unearthly sheen. It was Mrs. Chapman and one of the housemaids who washed and dressed her, but it was Rum who chose the deep green satin and the tigereye earrings. Mrs. Chapman said pearls would be more suitable. He insisted, a bit forcefully. The tigereyes glint in the guttering light of the candles.

"I called Dr. Stanley," he says quietly.

He imagines her saying: *Good God, Rum. Anytime Stanley enters a house, he manages to leave behind a dead body.*

"I know. These things can't be helped. I hope you like the earrings." He pauses. "I thought you should have the things you love." His throat tightens. "Since you died for them."

He strokes her cheek with the back of his finger. Her skin is cool and gritty with powder. She'd seemed so warm and alive when he carried her outside and knelt on the front lawn, shaking her, slapping her cheek gently, then less gently, saying her name over and over until he realized he was saying it to himself.

Heavy boots clomp up the stairs. Rum takes a shuddering breath, collects himself.

Richard Selwyn halts in the doorway. His nightshirt is tucked halfway into his trousers. He steps forward, and, with a trembling hand, touches her wrist for a prolonged moment. "Who—" he says, then quickly retracts his hand. "Who started it? Was it a servant?"

Rum recounts being woken from bed by the sound of her shouting. "I assume it was by Lady Selwyn's hand—it all happened quickly."

"What about the Frenchwoman—where was she?"

"Sir, you suspect Miss Jehanne?"

"No one is outside the realm of possibility, Rum. Is the Frenchwoman still here?"

"Yes, sir."

"Then I want her questioned along with everyone else."

"Yes, sir."

Richard fixes a wary gaze on his mother's body, scanning it head to toe. He turns the hat in his hands. "You were with her?" he asks quietly.

"I was," Rum says, and adds: "She died in my arms."

He waits for Richard to react. Hopes for it, almost. But Richard only glances at him opaquely, as if the detail is inconsequential.

"I want you to be here when the constable arrives," Richard says before exiting the room.

Briskly Richard Selwyn descends the staircase, wincing at the charred smell in the air, ready to devote weeks, even months, to finding the culprit. The mystery will be resolved within the hour, when the fire chief discovers behind the curtains the remnants of a meerschaum pipe.

XII

Only the Peacock Room suffered damage from the fire, yet from Jehanne's view on the south lawn, Cloverpoint has a humbled gloom to it now, as if the whole house has shifted on its very foundations. She walks and gnaws on her lower lip, asking herself every few steps: *What have I done? What was it all for?*

No, the fire did not start by her hand, but her words had been scorching enough to keep Lady Selwyn awake and alone, smoking until she was too stupefied to hold her own pipe upright.

And the regrets go back farther still. What possessed her to throw herself down the grand staircase on the day of their first meeting? What sort of person would do such a thing?

A person who desperately wanted to disrupt the pattern of herself, a choice that has led here, to death, the final disruption.

When she can walk no longer, she sits on a white stone bench in the shape of an upright shell. It is an impractical, uncomfortable piece of furniture, but at least the curved back muffles most sounds, allowing the sitter to cry in relative quiet.

.   .   .

Rum sleeps three hours before startling awake, fresh from a nightmare in which the whole house is burning, Rum going room to fiery room, trying to follow Aggie's screams and yet never finding her.

In the late morning he discovers Jehanne sitting on the shell bench in the Pleasure Garden. She is bare-headed, a shawl wrapped around her shoulders. At the sight of him, she rises halfway, as if to vacate what is not hers.

He stops her with a raised palm. She scoots to make room.

Neither wishes to speak first, so they sit listening to the birds blather away. He touches the corner of his brow, where the hair was singed off. Somehow he cannot stop touching that spot; it feels something like touching his own skull.

Her voice, when she speaks, is a rasp: "I heard Lady Selwyn saved the automaton."

Rum nods.

"How did she do it?" Jehanne asks.

"Sheer will."

Jehanne shakes her head. "She was an extraordinary woman."

They look up at the quatrefoil window where the glass, invincible and intact, flashes with sky.

"I suppose I owe you the truth," Jehanne says.

"I don't care anymore," Rum says, not unkindly.

"You were right about Abbas—he is not my valet." She pauses. "He was once a woodcarver to Tipu Sultan. He and my guardian— Lucien Du Leze—they made the Musical Tiger together."

"Oh, good Lord."

"What?"

Rum gives her a sidelong look. "You really expect me to believe that cockalorum?"

She frowns at the word *cockalorum,* whatever it may mean. "I do not expect you to believe me. I only wish to confess that his hope— our hope—was to take the tiger back and restore it and . . ."

"Become wealthy and famous?"

"Yes, it sounds foolish when you say it like that." She picks at the pollen cones stuck to her skirt.

"If he isn't your valet, what is your relation? Who are you to him?"

He senses he has struck a nerve when she doesn't reply, her fingernails frittering a cone to pieces. "I wish I knew," she says finally.

Ah, he thinks. She loves him.

Jehanne brushes the detritus from her skirt. "We intend to leave for the inn this afternoon. In a week or so, we will begin the journey home."

"Mr. Palmer can take you into town—I shall arrange it."

"And you, Monsieur Rum? Will you be staying on at Cloverpoint?"

"As long as I am needed. And then . . . I don't know."

"Do you have people here?"

He shakes his head.

She looks at him for a long time, then says: "I am very sorry for your loss."

"Indeed Lady Selwyn's death is a great loss to all of England. But she leaves behind one of the greatest country houses in the land, not to mention her collection—"

"Monsieur Rum." She lays a hand on his forearm. "I am sorry for *your* loss."

He looks at her. Dread has him riveted.

Jehanne releases his arm, sits back. "She was lucky to have one as loyal as you."

Rum does not breathe. If he breathes, he will weep, and she will see clear into the vaulted part of his heart. Perhaps Jehanne can already see with those piercing gray eyes. What she might do with the information, he has no idea. But here it is, out in the open between them. Flexing its wings. Testing the air.

Abruptly Rum rises, thanks her, bids her safe journey.

He hurries through the garden, then swerves away from the house, hoping Jehanne isn't watching the erratic path he is making toward the footbridge. Stopping in the middle, he grips the rail, tries to regulate his breathing. His throat tightens. He shakes his head. "Ah, come on," he mutters at himself.

Though he is late in reporting to the new Lord Selwyn, Rum takes a basket from the gardener's shed and circles the house until he comes to the hedge directly beneath the china closet. There he gathers all the things Lady Selwyn tossed from her skirt. Some are whole, some are shattered beyond mending, and one makes him laugh like a lunatic until he is crying—the porcelain head of a Saracen, its nose broken off.

Rouen

In the beginning Abbas resumes his spartan life, repairing clocks in the back of the shop. He is polite to Jehanne, and though the memory of him mumbling into her hair can stun her at any odd moment, his courtesy leads her to believe he wants friendship, nothing more. So be it, she thinks.

Sometimes, when there is nothing to do, no earnings coming in, Abbas rests his mouth in his palm and taps on the surface of the table, a dent of worry between his brows.

"You could go back to making toys," she suggests one day, sweeping around him. "Those would sell."

He sucks his teeth at the idea, which privately delights her. Not since childhood has she heard that sound, usually from one of her exasperated aunts.

"The toys would take too much time," he says. "It's not sustainable."

"And yet here we are, sustaining ourselves. Feet." He lifts his feet so that she can thrust her broom beneath the stool and table. "We are fine."

"For now."

"Why, what do you mean? Are you going somewhere?"

"No." He looks at her, puzzled by her alarm. "I only mean that it would be better if we sold the sort of things that would be easier to produce, that would require less time for each piece."

"Like what?"

For weeks they volley possibilities. Hats. Spinning tops. Dolls. Nothing sparks, though of all their ideas, Jehanne keeps returning to the dolls. She tells him of the one she'd had as a little girl, no more than a stuffed bulb of muslin, with two kohl-drawn eyes and a mouth. How she rocked it devotedly, mimicking a cry, wishing it would make sounds of its own.

Abbas listens, his fingers laced atop his head. "Lucien used to say the sound is everything. He said that the French word for 'animal' comes from some other word—"

"*Animus.*" Proudly she adds: "I excelled in Latin."

"He said, sound is breath is life. Or something like that."

She follows the direction of his thoughts. A doll that can be quickly produced and made to cry. But made how?

Days he spends with Lucien's notebooks and blueprints, paging quickly until he finds useful diagrams of bellows and grunt pipes. Sitting beside him, she translates what he cannot understand, so that the education is mutual and intimate, which she has never known an education could be.

For a full week, Abbas puts off his clock repairs and throws himself into design and construction. On the table before him: his sketches, his pencil, a small saw, rubber gaskets of various sizes, and a number of wooden cylinders, which he has carved himself. He is making a small bellows, he says, to fit inside the chest of a cloth doll. He entrusts her with sewing the doll itself, with peg limbs, wide-set eyes, and a versatile O-shape for the mouth.

One day, while stitching, she hears a squeal that makes her prick her own hand. "Good heavens!"

Abbas is beaming, a small strange object in his palm.

Such a simple thing, or so it seems: a cylinder inside another cylinder, a hole poked in the center of the lid. He explains how turning the object over causes the inner cylinder to sink and air to flow up through the hole, passing across a pair of hidden metal tabs. A crybox, he calls it, to be sewn into a doll's chest.

By the end of eight months, they have made and sold fifty cry dolls in Rouen alone. Their success attracts the attention of Madame Gardam, a friend of Aunt Isabelle, who wants to make an investment. Over lunch with Madame Gardam, Jehanne talks incessantly: explaining how the cry dolls are appealing because of the softness of the body and limbs, easier to reproduce than the bisque dolls (*so yesterday*), and much more satisfying to embrace. And, of course, there is the remarkable crybox mechanism, the first of its kind in France, developed by Jehanne's business partner, Monsieur Mahmud Abbas.

"What kind of name is Abbas?" asks Madame Gardam, brow raised.

"Moorish," says Jehanne, and hurries on to detail her plans: a factory in Rouen and someday maybe a shop in Montmartre—

"My dear," says Madame Gardam. "You needn't try so hard. Unlike your dear aunt, I care more about money than Moors. Shall we eat?"

Jehanne will forever remember the meal: herbed soup and two kinds of fish, fowl, breadmeat pie, gooseberry pie, cherries, strawberries, grapes, figs, and a genoise sponge. She manages to swipe two or three chocolate truffles while Madame Gardam is turned away, and smuggles them into her purse.

Riding home in a coach, she dips her fingers into the purse pocket and comes away with melted chocolate. And in her finest purse! Although a new life is unfolding before her, one in which she can afford to buy an even finer purse. Maybe. She nibbles on the remainder of a truffle, tasting a compote of white chocolate, strawberry, and champagne.

Jehanne arrives at the shop to find Abbas nestling a crybox inside the back of a cloth doll. "So?" he asks.

"She said the brunettes were nice but the blondes will sell," says Jehanne, untying her hat.

"What else?"

"She asked about your nationality. I told her you were Moorish."

"You may tell her I am Jesus Christ if it will get her to open her pocketbook." He waits. "And? Did she?"

Unable to maintain the ruse, Jehanne grins.

Abbas releases a breath. "Good. That's very good."

"The only bad news," she says, peering into her purse, "is that I have melted chocolate all over the lining of my purse and—" She looks up to find, to her surprise, that he is walking toward her, that he is setting aside her purse and taking both her hands in his. "Under my nails."

He looks at her for what feels a long time, studying the different parts of her face. She is too stunned to wonder what he is contemplating beyond that concentrated expression. Then he kisses her mouth, dismissing all her other thoughts.

After the kiss, he courts her so slowly she isn't sure if she is being courted at all. He asks her to go for long walks, which end with nothing more than his lips brushing her knuckles. Then he departs to the shop, leaving her to retire to her room, wondering how to interpret the thrum of her heart.

In the meantime Madame Gardam buys an abandoned factory and hires a team to renovate the production floors. Cloth dolls on the first floor, crybox construction on the second. Jehanne brings the plans that Abbas painstakingly drew out; he has taught her how to train the workers herself. She finds she likes teaching the women. *The internal cylinder must sink at just the right speed. If it falls with a clunk, you have made the cylinder too small and must start again. Precision, ladies. If nothing else we must be precise.* In the beginning, the factory is an aviary of plaintive *kee*s and *coo*s, but a little cotton in the ears and the sounds are bearable.

Two weeks into production, a week before the dolls will be shipped to boutiques in Paris, Jehanne wakes early one morning to a knock on the door. Abbas asks if she'd like to go on a walk.

Another walk, she thinks. But she dons her pelisse and bonnet and takes his arm.

It is a short walk to the shop. Across the glass, in gold lettering, read the words:

Jehanne Du Leze.
Toys. Hats. Creations.

"You did this?" she asks, stepping toward the glass. She can smell the fresh paint.

"I did."

"But your name . . ."

"Never mind. The shop is yours."

He joins her by the window. In the reflection, she watches his hand find hers.

"I think this occasion deserves a toast," she says to his reflection, which is just vague enough that she finds the courage to say, offhand: "I have brandy at home."

"Your home? Now?"

She nods.

As he considers this, she imagines the earth opening up and swallowing her whole, a preferable outcome to waiting for his answer.

"Is it proper to do so before marriage?" he asks.

"Are we getting married?"

"I would like to. To you." He swallows audibly. "Then we could have brandy every day. Even twice a day."

"That sounds enjoyable."

They fall quiet, as if testing the temperature of the decision they've made.

"But why waste time?" he says, and she agrees, and they make haste for her door.

Jehanne learned the basics of sex from convent school—not from the nuns, of course, but from particularly adventurous girls, or girls with adventurous imaginations. One girl said there would be a smell like mushrooms. Another girl claimed that at the climactic moment, both parties would feel the need to pee. Such details amounted to an act that sounded animalistic and embarrassing.

The sound Abbas makes, when he enters her, does have an animal quality, but in a curious way. Somewhere between heaving and lowing. As she ponders this, her breath turns rhythmic and strange, and the hunger flares from her own body, boundless as light . . .

(But it is over quickly, this being his first time in a very long while.)

A round shock of red stains the sheet. The pain lessens drastically on the next go-round; he moves more slowly and looks at every part of her with a candor that overwhelms her even more than the sex itself. And when he collapses against her shoulder, she can regard him freely, the furrowed brow, the parted lips, the face of a boy who has fought sleep all his life and finally come to rest.

And so they go on for months, learning the contours of this new life, grateful and astounded at this chance at happiness. Not that they are always happy. But at least each of them bears a wound that the other understands, being severed from their bloodlines, their homeland. Each is all the other has, and this can sometimes be a burden, but mostly a solace.

Often Abbas wonders what has become of the automaton. Rum would know, but for a good long time, guilt stops Abbas from writing. He still remembers shaking the man's hand on the day of their departure. How broken Rum had looked as he stepped back from the coach. A man dispossessed.

As the coach drove off, Abbas waited for his own sense of loss to set in, yet all he experienced was a stunned sort of nothing. In time, he came to feel relieved. It was quite like tugging on a closed door for years, only to find that, in fact, the door opened the other way, with but a nudge. And on the other side: a new life.

On recent nights, Abbas has taken to lying awake, staring up at the ceiling, while Jehanne snores gently beside him. From the outside, he looks perfectly still. On the inside is a churning of dark and light, old memories and fresh senses. Something new is coming, and whether it comes by ink or chisel or gouge, for now it is limitless.

The Voyage

After another long winter and a chilly spring, summer has come to Twickenham. Gnats buzz in clouds; bees cling to blooms. Rum is leaving Cloverpoint Castle.

He resigned from his post two months before, via a letter posted to Richard's London address. The new Lord Selwyn had not visited the house in weeks, preferring for Rum to manage his business affairs and Fellowes to manage the household.

To Rum's surprise, Richard actually listened to his advice. It was Rum's idea to donate the Musical Tiger to the East India Museum, where it could be refurbished and displayed on a platform, with a plaque that would acknowledge Richard's generosity.

The curators discovered two names elegantly inscribed on the bottom of the head bellows—*Faite par L. Du Leze & Abbas*—and suggested adding these to the description. Rum had never noticed the inscription before, though he'd also never examined each piece at length. He knew only one other person who had—the faux-valet who had crept into the Peacock Room one night.

There were two possible explanations:

Abbas had slipped into the Peacock Room on his last day at the house, unnoticed, for no one else wanted to suffer the smoggy air, and had carved the words himself. Or—

The names had been there all along.

A con artist or an artist? The more closely Rum examined the letters—authoritative and elegant and perfectly scored—the more he leaned, awestruck, toward artist.

Without asking Richard, Rum wrote to the curators, saying that Lord Selwyn had accepted their suggestion to include both names on the plaque.

On the morning of Rum's departure, Fellowes meets him in the vestibule and hands over an envelope bearing the Selwyn seal. Inside are Rum's wages and severance. He touches the barbed quatrefoil before sliding the envelope into the lining of his suit jacket.

"You will be missed," says Fellowes, who has been one degree friendlier ever since learning of Rum's impending departure.

They acknowledge one another—and their years of service—with a curt nod. Rum takes one last look up the grand staircase, his gaze leaping from bust to bust, and up to the frieze where the Romans clash eternally with the Huns.

As Rum descends the front steps, Fellowes calls after him. "I expect you'll be passing the cliffs of Dover."

"I believe so," says Rum.

"My father worked in the watchtower. I used to run along those cliffs as a little boy. Never tired of looking at the sea from that height." Fellowes opens his mouth for a wordless moment, then says: "If you happen to stop there, you might ask about my mother, Mrs. Cruickshank."

"Cruickshank? Your name is Cruickshank?"

Fellowes winces and makes a quieting gesture with his hand. "I thought Fellowes sounded more butlery." He shrugs. "Never too late to reinvent yourself, I say."

For once they are in agreement. "I shall tell the cliffs you say hello."

·　·　·

The carriage takes Rum to London, where he boards the ten o'clock coach near Leadenhall Market. The air is thick with fumes and noise. Gracechurch Street to Kinghall Street. London Bridge. Southwark Cathedral. At the corner of Kent and Dunton, he says goodbye to London. The fields resume, with an occasional house hugging the road.

They stop at an inn to water the horses and eat, and then carry on down the road that the ancients took between London and Dover, crossing the heath behind Greenwich. The countryside unfolds, not a house in sight, seas of grass on both sides, here and there an oak or birch. It has been three hours since they left the inn, and in all that time, Rum has not spoken. No one in the coach has spoken to him. A man with the pallor of a boiled potato keeps checking him with a wary glance.

Rum doesn't mind keeping silent. He is thinking of Lady Selwyn. She was a pain in the rear. Pushy. Outright rude, sometimes. Tender at others. Sexy as anything. Even her pushiness had propped him up all these years, he can see that now. He feels weaker without her voice buffeting him about. Now it's the road that buffets him from down below, giving him the stirs as they cross the River Medway.

They pass through Sittingbourne and Faversham. Boughton under Blean. The road thins and widens and thins again, like a snake digesting a series of things. They reach Canterbury through the Westgate, and stop for dinner at an inn.

Inside, Rum finds himself sitting across from the pale-faced man, who spends an agonizing length of time explaining the historical significance of Canterbury. They eat rump steaks and potatoes with port. The man, named Bertie, asks where Rum is from.

"I am from India, originally."

"Ah, thought so."

"Where are you from?"

"Me?" Bertie laughs for some reason. "Here. Liverpool, to

be specific. So what brings you to England from all the way over there?"

Among all the possible answers, Rum does not say what first comes to mind: *I am here because you were there.*

Instead he says: "I was land agent to Lady Selwyn of Cloverpoint Castle for many years."

Bertie's eyes widen. "That's a fine house! You're lucky to get a job there."

Rum allows himself a modest smile and a sip of port. Yes, it is. Yes, he was.

"And where are you headed?" asks Bertie.

So far, Rum hasn't told anyone where he is going. He has spoken of a blurry future that consists of travel and leisure, as if the world is his. He hasn't felt that the world was his since he was five years old.

Maybe it's the port, but Rum, all of a sudden, decides to tell the truth.

"To a town in France called Rouen." Bertie chews blankly. Rum presses on. "I am taking another job, as a bookkeeper for a toy shop."

"A toy shop?" Bertie's forehead creases. "That's a far cry from Cloverpoint."

"At this age I wouldn't mind living with a cry."

Bertie heartily agrees. Newly widowed, he is bound for the south of France, where he plans to drink Muscat and sleep with French-women who don't mind their men of a riper vintage. Find them he will, along with a viral strain of syphilis that will nibble his brain down to the nodes, leaving him dead by All Saints.

"To living with a cry," Bertie says, raising his glass. Rum meets it with his own.

The water glitters and churns, rocking Rum's insides. The boat sees and saws. He shuts his eyes, which only worsens his nausea. He vomits over the side of the boat, his gut clenching tight as a fist, releasing, then tightening further still.

Once he has emptied himself, he feels slightly better. It also helps to pat his inside jacket pocket, as a reminder to himself that he does have a specific destination in mind. Tucked behind Richard's envelope is the letter from Jehanne Du Leze. He has read it so many times he no longer needs to look at the letter to recall the final paragraph:

> *Our cry dolls have gained in popularity, and our business continues to grow beyond our projections. We anticipate the need for a bookkeeper in the near future and would prefer someone sensible as you, Mr. Rum, with your fastidiousness and cast of mind. I do not know that you would find lodgings as fine as those at Cloverpoint Castle, but you would find the two of us, who would treat you as equals.*

Here are the cliffs of Dover, the place where little Cruickshank was born.

Rum used to roll his eyes whenever Fellowes began talking of his beloved cliffs. But now he understands: the cliffs are as astounding as Fellowes claimed them to be. It's impossible to look anywhere other than at that startling white rock, where faces rise from the marbled creases and fold into other shapes.

Strange to think of Fellowes as having a home other than Cloverpoint. Yet the cliffs seem somehow appropriate to his character—steady, serious, chiseled from English stone. A falcon sails across the sky. Rum imagines the little Cruickshank in breeches, galloping over the green. He finally realizes the depth of Fellowes's yearning, and why he could not express anything more about these cliffs, that watchtower, the sea.

Another day, another harbor. As the watchtower guides them into Bassin du Paradis, Rum wonders at how far he has come. Not only the distance he has crossed over the past six days, from Cloverpoint to Calais, but the past sixty years. He pens a mental biography containing these lines: *He was unusual for a man of his time. He traveled*

more than most. He saw many of the greatest wonders of the world.
He: a boy, then a clerk, then a sepoy, then a steward. Now what?
As the boat nears a dock where no man, woman, or child is waiting
or waving for Rum, it occurs to him—as it has before, but never
so acutely—that he has put himself in a precarious position. The
people on the dock speak in French and Flemish, all of it a pudding
to his ears. He feels the old flutter of panic as he disembarks along
the gangway, tightly gripping the handle of his small valise. Panic,
yet also admiration. A graceful city, this one, nothing like any in
England he has seen. The buildings and houses are of all different
heights, timeworn yet stately. He squints at a brass plaque on the cay,
the French words illegible to him, except for *Roi . . . Louis XVIII . . .*
pied . . . 1792. Likely this is where the king first set his royal foot
upon his return from exile, Napoleon left to rot in Corsica. Rum
takes a briny breath as the king must have done, and joins the flow
toward customs.

London, England

1859

A man steps foot inside the Oriental Repository of the East India House. He shivers within his woolen shawl, the draft piercing his cotton kameez. He finds most of the East India House distasteful and common, a warren of dark offices and weak-eyed clerks. The Oriental Repository is a pleasant contrast. He takes in the high-domed ceiling, its dazzling hues of azure and gold. In the center is a painting of a blackish bare-breasted woman offering up a platter of pearls to a toga-clad white woman. The man studies the painting so long his neck stiffens.

He drops his gaze to the walls, where the books of Tipu Sultan are arranged neatly on shelves. The man grazes his fingertips across a row of spines, inhaling their leather and dust, scents he used to hold sacred.

From the clerk, he requests several books not on these shelves, quarantined for safe-keeping. These are laid before him on a table: *The Dream Register of Tipu Sultan*, a treatise on letter-writing, and some of Tipu's personal Qurans. He touches the first foxed page of the dream register, vaguely looking for his name, which he doesn't find. This is a slight but predictable disappointment. After all, Tipu had twelve sons. He, Ghulam Muhammad, is remarkable only for the fact that he is the last one alive.

He pages through the middle of the dream register, whose honesty and vulnerability unnerve him. He never knew this version of his father. (Talking cows? Big-breasted men?) He imagines some common merchant, rooting through his father's secrets, laughing. His face grows hot with anger and shame. He shuts the register.

He must compose himself. In a few hours, he will be meeting with the Queen of England, to petition for an increase in his clan's monthly stipend. He wishes to express dignity, not self-pity, on behalf of the hundreds of descendants living in forced seclusion in the malarial suburbs of Calcutta.

For courage, he turns to a Quran he knows well, having seen it so many times in his father's hands. The leather is a warm reddish brown. Gilded vines blossom around the border, framing medallions and pendants of nastaliq. At the top is written: *the God-Given Government.* At the bottom: *Allah is sufficient.* Along the spine: *None may touch it except the purified.*

The last sentence gives him pause. Can a prince, pensioned off by the English, ever be pure? His father would have said no. Better to live two days as a tiger than two hundred days as a sheep, he used to say.

As a child, Ghulam Muhammad asked his mother, "Tiger or sheep, which one am I?"

He never forgot her reply, clear and firm:

"You are a boy."

A clerk is escorting him to the exit when he spots Tipu's Tiger, crouched in the shadows of another room. The clerk waits as he circles it slowly, peering into the hollows, squinting at the holes on the shoulders where the tiger's incisors are sunk like knives. He smiles, a boy again. He remembers a European playing the keys. And there was someone else, wasn't there? The woodcarver, yes, working with unblinking concentration, as if the entire turning of the earth depended on his turning of the crank.

Ghulam Muhammad rests a hand on the flat between the tiger's ears. He lets a feeling blow through him, the sensation of touching a tree that once grew in Mysore, a tree that shaded people who are now dead. Both places, both times, vibrating within.

Behind him, someone shifts. He turns, half expecting to see his father standing there, his hand on his patka, his attention absolute.

But it's only the clerk, whose stern presence causes Ghulam Muhammad to remove his hand.

He had thought it would pain him to part with his father's things. But as he passes through the dark room and out the double doors, the light comes as relief to his eyes.

A Note from the Author

The automaton at the center of this novel—Tipu's Tiger—was first commissioned by Tipu Sultan in the late eighteenth century. In reality, the makers of the automaton are unknown, but the carving style of the exterior and the mechanics of the interior suggest a collaboration between Mysorean and French craftsmen. I have taken great liberties in imagining these makers and the journey of the automaton itself.

Works by historians Mohibbul Hasan and Mir Hussain Ali Khan Kirmani were crucial to my rendering of late-eighteenth-century Mysore. I also kept the following books close at hand: *Tipu's Tigers* by Susan Stronge, *Historical Sketches of the South of India* by Mark Wilks, *The Old East Indiamen* by E. Keble Chatterton, *A Master Mariner: Being the Life and Adventures of Captain Robert William Eastwick* by Robert William Eastwick, and *Strawberry Hill and Horace Walpole* by John Iddon.

On three occasions, I embedded the words of other writers into the novel and would like to cite them here.

In *A Master Mariner,* Captain Eastwick recalls a piece of advice given to him as a young sailor, a version of which appears in the novel: "There is no justice or injustice on board ship, my lad. There are only two things: Duty and Mutiny—mind that. All that you are ordered to do is duty. All that you refuse to do is mutiny. And the punishment for mutiny on a king's frigate is the yard-arm."

I would also like to cite Ambalavaner Sivanandan, a British—

Sri Lankan activist and writer, who coined the line: "We are here because you were there."

And finally, a verse of poetry recurs throughout the novel:

Were an artist to choose me for his model—
How could he draw the form of a sigh?

This verse is attributed to Zeb-un-Nissa, a Sufi poet and patron of the arts, and daughter of the Mughal emperor Aurangzeb. It is believed that Zeb-un-Nissa authored a collection of poems under a pseudonym, *Diwan-i-Makhfi,* or *Book of the Hidden One.* By including her verse in this novel, I hope to invite inquiry into a figure, one among many, whose voice has gone before mine.

Acknowledgments

I am grateful to the people who guided me through their fields of expertise. Any mistakes are my own.

Thank you to Susan Stronge, senior curator in the Asian Department at the Victoria & Albert Museum, and to Robert Race, maker of extraordinary toys and automata, who helped me to speculate on the tiger's internal workings. Thank you to William Dalrymple for the conversation and excellent book recommendations.

Thank you to those who showed me around Mysore and Srirangapatna, and who answered every one of my questions with endless patience: Vinay Parameswarappa, Nidhin Olikara, and Pamela Sanath. My deepest thanks to Poorna Kemparajurs and K.G. Anantharaj Urs for pointing me in all the right directions.

Thank you to Alena Graedon and Joy Johannessen for careful feedback on early and later drafts. Thank you to Abdullah Elamari for providing helpful research assistance and to Matt Seidel for fielding all my French questions.

Thank you to George Mason University for the Faculty Research and Development Award, which allowed me to travel to Rouen, London, and Mysore. Thank you to my colleagues and students.

Thank you to my agent, Nicole Aragi, for your great big heart and steadying hand. How lucky I am to know you. Thank you to Grace Dietshe, Maya Solovej, and Kelsey Day. Thank you to Jordan Pavlin for the superb editorial guidance and friendship throughout my writing career. I am grateful to the whole team at Knopf, including Isabel Meyers, Josefine Kals, and Ellen Feldman, for bringing this book, and so many others I admire, into the world.

Thank you to my safety net of friends and family, near and far, especially Chintan Maru, Edwin Zhao, Indira Sarma, and Shankar Duraiswamy. Thank you to Andrea Olivas and Candice Brown, who cared for my children before, during, and after the pandemic, thereby allowing me to write this book.

Thank you to my Jackson Heights family: Hansraj and Usha Maru, Sheela and Duncan Maru, and Anand and Umed.

Thank you to my sisters, Neena and Christine, a coven I could not live without. All the nonallergenic flowers in the world to Raj, Revi, Mia, Aashiq, and Zahra.

Thank you to Luka and Sajan, for reminding me to play.

Thank you to my father, Koduvathara James, who, at the time of this writing, had just texted me a detail he'd discovered about the lining of Tipu's battle garments. Your restless curiosity is an inspiration.

Thank you to my mother, Mariamma James, who has always led with love and courage, and whose belief in us meant the world.

Thank you to my beloved grandmother, Rachel Kurian, for helping to raise us, and for gifting us with her artistry.

Thank you, Vivek, for making this life with me and fighting for the future.

A NOTE ON THE TYPE

This book was set in Adobe Garamond. Designed for the Adobe Corporation by Robert Slimbach, the fonts are based on types first cut by Claude Garamond (ca. 1480–1561). Garamond was a pupil of Geoffroy Tory and is believed to have followed the Venetian models, although he introduced a number of important differences, and it is to him that we owe the letter we now know as "old style." He gave to his letters a certain elegance and feeling of movement that won their creator an immediate reputation and the patronage of Francis I of France.

Composed by North Market Street Graphics,
Lancaster, Pennsylvania

Printed and bound by Berryville Graphics,
Berryville, Virginia

Designed by Soonyoung Kwon